FIVE HEROIC TALES OF ENCHANTMENT FROM MASTERS OF THE ART

The castle had completely vanished and large fissures had appeared in the slope. Above the summit of the mountain, two columns of smoke now stood—a dark one and a light one. The two columns had begun to move, slowly, toward one another . . .

—*Tower of Ice*
ROGER ZELAZNY

Gillian looked, where something like a rope of darkness twisted among the columns, above the blood which spattered the altar; a trick of the wind and lamps, perhaps. But it crossed the sky, where the stars paled to day, and moved against the ceiling. Her right hand was suddenly cold . . .

—*A Thief in Korianth*
C. J. CHERRYH

The burning of her tears and the more terrible burning of the cold breaking through her circle came together. Enraged and terrified, Sirronde lifted her Rod and slashed the air in front of her, striking the basilisk's power aside with a long whip of Flame . . .

—*Parting Gifts*
DIANE DUANE

The vines crept all about the wizard, but were only now pushing at his sorcerous robes, as if the animate vegetation somehow sensed that Ebenezum was a greater threat than either Hendrek or myself. A gnarled tendril crept toward the wizard's sleeve . . .

—*A Dealing with Demons*
CRAIG SHAW GARDNER

Her eyes were wide and intent. Without modesty and without invitation, they explored him. He saw again that curious expression of amazement below the surface of her eyes. He could not explain to himself what she represented. His heart hitting his breastbone, the sound of blood in his ears like the sea, he thought, *Why did I not meet you somewhere, sometime else? Not now, like this. Why now?*

—*The Dry Season*
TANITH LEE

Flashing Swords! No. 5:
DEMONS AND DAGGERS

Edited, with an Introduction
and notes, by Lin Carter

RECENT BOOKS BY LIN CARTER

Tara of the Twilight
Zanthodon
Lost Worlds (short stories)
The Year's Best Fantasy Stories 6 (Editor)
Weird Tales #1 (Editor)
Weird Tales #2 (Editor)
Hurok of the Stone Age
Weird Tales #3 (Editor)
Darya of the Bronze Age
Mysteries of the Worm (Editor)
Flashing Swords! #5 (Editor)

Flashing Swords! No. 5:

DEMONS AND DAGGERS

Edited by Lin Carter

A DELL BOOK

Published by
Dell Publishing Co., Inc.
1 Dag Hammarskjold Plaza
New York, New York 10017

Dell ® TM 681510, Dell Publishing Co., Inc.

ISBN: 0-440-12590-1

Printed in the United States of America

First printing—December 1981

Contents

Where Magic Reigns

This is the fifth volume I have edited in the *Flashing Swords!* sequence; like its predecessors, it is made up of brand-new tales especially commissioned for this book of Sword & Sorcery by some of the best living writers in the field.

For this fifth volume, my editor at Dell, Jim Frenkel, suggested I do something a little different. The previous volumes had been composed of stories written by members of SAGA, the private club of Sword & Sorcery writers. It was Jim's idea that I solicit stories for #5 from writers who have not yet become members of the club. So, herein, you will find new tales by such extraordinary fantasy writers as Tanith Lee, Craig Shaw Gardner, Diane Duane, C. J. Cherryh and Roger Zelazny. And terrific stories they are, I can promise you!

Incidentally, Sword & Sorcery, if you happen not to have yet encountered the term, describes a special province of fantasy literature that pits heroes of one sort or another against the forces of supernatural evil. The genre was originally founded by Robert E. Howard, with his famous tales of King Kull and Conan the Barbarian, and originally consisted pretty largely of pulp-style action stories laid in imaginary prehistoric fantasy kingdoms. But with the advent into the field of such unpredictable talents as Jack Vance, for instance, and Avram Davidson, that definition broadened in scope to include stories in which, instead of the burly barbarian as hero, we have elderly magicians, sly thieves, old women, even children. (And they aren't all *heroes*, either.)

I've long since given up trying to figure out why I prefer such fantasies to other kinds of fiction. It's not that I disapprove of social realism or science fiction or the formal historical or the mystery yarn or anything else. Perhaps it is quite simply that in the imaginary-world fantasy, the author has the widest possible room to swing his imagination: he can invent worlds where magic works and the hard sciences just plain don't; worlds ruled by gods or wizards or elves; flat worlds, hollow worlds, worlds that are real only in dream. In other words, Sword & Sorcery gives the broadest conceivable scope to the playfully inventive imagination. Maybe that's why I like it best.

It would seem, happily, that I am very far from being alone in my preference. For this sort of fantasy has become enormously popular in recent years, and even science-fiction writers (like John Brunner and Roger Zelazny and Chip Delaney and Larry Niven) are venturing across its shadowy borders. And even more happily, the enthusiasm of the audience remains insatiable for such tales when they are truly well done.

As in the five new stories that follow . . .

—LIN CARTER

Tower of Ice

by Roger Zelazny

I suppose that Roger Zelazny is best known for his, brilliant science fiction, such as the Hugo-winning novel *Lord of Light;* but he first came to our attention, back in the early 1960s, with a strangely powerful series of short fantasies in the magazine *Fantastic.* I refer to the Tales of Dilvish.

These were essentially Sword & Sorcery, of course, but they were certainly Sword & Sorcery of a different breed from anything that had been published in the genre up to that time. Written with crisp, taut economy, they were laconic rather than fulsome, sharp rather than lushly colorful, and each tale was informed with an originality of scene, character, situation and style that was exciting.

Zelazny soon moved into science fiction and very quickly rose to the forefront of practitioners of the craft. But in recent years he has returned again and again to chronicling the adventures of Dilvish, with such superb tales as the major novella that follows . . .

TOWER OF ICE

The dark, horse-shaped beast paused on the icy trail. Head turned to the left and upward, it regarded the castle atop the glistening mountain, as did its rider.

"No," the man finally stated.

The black beast continued on, ice cracking beneath its cloven metal hoofs, snow blowing about it.

"I'm beginning to suspect that there is no trail," the beast announced after a time. "We've come more than halfway around."

"I know," replied the muffled, green-booted rider. "I might be able to scale the thing, but that would mean leaving you behind."

"Risky," his mount replied. "You know my value in certain situations—especially the one you court."

"True. But if it should prove the only way . . ."

They moved on for some time, pausing periodically to study the prominence.

"Dilvish, there was a gentler part of the slope—some distance back," the beast announced. "If I'd a good start, I could bear you quite a distance up it. Not all of the way to the top, but near."

"If that should prove the only way, Black, we'll go that route," the rider replied, breath steaming before him to be whipped away by the wind. "We might as well check further first, though. Hello! What is—"

A dark form came hurtling down the side of the mountain. When it seemed that it was about to strike the ice before them, it spread pale green, batlike wings and pulled itself aloft. It circled quickly, gaining altitude, then dove toward them.

Immediately his blade was in his hand, held vertically before him. Dilvish leaned back, eyes on the approaching creature. At the sight of his weapon, it veered off, to return again. He swung at it and missed. It darted away again.

"Obviously our presence is no longer a secret," Black commented, turning so as to face the flying thing.

The creature dove once more, and Dilvish swung again. It turned at the last moment, to be struck by the side of his blade. It fell then, fluttered, rose into the air again, circled several times, climbed higher, turned away. It began to fly back up along the side of the tower of ice.

"Yes, it would seem we have lost the advantage of surprise," Dilvish observed. "Actually I'd thought he would have noted us sooner."

He sheathed his blade.

"Let's go find that trail—if there is one."

They continued on their way about the base of the mountain.

Corpselike, the green and white face stared out of the mirror. No one stood before it to cast such an image. The high stone hall was reflected behind it; threadbare tapestries on its walls; several narrow windows; the long, heavy dining table; a candelabrum flickering at its further end. The wind made moaning noises down a nearby chimney, alternately flattening and drawing the flames in the wide fireplace.

The face seemed to be regarding the diners—a thin, dark-haired, dark-eyed young man in a black doublet lined with green, who toyed with his food and whose nervous gestures carried his fingers time and again to the heavy, black metal ring with the pale pink stone that depended from a chain about his neck; and a girl, whose hair and eyes matched the man's, whose generous mouth quirked into occasional odd, quick smiles as she ate with better appetite. She had a brown and red cloak thrown about her shoulders, its ends folded across her lap. Her eyes were not so deep-set as the man's and they did not dart as his did.

The thing in the mirror moved its pale lips.

"The time is coming," it announced in a deep, expressionless voice.

The man leaned forward and cut a piece of meat. The girl raised her wineglass. Something seemed to flutter against one of the windows for a moment.

From somewhere far up the long corridor to the girl's right, an agonized voice rang out:

"Release me! Oh, please don't do this! Please! It hurts so much!"

The girl sipped her wine.

"The time is coming," the thing in the mirror repeated.

"Ridley, would you pass the bread?" the girl asked.

"Here."

"Thank you."

She broke off a piece and dipped it into the gravy. The man watched her eat, as if fascinated by the act.

"The time is coming," the thing said again.

Suddenly Ridley slapped the table. His cutlery rattled. Beads of wine fell across his plate.

"Reena, can't you shut that damned thing off?" he asked.

"Why, you summoned it," she said sweetly. "Can't you just wave your wand or snap your fingers and give it the proper words—?"

He slapped the table again, half-rising from his seat.

"I will not be mocked!" he said. "Shut it off!"

She shook her head slowly. "Not my sort of magic," she replied, less sweetly. "I don't fool with things like that."

From up the hall came more cries: "It hurts! Oh, please! It hurts so . . ."

"—Or that," she said more sternly. "Besides, you told me at the time that it was serving a useful purpose."

Ridley lowered himself into his seat.

"I was not—myself," he said softly, taking up his wineglass and draining it.

A mummy-faced individual in dark livery immediately rushed forward from the shadowy corner beside the fireplace to refill his glass.

Faintly and from a great distance there came a rattling, as of chains. A shadowy form fluttered against a different window. Ridley fingered his neck chain and drank again.

"The time is coming," announced the corpse-colored face under glass.

Ridley hurled his wineglass at it. It shattered, but the mirror remained intact. Perhaps the faintest of smiles touched the corners of that ghastly mouth. The servant hurried to bring him another glass.

There came more cries from up the hall.

"It's no good," Dilvish stated. "We've more than circled it. I don't see any easy way up."

"You know how sorcerers can be. Especially this one."

"True."

"You should have asked that werewolf you met awhile back about it."

"Too late now. If we just keep going, we should come to that slope you mentioned pretty soon, shouldn't we?"

"Eventually," Black replied, trudging on. "I could use a bucket of demonjuice. I'd even settle for wine."

"I wish I had some wine here myself. I haven't sighted that flying thing again." He looked up into the darkening sky to where the snow- and ice-decked castle stood with a high window illuminated. "Unless I've glimpsed it darting about up there," he said. "Hard to tell, with the snow and shadows."

"Strange that he didn't send something a lot more deadly."

"I've thought of that."

They continued on for a long while. The lines of the slope softened as they advanced, the icy wall dipping toward a slightly gentler inclination. Dilvish recognized the area as one they had passed before, though Black's earlier hoofprints had been completely obliterated.

"You're pretty low on supplies, aren't you?" Black asked.

"Yes."

"Then I guess we'd better do something—soon."

Dilvish studied the slope as they moved along its foot.

"It gets a little better, further ahead," Black remarked. Then, "That sorcerer we met—Strodd—had the right idea."

"What do you mean?"

"He headed south. I hate this cold."

"I didn't realize it bothered you, too."

"It's a lot hotter where I come from."

"Would you rather be back there?"

"Now that you mention it, no."

Several minutes later they rounded an icy mass. Black halted and turned his head. "That's the route I'd choose—over there. You can judge it best from here."

Dilvish followed the slope upward with his eyes. It reached about three-quarters of the way up to the castle. Above it the wall rose sheer and sharp.

"How far up do you think you can get me?" he asked.

"I'll have to stop when it goes vertical. Can you scale the rest?"

Dilvish shaded his eyes and squinted. "I don't know. It looks bad. But then so does the grade. Are you sure you can make it that far?"

Black was silent for a time, then, "No, I'm not," he said. "But we've been all the way around, and this is the only place where I think we've got a chance."

Dilvish lowered his eyes.

"What do you say?"

"Let's do it."

"I don't see how you can sit there eating like that!" Ridley declared, throwing down his knife. "It's disgusting!"

"One must keep up one's strength in the face of calamities," Reena replied, taking another mouthful. "Besides, the food is exceptionally good tonight. Which one prepared it?"

"I don't know. I can't tell the staff apart. I just give them orders."

"The time is coming," stated the mirror.

Something fluttered against the window again and stopped, hanging there, a dark outline. Reena sighed, lowered her utensils, rose. She rounded the table and crossed to the window.

"I am not going to open the window in weather like this!" she shouted. "I told you that before! If you want to come in, you can fly down one of the chimneys! Or not, as you please!"

She listened a moment to a rapid chittering noise from beyond the pane.

"No, not just this once!" she said then. "I told you that before you went out in it!"

She turned and stalked back to her seat, her shadow dancing on a tapestry as the candles flickered.

"Oh, don't . . . Please, don't . . . Oh!" came a cry from up the hall.

She settled into her chair once more, ate a final mouthful, took another sip of wine.

"We've got to do something," Ridley said, stroking the ring on the chain. "We can't just sit here."

"I'm quite comfortable," she answered.

"You're in this as much as I am."

"Hardly."

"He's not going to look at it that way."

"I wouldn't be too sure."

Ridley snorted. "Your charms won't save you from the reckoning."

She protruded her lower lip in a mock pout. "On top of everything else, you insult my femininity."

"You're pushing me, Reena!"

"You know what to do about it, don't you?"

"No!" He slammed his fist against the table. "I won't!"

"The time is coming," said the mirror.

He covered his face with his hands and lowered his head. "I—I'm afraid . . ." he said softly.

Now out of his sight, a look of concern tightened her brow, narrowed her eyes.

"I'm afraid of—the other," he said.

"Can you think of any other course?"

"You do something! You've got powers!"

"Not on that level," she said. "The other is the only one I can think of who would have a chance."

"But he's untrustworthy! I can't anticipate him anymore!"

"But he gets stronger all the time. Soon he may be strong enough."

"I—I don't know . . ."

"Who got us into this mess?"

"That's not fair!"

He lowered his hands and raised his head just as a rattling began within the chimney. Particles of soot and mortar fell upon the flames.

"Oh, really!" she said.

"That crazy old bat—" he began, turning his head.

"Now that isn't nice either," Reena stated. "After all—"

Ashes were scattered as a small body crashed into the flaming logs, bounced away, hopped about the floor flapping long, green, membranous wings, beating sparks from its body fur. It was the size of a small ape, with a shriveled, nearly human face. It squeaked as it hopped, some of its noises sounding strangely like human curses. Finally it came to a stooped standstill, raised its head, turned burning eyes upon them.

". . . Try to set fire to me!" it chirped shrilly.

"Come on now! Nobody tried to set fire to you," Reena said.

". . . Said 'chimney'!" it cried.

"There are plenty of chimneys up there," Reena stated. "It's pretty stupid to choose a smoking one."

". . . Not stupid!"

"What else can you call it?"

The creature sniffed several times.

"I'm sorry," Reena said. "But you could have been more careful."

"The time is coming," said the mirror.

The creature turned its small head, stuck out its tongue. ". . . Lot you know," it said. "He . . . He beat me!"

"Who? Who beat you?" Ridley asked.

". . . The avenger." It made a sweeping, downward gesture with its right wing. ". . . He's down there."

"Oh, my!" Ridley paled. "You're quite certain?"

". . . He beat me," the creature repeated. Then it began to bounce along the floor, beat at the air with its wings and flew to the center of the table.

Somewhere, faintly, a chain was rattled.

"How—how do you know he is the avenger?" Ridley asked.

The creature hopped along the table, tore at the bread with its talons, stuffed a piece into its mouth, chewed noisily.

". . . My little ones, my pretty ones," it chanted after a time, glancing about the hall.

"Stop that!" Reena said. "Answer his question! How do you know who it is?"

It raised its wings to its ears. "Don't shout! Don't shout!" it cried. ". . . I saw! I know! He beat me— poor side!—with a sword!" It paused to hug itself with its wings. ". . . I only went to look up close. My eyes are not so good . . . He rides a demon-beast! Circling, circling—the mountain! Coming, coming—here!"

Ridley shot a look at Reena. She compressed her lips, then shook her head.

"Unless it is airborne it will never make it up the tower," she said. "It wasn't a winged beast, was it?"

". . . No. A horse," the creature replied, tearing at the bread again.

"There was a slide near the south face," Ridley said. "But no. Even so. Not with a horse . . ."

". . . A demon-horse."

"Even with a demon-horse!"

"The pain! The pain! I can't stand it!" came a shrill cry.

Reena raised her wineglass, saw that it was empty, lowered it again. The mummy-faced man rushed from the shadows to fill it.

For several moments they watched the winged creature eat. Then, "I don't like this," Reena said. "You know how devious he can be."

"I know."

". . . . And green boots," chirped the creature. ". . . Elfboots. Always to land on his feet. You burned me, he beat me . . . Poor Meg! Poor Meg! He'll get you, too . . ."

It hopped down and skittered across the floor. ". . . My little ones, my pretty ones!" it called.

"Not here! Get out of here!" Ridley cried. "Change or go away! Keep them out of here!"

". . . Little ones! Pretties!" came the fading voice as Meg ran up the corridor in the direction of the screams.

Reena swirled the wine in her glass, took a drink, licked her lips.

"The time has come," the mirror suddenly announced.

"Now what are you going to do?" Reena asked.

"I don't feel well," Ridley said.

When they came to the foot of the slope, Black halted and stood like a statue for a long while, studying it. The snow continued to fall. The wind drove the flakes past them.

After several minutes Black advanced and tested the grade, climbing several paces, standing with his full weight upon it, stamping and digging with his hoofs, head lowered.

Finally he backed down the slope and turned away.

"What is the verdict?" Dilvish inquired.

"I am still willing to try. My estimate of our chances is unchanged. Have you given any thought to what you are going to do if—rather, when—you make it to the top?"

"Look for trouble," Dilvish said. "Defend myself at all times. Strike instantly if I see the enemy."

Black began to walk slowly away from the mountain.

"Almost all of your spells are of the offensive variety," Black stated, "and most are too terrible to be used, except in final extremes. You should really take the time to learn some lesser and intermediate ones, you know."

"I know. This is a fine time for a lecture on the state of the art."

"What I am trying to say is that if you get trapped up there, you know how to level the whole damned place and yourself with it. But you don't know how to charm the lock on a door—"

"That is *not* a simple spell!"

"No one said that it was. I am merely pointing out your deficiencies."

"It is a little late for that, isn't it?"

"I am afraid so," Black replied. "So, there are three good general spells of protection against magical attack. You know as well as I do that your enemy can break through any of them. The stronger ones, though, might slow him long enough for you to do something. I can't let you go up there without one of them holding you."

"Then lay the strongest upon me."

"It takes a full day to do it."

Dilvish shook his head. "In this cold? Too long. What about the others?"

"The first one we may dismiss as insufficient against any decent operator in the arts. The second takes the better part of an hour to call into being. It will give you good protection for about half a day."

Dilvish was silent for a moment. Then, "Let's be about it," he said.

"All right. But even so, there must be servants, to keep the place running. You are probably going to find yourself physically outnumbered."

Dilvish shrugged. "It may not be much of a staff," he said, "and there'd be no need to maintain a great guard in an inaccessible spot like this. I'll take my chances."

Black came to the place he deemed sufficiently distant from the slope. He turned and faced the tower.

"Get your rest now, then," he stated, "while I work your protection. It will probably be the last you have for a while."

Dilvish sighed and leaned forward. Black began speaking in a strange voice. His words seemed to crackle in the icy air.

* * *

The latest scream ceased on a weakened note. Ridley got to his feet and moved across the hall to a window. He rubbed at the frosted pane with the palm of his hand, a quick, circular motion. He placed his face near the area he had cleared, holding his breath.

Finally, "What do you see?" Reena asked him.

"Snow," he muttered, "ice . . ."

"Anything else?"

"My reflection," he answered angrily, turning away.

He began to pace. When he passed the face in the mirror, its lips moved.

"The time is come," it said.

He replied with an obscenity. He continued pacing, hands clasped behind his back.

"You think Meg really saw something down there?" he asked.

"Yes. Even the mirror has changed its tune."

"What do you think it is?"

"A man on a strange mount."

"Perhaps he's not actually coming here. Maybe he's on his way someplace else."

She laughed softly. "Just on his way to the neighborhood tavern for a few drinks," she said.

"All right! All right! I'm not thinking clearly! I'm upset! Supposing—just supposing—he does make it up here. He's only one man."

"With a sword. When was the last time you had one in your hands?"

Ridley licked his lips.

"And he most be fairly sturdy," she said, "to have come so far across these wastes."

"There are the servants. They obey me. Since they

are already dead, he'd have a hard time killing them."

"That would tend to follow. On the other hand, they're a bit slower and clumsier than ordinary folk—and they can be dismembered."

"You don't do much to cheer a man up, you know."

"I am trying to be realistic. If there is a man out there wearing elfboots, he has a chance of making it up here. If he is of the hardy sort and a decent swordsman, then he has a chance of doing what he was sent to do."

"And you'll still be mocking and bitching while he lops off my head! Just remember that yours will roll, too!"

She smiled. "I am in no way responsible for what happened."

"Do you really think he'll see it that way? Or care?"

She looked away.

"You had a chance," she said slowly, "to be one of the truly great ones. But you wouldn't follow the normal courses of development. You were greedy for power. You rushed things. You took risks. You created a doubly dangerous situation. You could have explained the sealing as an experiment that went bad. You could have apologized. He would have been irritated, but he would have accepted it. Now, though, when you can't undo what you did—or do much of anything else, for that matter—he is going to know what happened. He is going to know that you were trying to multiply your power to the point where you could even challenge him. You know what his response has to be under the circumstances. I can almost sympathize with him. If it were me, I would have to do the same thing—destroy you before you get control of the other. You've become an extremely dangerous man."

"But I am powerless! There isn't a damned thing I can do! Not even shut off that simple mirror!" he cried, gesturing toward the face, which had just spoken again. "In this state I'm no threat to anybody!"

"Outside of his being inconvenienced by your having cut off his access to one of his strongholds," she said, "he would have to consider the possibility that you keep drawing back from—namely that if you gain control of the other, you will be one of the most powerful sorcerers in the world. As his apprentice—pardon me, ex-apprentice—who has just apparently usurped a part of his domain, only one thing can follow—a sorcerous duel in which you will actually have a chance of destroying him. Since such a duel has not yet commenced, he must have guessed that you are not ready—or that you are playing some sort of waiting game. So he has sent a human avenger rather than run the risk that you've turned this place into some sort of magical trap."

"The whole thing could simply have been an accident. He'd have to consider that possibility, too . . ."

"Under the circumstances, would *you* take the risk of assuming that and waiting? You know the answer. You'd dispatch an assassin."

"I've been a good servant. I've taken care of this place for him . . ."

"Be sure to petition him for mercy on that count the next time you see him."

Ridley halted and wrung his hands. "Perhaps you could seduce him. You're comely enough . . ."

Reena smiled again. "I'd lay him on an iceberg and not complain," she said. "If it would get us off the hook, I'd give him the high ride of his long life. But a sorcerer like that—"

"Not him. The avenger."

"Oh." She blushed suddenly. Then she shook her head.

"I can't believe that anyone who has come all this way could be dissuaded from his purposes by a bit of dalliance, even with someone of my admitted charms. Not to mention the thought of the penalty for his failure. No. You are skirting the real issue again. There is only one way out for you, and you know what that is."

He dropped his eyes, fingered the ring on the chain.

"The other . . ." he said. "If I had control of the other, all of our problems would be over . . ."

He stared at the ring as if hypnotized by it.

"That's right," she said. "It's the only real chance."

"But you know what I fear . . ."

"Yes. I fear it, too."

". . . That it may not work—that the other may gain control of *me*!"

"So, either way you are doomed? Just remember, one way it is certain. The other . . . That way there is still a chance."

"Yes," he said, still not looking at her. "But you don't know the horror of it!"

"I can guess."

"But you don't have to go through it!"

"I didn't create the situation, either."

He glared at her. "I'm sick of hearing you protest your innocence just because the other is not your creation! I went to you first and told you everything I proposed to do! Did you try to talk me out of it? No!

You saw the gains in store for us! You went along with my doing it!"

She covered her mouth with her fingertips and yawned delicately.

"Brother," she said, "I suppose that you are right. It doesn't change anything, though, does it? Anything that has to be done. . . ?"

He gnashed his teeth and turned away. "I won't do it. I can't!"

"You may feel differently about it when he comes knocking at your door."

"We have plenty of ways to deal with a single man—even a skilled swordsman!"

"But don't you see? Even if you succeed you are only postponing the decision, not solving the problem."

"I want the time. Maybe I can think of some way to gain an edge over the other."

Reena's features softened. "Do you really believe that?"

"Anything is possible, I suppose . . ."

She sighed and stood. She moved toward him. "Ridley, you are deceiving yourself," she said. "You will never be any stronger than you are now."

"Not true!" he cried, beginning to pace again. "Not true!"

Another scream came from up the hall. The mirror repeated its message.

"Stop him! We have to stop him! *Then* I'll worry about the other!"

He turned and tore out of the room. Reena lowered the hand she had raised toward him and returned to the table to finish her wine. The fireplace continued to sigh.

*　　*　　*

Black completed the spell. They remained motionless for a brief while after that.

Then, "That's it?" Dilvish asked.

"It is. You are now protected through the second level."

"I don't feel any different."

"That's how you should feel."

"Is there anything special that I should do to invoke its defense, should the need arise?"

"No, it is entirely automatic. But do not let that dissuade you from exercising normal caution about things magical. Any system has its weak points. But that was the best I could do in the time that we had."

Dilvish nodded and looked toward the tower of ice. Black raised his head and faced it also.

"Then I guess that all of the preliminaries are out of the way," Dilvish said.

"So it would seem. Are you ready?"

"Yes."

Black began to move forward. Glancing down, Dilvish noted that his hoofs seemed larger now, flatter. He wanted to ask about it, but the wind came faster as they gained speed and he decided to save his breath. The snow stung his cheeks, his hands. He squinted and leaned further forward.

Still running on a level surface, Black's pace increased steadily, one hoof giving an almost bell-like tone as it struck some pebble. Soon they were moving faster than any horse could run. Everything on both sides became a snowy blur. Dilvish tried not to look ahead, to protect his eyes, his face. He clung tightly and thought about the course he had come.

He had escaped from Hell itself, after two centuries' torment. Most of the humans he had known were long dead, and the world somewhat changed.

Yet the one who had banished him, damning him as he did, remained—the ancient sorcerer Jelerak. In the months since his return, he had sought that one, once the call of an ancient duty had been discharged before the walls of Portaroy. Now, he told himself, he lived but for vengeance. And this, this tower of ice, one of the seven strongholds of Jelerak, was the closest he had yet come to his enemy. From Hell he had brought a collection of Awful Sayings—spells of such deadly potency as to place the speaker in as great jeopardy as the victim should their rendering be even slightly less than flawless. He had only used one since his return and had been successful in leveling an entire small city with it. His shudder was for the memory of that day on that hilltop rather than for the icy blasts that now assailed him.

A shift in equilibrium told him that Black had reached the slope and commenced the ascent. The wind was making a roaring sound. His head was bowed and turned against the icy pelting. He could feel the rapid crunching of Black's hoofs beneath him, steady, all of the movements extraordinarily powerful. If Black should slip, he knew that it would be all over for him . . . goodbye again, world—and Jelerak still unpunished . . .

As the gleaming surface fled by beneath him, he tried to push all thoughts of Jelerak and death and vengeance from his mind. As he listened to the wind and cracking ice, his thoughts came free of the moment, drifting back over the unhappy years, past the days of his campaigns, his wanderings, coming to rest on a misty morning in the glades of far Elfland as he rode to the hunt near the Castle Mirata. The sun was big and golden, the breezes cool, and everywhere— green. He could almost smell the earth, feel the texture of tree bark . . . Would he ever know that again, the way that he once had?

An inarticulate cry escaped him, hurled against the wind and destiny and the task he had set himself. He cursed then and squeezed harder with his legs as his equilibrium shifted again and he knew that the course had steepened.

Black's hoofs pounded perhaps a trifle more slowly. Dilvish's hands and feet and face were growing numb. He wondered how far up they were. He risked a glance forward but saw only rushing snow. We've come a long way, he decided. Where will it end?

He called back his memory of the slope as seen from below, tried to judge their position. Surely they were near the halfway point. Perhaps they had even passed it.

He counted his heartbeats, counted Black's hoof falls. Yes, it did seem that the great beast was slowing.

He chanced another look ahead.

This time he caught the barest glimpse of the towering rise above and before him, sparkling through the evening, sheer, glassy. It obliterated most of the sky now, so he knew that they must be close.

Black continued to slow. The roaring wind lowered its voice. The snow came against him with slightly diminished force.

He looked back over his shoulder. He could see the great slope spread out behind them, glistening like the mosaic tiles in the baths of Ankyra. Down, down and back . . . They *had* come a great distance.

Black slowed even more. Now Dilvish could hear as well as feel the crunching of crusted snow and ice beneath them. He eased his grip slightly, leaned back a little, raised his head. There was the last stage of the tower, glistening darkly, much nearer now.

Abruptly the winds ceased. The monolith must be blocking them, he decided. The snow drifted far more gently here. Black's pace had become a canter, though he was laboring no less diligently than before. The journey up the white-smeared tunnel was nearing its end.

Dilvish adjusted his position again to better study the high escarpment. At this quarter its surface had resolved itself into a thing of textures. From the play of shadow he could make out prominences, crevices. Bare rock jutted in numerous places. Quickly he began tracing possible routes to the top..

Black slowed further, almost to a walk, but they now were near to the place where the greatest steepness began. Dilvish cast about for a stopping point.

"What do you think of that ledge off to the right, Black?" he asked.

"Not much," came the reply, "but that's where we're headed. The trickiest part will be making it up onto the shelf. Don't let go yet."

Dilvish clung tightly as Black negotiated a hundred paces, a hundred more.

"It looks wider from here than it did from back there," he observed.

"Yes. Higher, too. Hang on. If we slip here it's a long way back down."

Black's pace increased slightly as he approached the ledge that stood at nearly the height of a man above the slope. It was indented several spans into the cliff face.

Black leaped.

His hind hoofs struck a waist-high prominence, a bare wrinkle of icy rock running horizontally below the ledge. His momentum bore him up past it. It cracked and fell away, but by then his forelegs were on the shelf and his rear ones had straightened with a tiny spring. He scrambled up over the ledge and found his footing.

"You all right?" he asked.

"Yes," said Dilvish.

Simultaneously they turned their heads, slowly, and looked back down to where the winds whipped billows of white like clouds of smoke across the sparkling way. Dilvish reached out and patted Black's shoulder.

"Well done," he said. "Here and there, I was a little worried."

"Did you think you were the only one?"

"No. Can we make it back down again?"

Black nodded. "We'll have to move a lot more slowly than we did coming up, though. You may even have to walk beside me, holding on. We'll see. This ledge seems to go back a little way. I'll explore it while you are about your business. There may be a slighly better route down. It should be easier to tell from up here."

"All right," Dilvish said, dismounting on the side nearest the cliff face.

He removed his gloves and massaged his hands, blew on them, tucked them into his armpits for a time.

"Have you decided upon the place for your ascent?"

"Off to the left." Dilvish gestured with his head. "That crevice runs most of the way up and it is somewhat irregular on both sides."

"Looks to be a good choice. How will you get to it?"

"I'll begin climbing here. These handholds look good enough. I'll meet it at that first big break."

Dilvish unfastened his sword belt, slung his blade over his back. He chafed his hands again, then drew on his gloves.

"I might as well get started," he said. "Thanks, Black. I'll be seeing you."

"Good thing you're wearing those elfboots," Black said. "If you slip you know that you'll land on your feet—eventually."

Dilvish snorted and reached for the first handhold.

Wearing a dark dress, wrapped in a green shawl, the crone sat upon a small stool in the corner of the long underground chamber. Torches flamed and smoked in two wall sockets, melting, above and behind them, portions of the icy glaze that covered the walls and the ceiling. An oil lamp burned near her feet on the strawstrewn stone of the floor. She hummed to herself, fondling one of the loaves she bore in her shawl.

Across from her were three heavy wooden doors bound with straps of rusted metal, small, barred windows set high within them. A few faint sounds of movement emerged from the one in the middle, but she was oblivious to this. The water that dripped from the irregular stone ceiling above the torches had formed small pools that spread into the straw and lost their boundaries. The dripping sounds kept syncopated accompaniment to her crooning.

" . . . My little ones, my pretty ones," she sang. ". . . Come to Meg. Come to Mommy Meg."

There was a scurrying noise in the straw in the dim corner near the lefthand door. Hastily she broke off a piece of bread and tossed it in that direction. There followed a fresh rustling and a small movement. She nodded, rocked back on her seat and smiled.

From across the way—possibly from behind the middle door—there came a low moan. She cocked her head for a moment, but it was followed by silence.

She cast another piece of bread into the same corner. The sounds that followed were more rapid, more pronounced. The straw rose and fell. She threw another piece, puckered her lips and made a small chirping noise.

She threw more.

". . . My little ones," she sang again, as over a dozen rats moved nearer, springing upon the bread, tearing at it, swallowing it. More emerged from dark places to join them, to contest for the food. Isolated squeaks occurred, increased in frequency, gradually merged into a chorus.

She chuckled. She threw more bread, nearer. Thirty or forty rats now fought over it.

From behind the middle door came a clinking of chain links, followed by another moan. Her attention, though, was on her little ones.

She leaned forward and moved the lamp to a position near the wall to her right. She broke another loaf and scattered its pieces on the floor before her feet. Small bodies rustled over the straw, approaching. The squeaking grew louder.

There came a heavy rattling of chains, a much louder moan. Something moved within the cell and crashed against the door. It rattled, and another moan rose above the noises of the rats.

She turned her head in that direction, frowning slightly.

The next blow upon the door made a booming

sound. For a moment something like a massive eye seemed to peer out past the bars.

The moaning sound came again, almost seeming to shape itself into words.

". . . Meg! Meg . . ."

She half-rose from her seat, staring at the cell door. The next crash—the loudest thus far—rattled it heavily. By then the rats were brushing against her legs, standing upon their hind paws, dancing. She reached out to stroke one, another . . . She fed them from her hands.

From within the cell the moaning rose again, this time working itself into strange patterns.

". . . Mmmmegg . . . Mmeg . . ." came the sound.

She raised her head once more and looked in that direction. She moved as if about to rise.

Just then, however, a rat jumped into her lap. Another ran up her back and perched upon her right shoulder.

"Pretty ones . . ." she said, rubbing her cheek against the one and stroking the other. "Pretty . . ."

There came a sound as of the snapping of a chain, followed by a terrific crash against the door across from her. She ignored it, however, for her pretty ones were dancing and playing for her.

Reena drew garment after garment from her wardrobe. Her room was full of dresses and cloaks, mufflers and hats, coats and boots, underthings and gloves. They lay across the bed and all of the chairs and two wall benches.

Shaking her head, she turned in a slow circle, surveying the lot. The second time around she withdrew a dress from one of the heaps and draped it over her left arm. Then she took a heavy fur wrap down from a hook. She handed both to the tall, sallow, silent man who stood beside the door. His heavily wrinkled face resembled that of the man who had served her dinner—expressionless, vacant-eyed.

He received the garments from her and began folding them. She passed him a second dress, a hat, hose and underthings. Gloves . . . He accepted two heavy blankets she took down from a shelf. More hose . . . He placed everything within a dufflelike sack.

"Bring it along—and one empty one," she said, and she moved toward the door.

She passed through and crossed the hallway to a stair, which she began to descend. The servant followed her, holding the sack by its neck with one hand before him. He bore another one, folded, beneath his other arm, which hung stiffly at his side.

Reena made her way through corridors to a large, deserted kitchen, where a fire still smoldered beneath a grate. The wind made a whistling noise down the chimney.

She passed the large chopping block and turned left into the pantry. She checked shelves, bins and cabinets, pausing only to munch a cookie as she looked.

"Give me the bag," she said. "No, not that one. The empty one."

She shook out the bag and began filling it with dried meats, heads of cheese, wine bottles, loaves of bread. Pausing, she looked about again, then added a sack of tea and a sack of sugar. She also put in a small pot and some utensils.

"Bring this one, too," she said finally, turning and leaving the pantry.

She moved more cautiously now, the servant treading silently at her heels, a bag in either hand. She paused and listened at corners and stairwells before moving on. The only things she heard, though, were the screams from far above.

At length she came to a long, narrow stair leading down, vanishing into the darkness.

"Wait," she said softly, and she raised her hands, cupping them before her face, blowing gently upon them, staring at them.

A faint spark occurred between her palms, faded, grew again as she whispered soft words over it.

She drew her hands apart, her lips still moving. The tiny light hung in the air before her, growing in size, increasing in brilliance. It was blue-white, and it reached the intensity of several candles.

She uttered a final word and it began to move, drifting before her down the stairwell. She followed it. The servant followed her.

They descended for a long while. The stair spiraled down, with no terminus in sight. The light seemed to lead them. The walls grew damp, cold, colder, coming to be covered with a fine patina of frost figures. She drew her cloak further forward over her shoulders. The minutes passed.

Finally they reached a landing. Distant walls were barely visible in the blackness beyond her light. She turned to her left, and the light moved to precede her.

They passed through a long corridor that sloped gently downward, coming after a time to another stair at a place where the walls widened on either hand and the rocky ceiling maintained its level, to vanish from sight as they descended.

The full dimensions of the chamber into which

they came were not discernible. It seemed more a cavern than a room. The floor was less regular than any over which they had so far passed, and it was by far the coldest spot they had yet come to.

Holding her cloak fully closed before her now, hands beneath it, Reena proceeded into the chamber, moving diagonally to her right.

Finally a large, boxlike sled came into view, a waxy rag hanging from the point of its left runner. It stood near the wall at the mouth of a tunnel through which an icy wind roared. The light came to hover above it.

Reena halted and turned to the servant.

"Put them in there," she said, gesturing, "toward the front."

She sighed as this was done, then leaned forward and covered them over with a pelt of white fur, which had lain folded upon the vehicle's seat.

"All right," she said, turning away, "we'd better be getting back now."

She pointed in the direction from which they had come, and the floating light moved to follow her finger.

In the circular room at the top of the highest tower, Ridley turned the pages in one of the great books. The wind howled like a banshee above the pitched roof, which sometimes vibrated with the force of its passage. The entire tower even had a barely perceptible sway to it.

Ridley muttered softly to himself as he fingered the leather binding, casting his eyes down the creamy sheets. The chain with the ring on it now rested atop a small chest of drawers by the wall near the door. A high, narrow mirror above it caught their image, the stone glowing palely within it.

Still muttering, he turned a page, then another, and paused. He closed his eyes for a moment, then turned away, leaving the book on the reading stand. He moved to the exact center of the room and stood there for a long while, at the middle of a red diagram drawn upon the floor. He continued to mutter.

He turned abruptly and walked to the chest of drawers. He picked up the ring and chain. He unfastened the chain and removed it.

Holding the ring between the thumb and forefinger of his right hand, he extended his left forefinger and quickly slipped the ring over it. He withdrew it almost immediately and took a deep breath. He regarded his reflection in the mirror. Quickly he slipped the ring on again, and after several moments withdrew it again, more slowly.

He turned the ring and studied it. Its stone seemed to shine a little more brightly now. He fitted it over his finger once more, withdrew it, paused, refitted it, withdrew it, refitted it, paused, withdrew it, replaced it, paused longer, slowly slid it partway off, then back again.

Had he been looking ahead into the mirror, he might have noticed that each manipulation of the ring caused a change in expression to flit across his face. He cycled between bafflement and pleasure, fear and satisfaction as the ring came on and off.

He slipped it off again and placed it atop the chest. He massaged his finger. He glanced at himself in the mirror, looked back down, staring deep into the depths of the stone. He licked his lips.

He turned away, walked several paces across the pattern, halted. He turned and looked back at the

ring. He returned and picked it up, weighing it in
the palm of his right hand.

He placed it on his finger again and stood there
wearing it, still gripping it tightly with the fingers of
his other hand. This time his teeth were clenched and
his brow furrowed.

As he stood there, the mirror clouded and a new
image began to take shape within it. Rock and snow
. . . Some sort of movement across it . . . A man
. . . The man was crawling through the snow
. . . No.

The man's hands grasped at holds. He drew himself upward, not forward! He was climbing, not
crawling!

The picture came clearer.

As the man drew himself up and located a fresh
foothold, Ridley saw that he had on green boots.
Then . . .

He snapped an order. There was a distancing effect. The man grew smaller, the cliff face wider and
higher. There, above the climbing man, stood the
castle, this castle, his own light gleaming through this
tower window!

With a curse he tore the ring from his finger. The
picture immediately faded, to be replaced by his own
angry expression.

"No!" he cried, striding to the door and unfastening it. "No!"

He flung the door open and tore off down the
winding stair.

Dilvish rested for a time, back and legs braced
against the sides of the rock chimney, gloves in his
lap, blowing on his hands, rubbing them. The chimney ended a small distance above his head. There

would be no more resting after this until he reached the top, and then—who could tell?

A few flakes of snow drifted past him. He searched the dark sky, as he had been doing regularly, for a return of the flying creature, but saw nothing. The thought of it catching him in a vulnerable position had caused him considerable concern.

He continued to rub his hands until they tingled, until he felt some warmth returning. Then he donned his gloves again to preserve it. He leaned his head as far back as it would go and looked upward.

He had come over two-thirds of the way up the vertical face. He sought and located his next handholds. He listened to his heartbeat, now returned to normal. Slowly, cautiously, he extended himself again, reaching.

He pushed himself upward. Leaving the chimney, he caught hold of a ledge and drew himself higher. His feet found purchase below him, and he reached again with one hand. He wondered whether Black had located a good way down. He thought of his last meal, cold and dry, almost freezing to his tongue. He recalled better fare from earlier days and felt his mouth begin to water.

He came to a slippery place, worked his way about it. He wondered at the strange feeling he had had earlier, as if someone had been watching him. He had sought in the sky hurriedly, but the flying creature had been nowhere about.

Drawing himself over a thick, rocky projection, he smiled, seeing that the wall began to slant inward above it. He found his footing and leaned into the climb.

He advanced more rapidly now, and before very long a sharp edge that could be the top came into view. He scrambled toward it as the slope increased, giving thought now to his movements immediately upon reaching it.

He drew himself up faster and faster, finally rising into a low crouch as the grade grew more gentle. Nearing what he took to be the top, he slowed again, finally casting himself flat a little more than a body length below the rim. For a time he listened, but there were no sounds other than those of the wind.

Carefully, gloves in his teeth, he drew his sword belt over an arm and shoulder, up over his head. He unfastened it and lowered it. He adjusted his garments, then fitted it in place about his waist once again.

As he approached the rim, he moved very slowly. When he finally raised his head above it his eyes were filled with the gleaming white of the castle, standing like a sugary confection not too far in the distance.

Several minutes passed as he studied the scene. Nothing moved but the snow. He looked for a side door, a low window, any indirect entrance.

When he thought he had found what he was seeking, he drew himself up over the edge and began his advance.

Meg sang to the dancing rats. The torches flickered. The walls ran wet. She teased the creatures with bits of bread. She stroked them and scratched them and chuckled over them.

There came another heavy crash against the central door. This time the wood splintered somewhat about the hinges.

"Mmeg . . . Mmeg . . . !" came from beyond it, and again the large eye appeared behind the bars.

She looked up, meeting the moist blue gaze. A troubled expression came over her face.

"Yes?" she said softly.

"Meg!"

There followed another crash. The door shuddered. Cracks appeared along its edge.

"Meg!"

Another crash. The door creaked and protruded beyond its frame, the cracks widened.

She shook her head.

"Yes?" she said more loudly, a touch of excitement coming into her voice.

The rats jumped down from her lap, her shoulders, her knees, racing back and forth across the straw.

The next crash tore the door free of its hinges, pushing it a full foot outward. A large, clawed, dead-white hand appeared about its edge, chain dangling from a metal cuff about its wrist, rattling against the wall, the door.

"Meg?"

She rose to her feet, dropping the remainder of the bread from within her shawl. A black whirlwind of furry bodies moved about it, the squeaking smothering her reply. She moved forward through it.

The door was thrust further outward. A gigantic, hairless white head with a drooping carrot of a nose looked out around it. Its neck was so thick that it seemed to reach out to the points of its wide shoulders. Its arms were as big around as a man's thighs, its skin a grease-splotched albino. It shouldered the door aside and emerged, back bent at an unnatural angle, head thrust forward, moving on legs like pillars. It wore the tatters of a shirt and the rent remains of a pair of breeches which, like their owner, had lost all color. Its blue eyes, blinking and watering against the torchlight, fixed upon Meg.

"Mack . . . ?" she said.

"Meg . . . ?"

"Mack!"

"Meg!"

She rushed to embrace the quarter-ton of snowy muscle, her own eyes growing moist as he managed to hold her gently. They mumbled softly at one another.

Finally she took hold of his huge arm with her small hand.

"Come. Come, Mack," she said. " Food for you. Warm. Be free. Come."

She led him toward the chamber's exit, her pretty ones forgotten.

Ignored, the parchment-skinned servant moved about Reena's chambers on silent feet, gathering up strewn garments, restoring them to drawers and wardrobe. Reena sat at her dressing table, brushing her hair. When the servant had finished putting the room in order, he came and stood beside her. She glanced up, looked about.

"Very good," she said. "I have no further need of you. You may return to your coffin."

The dark-liveried figure turned and departed.

Reena rose and removed a basin from beneath the bed. Taking it to her nightstand, she added some water from a blue pitcher and stood there. Moving back to her dresser, she took up one of the candles from near the mirror and transferred it to a position to the left of the basin. Then she leaned forward and stared down at the moist surface.

Images darted there. As she watched, they flowed together, fell apart, recombined . . .

The man was nearing the top. She shuddered slightly as she watched him pause to unsling his blade and fasten it about his waist. She saw him rise further, to the very edge. She saw him survey the castle for a long while. Then he drew himself up, to move across the snow. Where? Where would he seek entry?

Toward the north and coming in closer, up toward the windows of that darkened storage room in back. Of course! The snow was banked highest there, and heavily crusted. He could reach the sill, draw himself up to climb upon it. It would only be the work of a few moments to knock a hole near the latch with the hilt of his weapon, reach through and unfasten it. Then several long minutes with the blade to chip away all the ice that crusted the frame. More time to open it. Additional moments to locate the juncture of the shutters within, to slide the blade between them, lift upward, raise their latch . . . Then he would be disoriented in a dark room filled with clutter. It would take minutes more for him to negotiate that.

She blew gently upon the surface of the water, and the picture was gone among ripples. Taking up the candle, she bore it back to her dressing table, set it where it had been. She restored the basin to its former locale.

Seating herself before the mirror, she took up a tiny brush and a small metal box, to add a touch of color to her lips.

Ridley roused one of the servants and took him upstairs, to move along the corridor toward the room from which the screams still came. Halting before that door, he located the proper key upon a ring at his belt and unlocked it.

"At last!" came the voice from within. "Please! Now—"

"Shut up!" he said, and turned away, taking the servant by the arm and turning him toward the open doorway immediately across the corridor.

He pushed the servant into the darkened room.

"Off to the side," he directed. "Stand there." He guided him further. "There—where you will be out of sight of anyone coming this way but can still keep an eye on him. Now take this key and listen carefully. Should anyone come along to investigate those screams, you must be ready. As soon as he begins to open that door, you are to emerge behind him quickly, strike him and push him in through it—hard! Then close the door again quickly and lock it. After that you may return to your coffin."

Ridley left him, stepping out into the corridor, where he hesitated a moment, then stalked off in the direction of the dining hall.

"The time is come," the face in the mirror announced just as he entered.

He walked up to it, stared back at the grim visage. He took the ring into his hand and slipped it on.

"Silence!" he said. "You have served your purpose. Begone now!"

The face vanished just as its lips were beginning to form the familiar words anew, leaving Ridley to regard his own shadowy reflection surrounded by the ornate frame.

He smirked for an instant; then his face grew serious. His eyes narrowed, his image wavered. The mirror clouded and cleared again. He beheld the green-booted man standing upon a window ledge, chipping away at ice . . .

He began to twist the ring. Slowly he turned it

around and around, biting his lip the while. Then, with a jerk, he tore it from his finger and sighed deeply. The smirk returned to his reflected face.

He turned on his heel and crossed the room, where he passed through a sliding panel, a trapdoor and down a ladder. Moving rapidly down every shortcut he knew, he took his way once more to the servants' room.

Pushing the shutters aside, Dilvish stepped down into the room. A little light from the window at his back showed him something of the litter that resided there. He paused for several moments to memorize its disposition as best he could, then turned and drew the window shut, not closing it entirely. The heavily frosted panes blocked much of the light, but he did not want to risk betrayal by a telltale draft.

He moved silently along the map in his mind. He had sheathed his long blade and now held only a dagger in his hand. He stumbled once before he reached the door—against a jutting chair leg—but was moving so slowly that no noise ensued.

He inched the door open, looked at his right. A corridor, dark . . .

He stepped out into it and looked to the left. There was some light from that direction. He headed toward it. As he advanced he saw that it came from the right—either a side corridor or an open room.

The air grew warmer as he approached—the most welcome sensation he had experienced in weeks. He halted, both to listen for telltale sounds and to relish the feeling. After several moments there came the tiniest clinking from around the corner. He edged nearer and waited again. It was not repeated.

Knife held low, he stepped forward, saw that it was

the entrance to a room, saw a woman seated within it, reading a book, a glass of some beverage on the small table to her right. He looked to both the right and the left inside the doorway, saw that she was alone, stepped inside.

"You'd better not scream," he said.

She lowered her book and stared at him. "I won't," she replied. "Who are you?"

He hesitated, then, "Call me Dilvish," he said.

"My name is Reena. What do you want?"

He lowered the blade slightly. "I have come here to kill. Stay out of my way and you won't be harmed. Get in it and you will. What is your place in this household?"

She paled. She studied his face. "I am—a prisoner," she said.

"Why?"

"Our means of departure has been blocked, as has the normal means of entrance here."

"How?"

"It was an accident—of sorts. But I don't suppose you'd believe that."

"Why not? Accidents happen."

She looked at him strangely. "That is what brought you, is it not?"

He shook his head slowly. "I am afraid that I do not understand you."

"When he discovered that the mirror would no longer transport him to this place, he sent you to slay the person responsible, did he not?"

"I was not sent," Dilvish said. "I have come here of my own will and desire."

"Now it is I who do not understand you," said Reena. "You say that you have come here to kill, and

Ridley has been expecting someone to come to kill him. Naturally—"

"Who is Ridley?"

"My brother, the apprentice sorcerer who holds this place for his master."

"Your brother is apprentice to Jelerak?"

"Please! That name!"

"I am tired of whispering it! Jelerak! Jelerak! Jelerak! If you can hear me, Jelerak, come around for a closer look! I'm ready! Let's have this out!" he called.

They were both silent for several moments, as if expecting a reply or some manifestation. Nothing happened.

Finally Reena cleared her throat.

"Your quarrel, then, is entirely with the master? Not with his servant?"

"That is correct. Your brother's doings are nothing to me so long as they do not cross my own purposes. Inadvertently, perhaps, they have—if he has barred my enemy's way to this place. But I can't see that as a cause for vengeance. What is this transport mirror you spoke of? Has he broken it?"

"No," she replied, "it is physically intact. Though he might as well have broken it. He has somehow placed its transport spell in abeyance. It is a gateway used by the master. He employed it to bring himself here—and from here he could also use it to travel to any of his other strongholds, and probably to some other places as well. Ridley turned it off when he was—not himself."

"Perhaps he can be persuaded to turn it back on again. Then when Jelerak comes through to learn the cause of the trouble, I will be waiting for him."

She shook her head. "It is not that simple," she said. Then, "You must be uncomfortable, standing there in a knife-fighter's crouch. I know that it makes me uncomfortable just looking at you. Won't you sit down? Would you care for a glass of wine?"

Dilvish glanced over his shoulder. "Nothing personal," he said, "but I prefer to remain on my feet."

He sheathed his dagger, however, and moved toward the sideboard, where an open wine bottle and several glasses stood. "Is this what you are drinking?"

She smiled and rose to her feet. She crossed the room to stand beside him, where she took up the bottle and filled two glasses from it.

"Serve me one, sir."

He took up a glass and passed it to her with a courtly nod. Her eyes met his as she accepted it, raised it and drank.

He held the other glass, sniffed it, tasted it.

"Very good."

"My brother's stock," she said. "He likes the best."

"Tell me about your brother."

She turned partly and leaned back against the sideboard.

"He was chosen as apprentice from among many candidates," she said, "because he possessed great natural aptitude for the work. Are you aware that in its higher workings, sorcery requires the assumption of an artificially constructed personality—carefully trained, disciplined, worn like a glove when doing the work?"

"Yes," Dilvish replied.

She gave him a sidelong look and continued. "But Ridley was always different from most other people in that he already possessed two personalities. Most of the time he is amiable, witty, interesting. Occasionally his other nature would come over him, though, and it was just the opposite—cruel, violent, cunning. After he began his work with the higher magics, this other side of himself somehow merged with his magical personality. When he would assume the necessary mental and emotional stances for his workings, it would somehow be present. He was well on his way to becoming a fine sorcerer, but whenever he worked at it he changed into something—quite unlikeable. Still, this would be no great handicap if he could put it off again as easily as he took it on—with the ring he had made for this purpose. But after a time this—other—began to resist such a restoration. Ridley came to believe that *it* was attempting to control *him*."

"I have heard of people like that, with more than one nature and character," Dilvish said. "What finally happened? Which side of him came to dominate?"

"The struggle goes on. He is his better self now. But he fears to face the other, which has become a personal demon to him."

Dilvish nodded and finished his wine. She gestured toward the bottle. He refilled his glass.

"So the other was in control," Dilvish said, "when he nullified the spell on the mirror."

"Yes. The other likes to leave him with bits of unfinished work, so that he will have to call him back . . ."

"But when he was—this other—did he say why he had done what he did to the mirror? This would seem more than part of a mental struggle. He must have realized that he would be inviting trouble of the most dangerous sort—from elsewhere."

"He knew what he was doing," she said. "The other is an extraordinary egotist. He feels that he is ready to meet the master himself in a struggle for power. The denatured mirror was meant to be a challenge. Actually he told me at the time that it was meant to resolve two situations at once."

"I believe that I can guess at the second one," Dilvish said.

"Yes," she replied. "The other feels that in winning such a contest, he will also emerge as the dominant personality."

"What do you think?"

She paced slowly across the room and turned back toward him.

"Perhaps so," she said, "but I do not believe that he would win."

Dilvish drained his glass and set it aside. He folded his arms across his breast.

"Is there a possibility," he asked, "that Ridley may gain control of the other before any such conflict comes to pass?"

"I don't know. He has been trying—but he fears the other so."

"And if he should succeed? Do you feel that this might increase his chances?"

"Who can say? Not I, certainly. I'm sick of this whole business and I hate this place! I wish that I were someplace warm, like Tooma or Ankyra!"

"What would you do there?"

"I would like to be the highest-paid courtesan in town, and when I grew tired of that perhaps marry some nobleman. I'd like a life of indolence and luxury and warmth, far from the battles of adepts!"

She stared at Dilvish. "You've some Elvish blood, haven't you?"

"Yes."

"And you seem to know something of these matters. So you must have come with more than a sword to face the master."

Dilvish smiled. "I bring him a gift from Hell."

"Are you a sorcerer?"

"My knowledge of these matters is highly specialized. Why?"

"I was thinking that if you were sufficiently skilled to repair the mirror, I could use it to depart and get out of everyone's way."

Dilvish shook his head. "Magic mirrors are not my specialty. Would that they were. It is somewhat distressing to have come all this distance in search of an enemy and then to discover that his way here is barred."

Reena laughed. "Surely you do not believe that something like that will stop him?"

Dilvish looked up, dropped his arms, looked about him. "What do you mean?"

"The one you seek will be inconvenienced by this state of affairs, true. But it would hardly represent an insuperable barrier. He will simply leave his body behind."

Dilvish began to pace. "Then what's keeping him?" he asked.

"It will first be necessary for him to build his power. If he is to come here in a disembodied state, he would be at a slight disadvantage in whatever conflict ensues. It becomes necessary that he accumulate power to compensate for this."

Dilvish turned on his heel and faced her, his back to the wall. "This is not at all to my liking," he said. "Ultimately I want something that I can cut. Not some disembodied wraith! How long will this power building go on, do you think? When might he arrive here?"

"I cannot hear the vibrations on that plane. I do not know."

"Is there some way that we could get your brother to—"

A panel behind Dilvish slid open and a mummy-faced servant with a club struck him across the back of the head. Staggered, Dilvish began to turn. The club rose and fell again. He sank to his knees, then slumped forward onto the floor.

Ridley pushed his way past the servant and entered the room. The club-wielder and a second servant came in behind him.

"Very good, Sister. Very good," Ridley observed, "to detain him here until he could be dealt with."

Ridley knelt and drew the long blade from the sheath at Dilvish's side. He threw it across the room. Turning Dilvish over, he drew the dagger from the smaller sheath and raised it. "Might as well finish things," he said.

"You're a fool!" she stated, moving to his side and taking hold of his wrist. "That man could have been an ally! He's not after you! It is the master he wants to slay! He has some personal grudge against him."

Ridley lowered the blade. She did not release his wrist.

"And you believed that?" he said. "You've been up here too long. The first man who comes along gets you to believe—"

She slapped him.

"You've no call to talk to me like that! He didn't even know who you were! He might have helped! Now he won't trust us!"

Ridley regarded Dilvish's face. Then he rose to his feet, his arm falling. He let go the dagger and kicked it across the floor. She released her grip on his wrist.

"You want his life?" he said. "All right. But if he can't trust us, we can't trust him, either, now." He turned to the servants who stood motionless at his back. "Take him away," he told them, "and throw him down the hole to join Mack."

"You are compounding your mistakes," she said.

He met her gaze with a glare. "And I am tired of your mocking," he said. "I have given you his life. Leave it at that, before I change my mind."

The servants bent and raised Dilvish's limp form between them. They bore him toward the door.

"Whether I was wrong or right about him," Ridley said, gesturing after them, "an attack will come. You know it. In one form or another. Probably soon. I have preparations to make, and I do not wish to be disturbed." He turned as if to go.

Reena bit her lip, then said, "How close are you to some sort of—accommodation?"

He halted, not looking back. "Further than I'd thought I might be," he replied, "at this point. I feel now that I do have a chance at dominating. That is why I can afford to take no risks here, and why I cannot brook any further interruptions or delays. I am returning to the tower now."

He moved toward the door, out of which Dilvish's form had just passed.

Reena lowered her head. "Good luck," she said softly.

Ridley stalked out of the room.

The silent servants bore Dilvish along a dimly lit corridor. When they reached an indentation in the wall, they halted and lowered him to the floor. One of them entered the niche and raised a trapdoor. Returning to the still form, he helped lift it then, and they lowered Dilvish, feet first, into the dark opening that had been revealed. They released him, and he vanished from sight. One of them closed the trapdoor. They turned away and moved back along the corridor.

Dilvish was aware that he was sliding down an inclined surface. For a moment he had visions of Black's having slipped on the way up the mountain. Now he was sliding down the tower of ice, and when he hit the bottom . . .

He opened his eyes. He was seized by instant claustrophobia. He moved through darkness. He had felt the wall close beside him when he had taken a turn. If he reached out with his hands, he felt that the flesh would be rubbed away.

His gloves! He had tucked them behind his belt.

He reached, drew them forth, began pulling them on. He leaned forward as he did so. His eyes discerned a feeble patch of light ahead.

He reached out to his sides with both hands, spreading his legs as he did so.

His right heel touched the passing wall just as the palms of his hands did. Then his left . . .

Head throbbing, he increased the pressure at all four points. The palms of his hands grew warm from the friction, but he slowed slightly. He pushed harder, he dug with his heels. He continued to slow.

He exerted his full strength now. The gloves were wearing through. The left one tore. His palm began to burn.

Ahead, the pale square grew larger. He realized that he was not going to be able to stop himself before he reached it. He pushed one more time. He smelled rotten straw, and then he was upon it.

He landed on his feet and immediately collapsed.

The stinging in his left hand kept him from passing out. He breathed deeply of the fetid air. He was still dazed. The back of his head was one big ache. He could not recall what had happened.

He lay there panting as his heartbeat slowed. The floor was cold beneath him. Piece by piece, the memories began to return . . .

He recalled his climb to the castle, his entry . . . The woman Reena . . . They had been talking . . .

Anger flared within his breast. She had tricked him. Delayed him until help arrived for dealing with him.

But her story had been so elaborately constructed, full of unnecessary detail . . . He wondered. Was there more to this than a simple betrayal?

He sighed.

He was not ready to think yet. Where was he?

Soft sounds came to him across the straw. Some sort of cell, perhaps. Was there another inmate?

Something ran across his back.

He jerked partway upright, felt himself collapsing, turned to his side as he did. He saw the small, dark forms in the dim light. Rats. That was what it had been. He looked about the half of the cell that he faced. Nothing else.

Rolling over onto his other side, he saw the broken door.

He sat up, more carefully than before. He rubbed his head and blinked at the light. A rat drew back at the movement.

He climbed to his feet, brushed himself off. He felt after his weapons, was not surprised to find them missing.

A wave of dizziness came and went. He advanced upon the broken door, touched it.

Leaning against the frame, he peered out into the large room with frosty walls. Torches flickered in brackets at either end of it. There was an open doorway diagonally across from him, darkness beyond it.

He passed between the door and its frame, continuing to look about. There were no sounds other than the soft rat-noises behind him and the dripping of water.

He regarded the torches. The one to his left was slightly larger. He crossed to it and removed it from its bracket. Then he headed for the dark doorway.

A cold draft stirred the flames as he passed through. He was in another chamber, smaller than the one he had just quitted. Ahead, he saw a stair. He advanced upon it and began to climb.

The stair took a single turn as he mounted it. At its top he found a blank wall to his right, a wide, low-ceilinged corridor to his left. He followed the corridor.

After perhaps half a minute he beheld what appeared to be a landing, a handrail jutting out of the wall above it. As he neared he saw that there was an opening from which the railing emerged. Cautiously he mounted the landing, listened for a time, peered around the corner.

Nothing. No one. Only a long, dark stair leading upward.

He transferred the torch, which was burning low, to his other hand and began to climb quickly. This stair was much higher than the previous one, spiraling upward for a long while. He came to its ending suddenly, dropped the torch and stepped upon its flame for a moment.

After listening at the top stair he emerged into a hallway. This one had a long rug and wall decorations. Large tapers burned in standing holders along it. Off to his right there was a wide stairway leading up. He moved to its foot, certain that he had come into a more frequented area of the castle.

He brushed his garments again, removed his gloves and restored them to his belt. He ran his hand through his hair while looking about for anything that might serve as a weapon. Seeing nothing suitable, he commenced climbing.

As he reached a landing he heard a blood-chilling shriek from above.

"Please! Oh, please! The pain!"

He froze, one hand on the railing, the other reaching for a blade that was not there.

A full minute passed. Another began. The cry was not repeated. There were no further sounds of any sort from that direction.

Alert, he began to move again, staying close to the wall, testing each step before placing his full weight upon it.

When he reached the head of the stair, he checked the corridor in both directions. It appeared to be empty. The cry had seemed to come from somewhere off to the right. He went that way.

As he advanced a sudden soft sobbing began from some point to his left and ahead. He approached the slightly ajar door from behind which it seemed to be occurring. Stooping, he applied his eye to the large keyhole. There was illumination within, but nothing to view save for an undecorated section of wall and the edge of a small window.

Straightening, he turned to search again for some weapon.

The large servant's approach had been totally soundless, and he towered above him now, club already descending.

Dilvish blocked the blow with his left forearm. The

other's rush carried him forward to collide with him, however, bearing him backward against the door which flew wide, and through it into the room beyond.

Dilvish heard a cry from behind him as he strove to rise. At the same time the door was drawn shut and he heard a key slipped into the lock.

"A victim! He sends me a victim when what I want is release!" There followed a sigh. "Very well . . ."

Dilvish turned as soon as he heard the voice, his memory instantly drawing him back to another place.

Bright red body; long, thin limbs; a claw upon each digit; it had pointed ears, backward-curving horns and slitted yellow eyes. It crouched at the center of a pentacle, constantly shuffling its feet this way and that, reaching for him.

"Stupid wight!" Dilvish snapped, lapsing into another tongue. "Would you destroy your deliverer!"

The demon drew back its arms, and the pupils of its eyes expanded. "Brother! I did not know you in human form!" it answered in Mabrahoring, the language of demons. "Forgive me!"

Dilvish climbed slowly to his feet.

"I've a mind to let you rot there, for such a reception!" he replied, looking around the chamber.

The room was done up for such work, Dilvish now saw, everything still in its place. Upon the far wall there was a large mirror within an intricately worked metal frame.

"Forgive!" the demon cried, bowing low. "See how I abase myself! Can you really free me? Will you?"

"First tell me how you came into this unhappy state," Dilvish said.

"Ah! It was the young sorcerer in this place! He is mad! Even now I see him in his tower, toying with his madness! He is two people in one! One day, one must win over the other. But until then, he begins works and leaves them undone—such as summoning my poor self to this accursed place, forcing me upon this doubly accursed pentacle and taking his thrice-accursed self away without dismissing me! Oh, were I free to rend him! Please! The pain! Release me!"

"I, too, have known something of pain," said Dilvish, "and you will endure this for more questioning."

He gestured. "Is that the mirror used for travel?"

"Yes! Yes, it is!"

"Could you repair the damage it has endured?"

"Not without the aid of the human operator who laid the counterspell. It is too strong."

"Very well. Rehearse your oaths of dismissal now and I will do the things necessary to release you."

"Oaths? Between us? Ah! I see! You fear I envy you that body you wear! Perhaps you are wise . . . As you would. My oaths . . ."

". . . To include everyone in this household," Dilvish said.

"Ah!" it howled. "You would deprive me of my vengeance on the crazy sorcerer!"

"They are all mine now," Dilvish said. "Do not try to bargain with me!"

A crafty look came over the demon's face.

"Oh . . . ?" he said. "Oh! I see! Yours . . . Well, at least there will be vengeance—with much good rending and shrieking, I trust. That will be sufficient. Knowing that makes it much easier to renounce all claims. My oaths . . ."

He began the grisly litany, and Dilvish listened carefully for deviations from the necessary format. There were none.

Dilvish commenced speaking the words of dismissal. The demon hugged itself and bowed its head.

When he had finished, Dilvish looked back at the pentacle. The demon was gone from that place, but he was still present in the room. He stood in a corner, smiling an ingratiating smile.

Dilvish cocked his head. "You are free," he said. "Go!"

"A moment, great lord!" it said, cowering. "It is good to be free, and I thank you. I know, too, that only one of the greater ones of Below could have worked this release in the absence of a human sorcerer. So I would grovel and curry your favor a moment longer in the way of warning you. The flesh may have dulled your normal senses, and I bid you know that I feel the vibrations on another plane now. Something terrible is coming this way—and unless you are a part of its workings, or it of yours—I felt that you must be warned, great one!"

"I knew of it," Dilvish said, "but I am pleased that you have told me. Blast the door's lock if you would do me a final service. Then you may go."

"Thank you! Remember Quennel in the days of your wrath, and that he served you here!"

The demon turned and seemed to blow apart like fog in a wind, to the accompaniment of a dull, roaring sound. A moment later there came a sharp, snapping noise from the direction of the door.

Dilvish crossed the room. The lock had been shattered.

He opened the door and looked out. The corridor was empty. He hesitated as he considered both directions. Then with a slight shrugging movement he turned to the right and headed that way.

He came, after a time, to a great, empty dining

hall, a fire still smoldering upon its hearth, wind whistling down the chimney. He circled the entire room, moving along the walls, past the windows, the mirror, returning to the spot from which he had begun, none of the wall niches proving doorways to anywhere else.

He turned and headed back up the corridor. As he did he heard his name spoken in a whisper. He halted. The door to his left was partly ajar. He turned his head in that direction. It had been a woman's voice.

"It's me, Reena."

The door opened farther. He saw her standing there holding a long blade. She extended her arm.

"Your sword. Take it!" she said.

He took the weapon into his hands, inspected it, sheathed it.

"And your dagger."

He repeated the process.

"I am sorry," she said, "about what happened. I was as surprised as you. It was my brother's doing, not mine."

"I think I am willing to believe you," he said. "How did you locate me?"

"I waited until I was certain that Ridley was back in his tower. Then I sought you in the cells below, but you had already gone. How did you get out?"

"Walked out."

"You mean you found the door that way?"

"Yes."

He heard her sharp intake of breath, almost a gasp. "That is not at all good," she said. "It means that Mack is certainly abroad."

"Who is Mack?"

"Ridley's predecessor as apprentice here. I am not

certain what happened to him—whether he tried some experiment that simply did not work out, or whether his transformation was a punishment of the master's for some indiscretion. Whichever, he was changed into a dull-witted beast and had to be imprisoned down there because of his great strength and occasional recollection of some noxious spell. His woman went barmy after that. She's still about. A minor adept herself at one time. We've got to get out of here."

"You may be right," he said, "but finish the story."

"Oh. I've been looking all over for you since then. As I was about it I noticed that the demon had stopped screaming. I came and investigated. I saw that he had been freed. I was fairly certain that Ridley was still in the tower. It *was* you, wasn't it?"

"Yes, I released it."

"I thought then that you might still be near, and I heard someone moving in the dining hall. So I hid in here and waited to see who it was. I brought you your weapons to show that I meant you no ill."

"I appreciate it. I am only now deciding what to do. I am sure you have some suggestions."

"Yes. I've a feeling that the master will come here soon and slay every living thing under these roofs. I do not want to be around when that occurs."

"As a matter of fact, he should be here very soon. The demon told me."

"It is hard to tell what you know and what you do not know," she said, "what you can do and what you cannot do. Obviously you know something of the arts. Do you intend to stay and face him?"

"That was my purpose in traveling all this distance," he replied. "But I meant to face him in the flesh, and if I did not find him here I meant to use whatever means of magical transportation might be present to seek him in others of his strongholds. I do not know how my special presents will affect him in a disembodied state. I know that my blade will not."

"You would be wise," she said, taking his arm, "very wise, to live to fight another day."

"Especially if you need my help in getting away from here?" he asked.

She nodded. "I do not know what your quarrel with him may be," she said, leaning against him, "and you are a strange man, but I do not think you can hope to win against him here. He will have amassed great power, fearing the worst. He will come in cautiously—so cautiously! I know a possible way away, if you will help. But we must hurry. He could even be here right now. He—"

"How very astute of you, dear girl," came a dry, throaty voice from back up the hall, whence Dilvish had come.

Recognizing it, he turned. A dark-cowled figure stood just beyond the entrance within the dining hall.

"And you," it stated, "Dilvish! You are a most difficult person to be rid of, bloodling of Selar, though it has been a long while between encounters."

Dilvish drew his blade. An Awful Saying rose to his lips but he refrained from speaking it, not certain that what he saw represented an actual physical presence.

"What new torment might I devise for you?" the other asked. "A transformation? A degeneration? A—"

Dilvish began to move toward him, ignoring his words. From behind him he heard Reena whisper, "Come back . . ."

He continued on toward the form of his enemy. "I was nothing to you . . ." Dilvish began.

"You disturbed an important rite."

". . . and you took my life and threw it away. You visited a terrible vengeance upon me as casually as another man might brush away a mosquito."

"I was annoyed, as another man might be at a mosquito."

"You treated me as if I were a thing, not a person. That I cannot forgive."

A soft chuckle emerged from within the cowl. "And it would seem that in my own defense now I must treat you that way again."

The figure raised its hand, pointing two fingers at him.

Dilvish broke into a run, raising his blade, recalling Black's spell of protection and still loath to commence his own.

The extended fingers seemed to glow for a moment, and Dilvish felt something like a passing wind. That was all.

"Are you but an illusion of this place?" the other asked, beginning to back away, a tiny quavering note apparent in his voice for the first time.

Dilvish swung his blade but encountered nothing. The figure was no longer before him. Now it stood among shadows at the far end of the dining hall.

"Is this thing yours, Ridley?" he heard it ask suddenly. "If so, you are to be commended for dredging up something I'd no desire whatever to recall. It shan't distract me, though, from the business at hand. Show yourself, if you dare!"

Dilvish heard a sliding sound from off to his left, and a panel opened there. He saw the slim figure of a younger man emerge, a shining ring upon the left forefinger.

"Very well. We shall dispense with these theatrics,"

came Ridley's voice. He seemed slightly out of breath and striving to control it. "I am master of myself and this place," he continued. He turned toward Dilvish. "You, wight! You have served me well. There is absolutely nothing more for you to do here, for it is between the two of us now. I give you leave to depart and assume your natural form. You may take the girl back with you as payment."

Dilvish hesitated.

"Go, I say! Now!"

Dilvish backed from the room.

"I see that you have cast aside all remorse," he heard Jelerak say, "and learned the necessary hardness. This should prove interesting."

Dilvish saw a low wall of fire spring up between the two of them. He heard laughter from the hall—whose, he was not certain. Then came a crackling sound and a wave of peculiar odors. Suddenly the room was a blaze of light. Just as suddenly it was plunged into darkness again. The laughter continued. He heard pieces of tile falling from the walls.

He turned away. Reena was still standing where he had left her.

"He did it," she said softly. "He has control of the other. He really did it . . ."

"We can do no good here," Dilvish stated. "It is, as he said, between them now."

"But his new strength may still not be sufficient!"

"I'd imagine he knows that, and that that is why he wants me to take you away."

The floor shook beneath them. A picture dropped from a nearby wall.

"I don't know that I can leave him like that, Dilvish."

"He may be giving his life for you, Reena. He

might have used his new powers to repair the mirror, or to escape this place by some other means. You heard how he put things. Would you throw away his gift?"

Her eyes filled with tears.

"He may never know," she said, "how much I really wanted him to succeed."

"I've a feeling he might," Dilvish said. "Now, how are we to save you?"

"Come this way," she said, taking his arm as a hideous scream came from the hall, followed by a thunderclap that seemed to shake the entire castle.

Colored lights glowed behind them as she led him along the corridor.

"I've a sled," she said, "in a cavern deep below here. It is filled with supplies."'

"How—" Dilvish began, and he halted, raising the blade that he bore.

An old woman stood before them at the head of the stair, glaring at him. But his eyes had slid beyond her to behold the great pale bulk that slowly mounted the last few stairs, head turned in their direction.

"There, Mack!" she screamed suddenly. "The man who hit me! Hurt my side! Crush him!"

Dilvish directed the point of his blade at the advancing creature's throat.

"If he attacks me, I will kill him," he said. "I do not want to, but the choice is not mine. It is yours. He may be big and strong, but he is not fast. I have seen him move. I will make a very big hole, and a lot of blood will come out of it. I heard that you once loved him, lady. What are you going to do?"

Forgotten emotions flickered across Meg's features. "Mack! Stop!" she cried. "He's not the one. I was wrong!"

Mack halted. "Not—the—one?" he said.

"No. I was—mistaken."

She turned her gaze up the hallway to where fountains of fires flashed and vanished and where multitudes of cries, as of two opposing armies, rang out.

"What," she said, gesturing, "is it?"

"The young master and the old master," Reena said, "are fighting."

"Why are you still afraid to say his name?" Dilvish asked. "He's just up the corridor. It's Jelerak."

"Jelerak?" A new light came into Mack's eyes as he gestured toward the awful room. "Jelerak?"

"Yes," Dilvish replied, and the pale one turned away from him and began shuffling in that direction.

Dilvish looked about for Meg, but she was gone. Then he heard a cry of "Jelerak! Kill!" from overhead.

He looked up and saw the green-winged creature that had attacked him—how long ago?—flapping off in the same direction.

"They are probably going to their deaths," Reena said.

"How long do you think they have waited for such an opportunity?" he said. "I am sure they know that they lost a long time ago. But just to have the chance now is winning, for them."

"Better in there than on your blade."

Dilvish turned away.

"I am not at all sure that *he* wouldn't have killed *me*," he said. "Where are we going?"

"This way."

She took him down the stair and up another corridor, heading toward the north end of the building. The entire place began shaking about them as they

went. Furniture toppled, windows shattered, a beam
fell. Then it was still again for a time. They hurried.

As they were nearing the kitchen the place shook
again with such violence that they were thrown to the
floor. A fine dust was drifting everywhere now, and
cracks had appeared in the walls. In the kitchen they
saw that hot ashes had been thrown from the grate to
lie strewn about the floor, smoking.

"It sounds as if Ridley is still holding his own."

"Yes, it does," she said, smiling.

Pots and pans were rattling and banging together
as they departed the kitchen, heading in the direction
of the stairwell. The cutlery danced in its drawers.

They paused at the stair's entrance just as a great,
inhuman moan swept through the entire castle. An
icy draft followed moments later. A rat flashed past
them from the direction of the kitchen.

Reena signaled Dilvish to halt and, leaning against
the wall, cupped her hands before her face. She
seemed to whisper within them, and a moment after
the small fire was born, to hover, growing, before her.
She moved her hands outward and it drifted toward
the stairwell.

"Come," she said to Dilvish, and she led the way
downward.

He moved behind her, and from time to time the
walls creaked ominously about them. When this happened the light danced for a moment, and occasionally it faded briefly. As they descended the sounds
from above grew more muffled. Dilvish paused once
to place his hand upon the wall.

"Is it far?" he asked.

"Yes. Why?"

"I can still feel the vibrations strongly," he said.

"We must be well below the level of the castle itself, down into the mountain by now."

"True," she replied, taking another turn.

"At first I feared that they might bring the castle down upon our heads . . ."

"They probably *will* destroy the place if this goes on much longer," she said. "I'm very proud of Ridley—despite the inconvenience."

"That wasn't exactly what I meant," Dilvish said as they continued their downward flight. "There! It's getting worse!" He put out a hand to steady himself as the stair shuddered from a passing shock wave. "Doesn't it seem to you that the entire mountain is shaking?"

"Yes, it does," she replied. "Then it must be true."

"What?"

"I'd heard it said that ages ago, at the height of his power, the ma—Jelerak—actually raised this mountain by his conjuring."

"So?"

"If he is sufficiently taxed in this place, I suppose that he might have to draw upon those ancient spells of his for more power. In which case—"

"The mountain might collapse as well as the castle?"

"There is that possibility. Oh, Ridley! Good show!"

"It won't be so good if we're under it!"

"True," she said, suddenly moving even faster. "As he's not *your* brother, I can see your point. Still, it must please you to see Jelerak so hard pressed."

"It does that," Dilvish admitted, "but you should really prepare yourself for any eventuality."

She was silent for a time.

Then, "Ridley's death?" she asked. "Yes. I've realized for some time now that there was a strong possibility of this, whatever the nature of their encounter. Still, to go out with such flare . . . That's something, too, you know."

"Yes," Dilvish replied. "I've thought of it many times myself."

Abruptly they reached the landing. She turned immediately and led him toward a tunnel. The rocky floor trembled beneath them. The light danced again. From somewhere there came a slow, grinding sound, lasting for perhaps ten seconds. They rushed into the tunnel.

"And you?" she said, as they hurried along it. "If Jelerak survives, will you still seek him?"

"Yes," he said. "I know for certain that he has at least six other citadels. I know the approximate locations of several of them. I would seek them as I did this place."

"I have been in three of the others," she said. "If we survive this, I can tell you something about them. They would not be easy to storm, either."

"It does not matter," Dilvish said. "I never thought that it would be easy. If he lives, I will go to them. If I cannot locate him, I will destroy them one by one, until he must needs come to me."

The grinding sound came again. Fragments of rocks fell about them. As this occurred the floating light vanished before them.

"Remain still," she said. "I'll do another."

Several moments later another light glowed between her hands.

They continued on, the sounds within the rock ceasing for a time.

"What will you do if Jelerak is dead?" she asked him.

Dilvish was silent awhile. Then, "Visit my homeland," he said. "It has been a long while since I have been back. What will you do if we make it away from here?"

"Tooma, Ankyra, Blostra," she replied, "as I'd said, if I could find some willing gentleman to escort me to one of them."

"I believe that could be arranged," Dilvish said.

As they neared the end of the tunnel, an enormous shudder ran through the entire mountain. Reena stumbled. Dilvish caught her and was thrown back against the wall. With his shoulders he felt the heavy vibrations within the stone. From behind them a steady crashing of falling rocks began.

"Hurry!" he said, propelling her forward.

The light darted drunkenly before them. They came into a cold cavern.

"This is the place," Reena said, pointing. "The sled is over there."

Dilvish saw the vehicle, took hold of her arm and headed toward it.

"How high up the mountain are we?" he asked her.

"Two-thirds of the way, perhaps," she said. "We are somewhat below the point where the rise steepens severely."

"That is still no gentle slope out there," he said, coming to a halt beside the vehicle and placing his hand upon its side. "How do you propose getting it down to ground level?"

"That will be the difficult part," she said, reaching within her bodice and withdrawing a folded piece of parchment. "I've removed this page from one of the books in the tower. When I had the servants build me this sled, I knew that I would need something strong to draw it. This is a fairly elaborate spell, but it will summon a demon beast to do our bidding."

"May I see it?"

She passed him the page. He unfolded it and held it near the hovering light.

"This spell requires fairly lengthy preparations," he said a little later. "I don't believe we have that kind of time remaining, the way things are shaking and crumbling here."

"But it is the only chance we have," she said. "We'll need these supplies. I had no way of knowing that the whole damned mountain was going to start coming apart. We are simply going to have to risk the delay."

Dilvish shook his head and returned the page.

"Wait here," he said, "and don't start that spell yet!"

He turned and made his way along the tunnel, down which icy blasts blew. Snow crystals lay upon the floor. After a single brief turn, he saw the wide cave mouth, pale light beyond it. The floor here had a heavy coating of snow over ice.

He walked to the entrance and looked out, looked down. The sled could be edged over the lip of the ridge at his feet at a low place off to his left. But then it would simply take off, achieving a killing speed long before it reached the foot of the mountain.

He moved forward to the very edge, looked up. An overhang prevented his seeing anything above. He moved a half-dozen paces to his left then, looked out, looked up, looked around. Then he crossed to the right-hand extremity of the ledge and looked up, shading his eyes against a blast of ice crystals.

There . . . ?

"Black!" he called to a darker patch of shadow above and to the side. "Black!"

It seemed to stir. He cupped his hands and shouted again.

"Diiil . . . viish!" rolled down the slope toward him, after his own cry had died away.

"Down here!" He waved both arms above his head.

"I . . . see . . . you!"

"Can you come to me?"

There was no answer, but the shadow moved. It came down from its ledge and began a slow, stiff-legged journey in his direction.

He remained in sight. He continued waving.

Soon Black's silhouette became clear through the swirling snow. He advanced steadily. He passed the halfway point, continued on.

As he came up beside him, Black pulsed heat for several moments and the snow melted upon him, trickling off down his sides.

"There are some amazing sorceries going on above," he stated, "well worth observing."

"Far better we do it from a distance," Dilvish said. "This whole mountain may be coming down."

"Yes, it will," Black said. "Something up there is drawing upon some very elemental, ancient spells woven all through here. It is most instructive. Get on my back and I'll take you down."

"It is not that simple."

"Oh?"

"There is a girl—and a sled—in the cave behind me."

Black placed his forefeet upon the ledge and heaved himself up to stand beside Dilvish.

"Then I had better have a look," he stated. "How did you fare up on top?"

Dilvish shrugged. "All of that would most likely have happened without me," he said, "but at least I've the pleasure of seeing someone giving Jelerak a hard time."

"That's him up there?"

They started back into the cave.

"His body is elsewhere, but the part that bites has paid a visit."

"Who is he fighting?"

"The brother of the lady you are about to meet. This way."

They took the turn and headed back into the larger cave. Reena still stood beside the sled. She had wrapped herself in a fur. Black's metal hoofs clicked upon the rock.

"You wanted a demon-beast?" Dilvish said to her. "Black, this is Reena. Reena, meet Black."

Black bowed his head.

"I am pleased," he said. "Your brother has been providing me with considerable amusement while I waited without."

Reena smiled and reached out to touch his neck. "Thank you," she said. "I am delighted to know you. Can you help us?"

Black turned and regarded the sled. "Backward," he said after a time. Then, "If I were hitched facing it, I could draw back slightly and let it precede me down the mountain. You would both have to walk, though—beside me, holding on. I don't believe I could do it with you in the thing. Even this way it will be difficult, but I see it to be the only way."

"Then we'd better push it out and get started," Dilvish said as the mountain shook again.

Reena and Dilvish each took hold of a side of the

vehicle. Black leaned against its rear. It began to move.

Once they reached the snow on the cave floor, it proceeded more easily. Finally they turned it about at the cave mouth and hitched Black between its traces.

Carefully, gently then, they edged its rear end over the ledge at the low place to the left as Black advanced slowly, maintaining tension on the traces.

Its runners struck the snow of the slope, and Black eased it down until it rested full-length upon it. Gingerly he followed it then, jerking stiffly upright to anchor it after he had jumped the last few feet.

"All right," he said. "Come down now and take hold of me on either side."

They followed him and took up their positions. Slowly he began to advance.

"Tricky," he said as they moved. "One day they will invent names for the properties of objects, such as the tendency of a thing to move once it is placed in motion."

"Of what use would that be?" Reena asked. "Everybody already knows that that's what happens."

"Ah! But one might put numbers to the amount of material involved and the amount of pushing required, and come up with wondrous and useful calculations."

"Sounds like a lot of trouble for a small return," she said. "Magic's a lot easier to figure."

"Perhaps you're right."

Steadily they descended, Black's hoofs crunching through the icy crust. Later, when they finally reached a place from which they could view the castle, they saw that the highest tower and several low ones had fallen. Even as they watched, a section of wall collapsed. Fragments of it fell over the edge, fortunately descending the slope far to their right.

Beneath the snow the mountain itself was shaking steadily now and had been for some time. Rocks and chunks of ice occasionally bounded past them.

They continued for what seemed an interminable time, Black edging the sled lower and lower with each step, Reena and Dilvish plodding numb-footed beside him.

As they neared the foot of the slope, a terrific crash echoed about them. Looking up, they saw the remains of the castle crumbling, shrinking, falling in upon itself.

Black increased his pace dangerously as small bits of debris began to rain about them.

"When we reach bottom," he said, "unhitch me immediately, but stay on the far side of the sled while you're doing it. I should be able to turn its side to the slope as we get there. Then, if you can hitch me properly in a hurry, do it. If the falling stuff becomes too severe, though, just crouch down on the far side and I will stand on the near one to help shield you. But if you can rehitch me, get in quickly and stay low."

They slid most of the final distance, and for a moment it seemed that the sled would turn over as Black maneuvered it. Picking himself up, Dilvish immediately set to work upon the harness.

Reena got behind the sled and looked upward.

"Dilvish! Look!" she cried.

Dilvish glanced upward as he finished the unfastening, and Black backed out from between the traces. The castle had completely vanished, and large fissures had appeared in the slope. Above the summit of the mountain, two columns of smoke now stood—a dark one and a light one—motionless despite the winds that must be lashing at them.

Black turned and backed in between the traces. Dilvish began harnessing him again. More debris was now descending the slope, off to their right.

"What is it?" Dilvish said.

"The dark column is Jelerak," Black replied.

Dilvish looked back periodically as he worked, seeing that the two columns had begun to move, slowly, toward one another. Soon they were intertwined, though not merging, twisting and knotting about one another like a pair of struggling serpents.

Dilvish completed the harnessing.

"Get in!" he cried to Reena as another part of the mountain fell away.

"You, too!" said Black, and Dilvish climbed in with her.

Soon they were moving, gathering speed. The top of the tower came apart as they watched, and still the billowing combatants rolled above it.

"Oh, no! Ridley seems to be weakening!" she said as they raced away.

Dilvish watched as the dark column seemed to bear the lighter one downward into the heart of the falling mountain.

Black's pace increased, though chunks of rubble still skidded and raced about them. Soon both smoky combatants were gone from sight, high above them. Black moved faster yet, heading south, outdistancing the pieces of the falling tower.

Perhaps a quarter of an hour passed with no change in the prospect behind them, save for its dwindling. But crouched beneath the furs, Dilvish and Reena still watched. An air of anticipation seemed to grow over the entire landscape.

When it came it rocked the ground, bouncing the sled from side to side, and its tremors continued for a long while after.

The top of the mountain blew off, peppering the sky with an expanding, dark cloud. The entire tower of ice fell, settling beneath it. Then the dusky smear was streaked, spread by the winds, sections of it reaching like slowly extending fingers to the west. After a time a mighty shock wave rolled over them.

Much later a single, attenuated, rough-edged cloud—the dark one—separated itself from the haze. Trailing ragged plumes, jounced by the winds, it moved like an old man stumbling, fleeing southward. It passed far to the right of them and did not pause.

"That's Jelerak," Black said. "He's hurt."

They watched the rough column until it jerked out of sight far to the south. Then they turned again toward the ruin in the north. They watched until it faded from view, but the white column did not rise again.

Finally Reena lowered her head. Dilvish put his arm about her shoulders. The runners of the sled sang softly on their way across the snow.

A Thief in Korianth

by C. J. Cherryh

For more years than I can recall, Donald A. Wollheim has made a career of discovering new writers of
extraordinary talent, such as Samuel R. Delaney and
Marion Zimmer Bradley and Thomas Burnett Swann.
One of his more remarkable recent discoveries is a
young woman who writes under the name of C. J.
Cherryh.

Her first novel, *Gate of Ivrel,* was an impressive de-
but (to say the least) : a fine first novel, which she
quickly followed with several more equally impressive. By now she has become (with Tanith Lee
and Katherine Kurtz) one of the best of the newer
generation of fantasy writers.

When I asked her for a novelette to include in this
special volume of *Flashing Swords!,* I had no idea of
what she would come up with. I suppose I had
thought she might do for me a tale of her Ivrel sequence; but no, she has launched a brand-new series
with the marvelous yarn that follows. In it she in-
troduces a heroine so unique that I am already in
love with her, and a city so rich and colorful that it
bears comparison only with Fritz Leiber's immortal
Lankhmar . . .

A THIEF IN KORIANTH

I

The Yliz River ran through Korianth, a sullen, muddy stream on its way to the nearby sea, with stone banks where it passed through the city . . . gray stone and yellow water, and gaudy ships which made a spider-tangle of masts and riggings above the drab jumbled roofs of the dockside. In fact all Korianth was built on pilings and cut with canals more frequent than streets, the whole pattern of the lower town dictated by old islands and channels, so that buildings took whatever turns and bends the canals dictated, huddled against each other, jammed one up under the eaves of the next—faded paint, buildings like aged crones remembering the brightness of their youths, decayed within from overmuch of wine and living, with dulled, shuttered eyes looking suspiciously on dim streets and scummed canals, where boat vendors and barge folk plied their craft, going to and fro from shabby warehouses. This was the Sink, which was indeed slowly subsiding into the River—but that took centuries, and the Sink used only the day, quick pleasures, momentary feast, customary famine. In spring rains the Yliz rose; tavern keepers mopped and dockmen and warehousers cursed and set merchandise up on blocks; then the town stank considerably. In summer heats the River sank, and the town stank worse.

There was a glittering world above this rhythm, the part of Korianth that had grown up later, inland, and beyond the zone of flood: palaces and town houses of hewn stone (which still sank, being too heavy for their foundations, and developed cracks, and whenever abandoned, decayed quickly). In this area too were temples . . . temples of gods and goddesses and whole pantheons local and foreign, ancient and modern, for Korianth was a trading city and offended no one permanently. The gods were transients, coming and going in favor like dukes and royal lovers. There was, more permanent than gods, a king in Korianth, Seithan XXIV, but Seithan was, if rumors might be believed, quite mad, having recovered after poisoning. At least he showed a certain bizarre turn of behavior, in which he played obscure and cruel jokes and took to strange religions, mostly such as promised sybaritic afterlives and conjured demons.

And central to that zone between, where town and dockside met on the canals, lay a rather pleasant zone of mild decay, of modest townsmen and a few dilapidated palaces. In this web of muddy waterways a grand bazaar transferred the wealth of the Sink (whose dark warrens honest citizens avoided) into higher-priced commerce of the Market of Korianth.

It was a profitable place for merchants, for proselytizing cults, for healers, interpreters of dreams, prostitutes of the better sort (two of the former palaces were brothels, and no few of the temples were), palm readers and sellers of drinks and smeetmeats, silver and fish, of caged birds and slaves, copper pots and amulets and minor sorceries. Even on a chill autumn day such as this, with the stench of hundreds of altars and the spices of the booths and the smokes of midtown, that of the River welled up. Humanity jostled shoulder to shoulder, armored guard against citizen, beggar against priest, and furnished ample opportunity for thieves.

Gillian glanced across that sea of bobbing heads and swirling colors, eased up against the twelve-year-old girl whose slim, dirty fingers had just deceived the fruit merchant and popped a first and a second handful of figs into the torn seam of her cleverly sewn skirt. Gillian pushed her own body into the way of sight and reached to twist her fingers into her sister's curls and jerk. Jensy yielded before it came out by the roots, let herself be dragged four paces into the woman-wide blackness of an alley, through which a sickly stream of something threaded between their feet.

"Hist," Gillian said. "Will you have us on the run for a fistful of sweets? You have no judgment."

Jensy's small face twisted into a grin. "Old Habershen's never seen me."

Gillian gave her a rap on the ear, not hard. The claim was truth: Jensy was deft. The double-sewn skirt picked up better than figs. "Not here," Gillian said. "Not in *this* market. There's high law here. They cut your hand off, stupid snipe."

Jensy grinned at her; everything slid off Jensy. Gillian gripped her sister by the wrist and jerked her out into the press, walked a few stalls down. It was never good to linger. They did not look the best of customers, she and Jensy, ragged curls bound up in scarves, coarse sacking skirts, blouses that had seen good days—before they had left some goodwoman's laundry. Docksiders did come here, frequent enough in the crowds. And their faces were not known outside the Sink; varying patterns of dirt were a tolerable disguise.

Lean days were at hand; they were not far from winter, when ships would be scant, save only the paltry, patched coasters. In late fall and winter the goods were here in midtown, being hauled out of warehouses and sold at profit. Dockside was slim pickings in winter; dockside was where she preferred to work—given choice. And with Jensy—

Midtown frightened her. This place was daylight and open, and at the moment she was not looking for trouble; rather she made for the corner of the fish market with its peculiar aromas and the perfumed reek of Agdalia's gilt temple and brothel.

"Don't want to," Jensy declared, planting her feet.

Gillian jerked her willy-nilly. "I'm not going to leave you there, mousekin. Not for long."

"I hate Sophonisba."

Gillian stopped short, jerked Jensy about by the shoulder and looked down into the dirty face. Jensy sobered at once, eyes wide. "Sophonisba never lets the customers near you."

Jensy shook her head, and Gillian let out a breath. *She* had started that way; Jensy would not. She dragged Jensy to the door, where Sophonisba held her usual post at the shrine of the tinsel goddess—legitimacy of a sort, more than Sophonisba had been born to. Gillian shoved Jensy into Sophonisba's hands . . . overblown and overpainted, all pastels and perfumes and swelling bosom—it was not lack of charms kept Sophonisba on the market street, by the Fish, but the unfortunate voice, a Sink accent and a nasal whine that would keep her here forever. *Dead ear,* Gillian reckoned of her in some pity, for accents came off and onto Gillian's tongue with polyglot facility; Sophonisba probably did not know her affliction—a creature of patterns, reliable to follow them.

"Not in daylight," Sophonisba complained, painted eyes distressed. "Double cut for daylight. Are you working *here*? I don't want any part of that. Take yourselves elsewhere."

"You know I wouldn't bring the king's men down on Jensy; mind her, old friend, or I'll break your nose."

"Hate you," Jensy muttered, and winced, for Sophonisba gripped her hair.

She meant Sophonisba. Gillian gave her a face and walked away, free. The warrens or the market—neither place was safe for a twelve-year-old female with light fingers and too much self-confidence; Sophonisba could still keep a string on her—and Sophonisba was right to worry: stakes were higher here, in all regards.

Gillian prowled the aisles, shopping customers as well as booths, lingering nowhere long, flowing with the traffic. It was the third winter coming, the third since she had had Jensy under her wing. Neither of them had known hunger often while her mother had been there to care for Jensy—but those days were gone, her mother gone, and Jensy—Jensy was falling into the pattern. Gillian saw it coming. She had nightmares, Jensy in the hands of the city watch, or knifed in some stupid brawl, like their mother. Or something happening to herself, and Jensy growing up in Sophonisba's hands.

Money. A large amount of gold: that was the way out she dreamed of, money that would buy Jensy into some respectable order, to come out polished and fit for midtown or better. But that kind of money did not often flow accessibly on dockside, in the Sink. It had to be hunted here; and she saw it—all about her—at the risk of King's-law, penalties greater than the dockside was likely to inflict: the Sink took care of its own problems, but it was apt to wink at pilferage and it was rarely so inventively cruel as King's-law. Whore she was not, no longer, never again; whore she had been, seeking out Genat, a thief among thieves; and the apprentice had passed the master. Genat had become blind Genat the beggar—dead Genat soon after—and Gillian was free, walking the market where Genat himself seldom dared pilfer.

If she had gold enough, then Jensy was out of the streets, out of the way of things that waited to happen.

Gold enough, and she could get more: gold was power, and she had studied power zealously, from street bravos to priests, listening to gossip, listening to rich folk talk, one with the alleys and the booths—she learned, did Gillian, how rich men stole, and she planned someday—she always had—to be rich.

Only three years of fending for two, and this third year that saw Jensy filling out into more than her own whipcord shape would ever be, *that* promised what Jensy would be the fourth year, when at thirteen she became a mark for any man on the docks—

This winter or never, for Jensy.

Gillian walked until her thin soles burned on the cobbles. She looked at jewelers' booths—too wary, the goldsmiths, who tended to have armed bullies about them. She had once—madly—entertained the idea of approaching a jeweler, proposing her own slight self as a guard: truth, no one on the streets could deceive her sharp eyes, and there would be no pilferage; but say to them, *I am a better thief than they, sirs?*—that was a way to end like Genat.

Mistress to such, instead? There seemed no young and handsome ones—even Genat had been that—and she, moreover, had no taste for more such years. She passed the jewelers, hoping forlornly for some indiscretion.

She hungered by afternoon and thought wistfully of the figs Jensy had fingered; Jensy had them, which meant Jensy would eat them. Gillian was not so rash as in her green years. She would not risk herself for a bit of bread or cheese. She kept prowling, turning down minor opportunities, bumped against a number of promising citizens, but each was a risk, and each deft fingering of their purses showed nothing of great substance.

The hours passed. The better classes began to wend homeward with their bodyguards and bullies. She began to see a few familiar faces on the edges of the crowd, rufflers and whores and such anticipating the night, which was theirs. Merchants with more expensive goods began folding up and withdrawing with their armed guards and their day's profits.

Nothing—no luck at all, and Sophonisba would not accept a cut of bad luck; Gillian had two coppers in her own purse, purloined days ago, and Sophonisba would expect one. It was the streets and no supper if she were not willing to take a risk.

Suddenly a strange face cut the crowd, making haste: that caught her eye, and like the reflex of a boxer, her body tended that way before her mind had quite weighed matters, so she should not lose him. This was a stranger; there was a fashion to faces in Korianth, and this one was not Korianthine—Abhizite, she reckoned, from upriver. Gillian warmed indeed; it was like summer, when gullible foreigners came onto the docks carrying their traveling funds with them and giving easy opportunity to the light-fingered trade.

She bumped him in the press at a corner, anticipating his move to dodge her, and her razor had the purse strings, her fingers at once aware of weight, her heart thudding with the old excitement as she eeled through the crowd and alleyward.

Heavy purse—it was too soon missed: her numbing blow had had short effect. She heard the bawl of outrage, and suddenly a general shriek of alarm. At the bend of the alley she looked back.

Armored men. Bodyguards!

Panic hit her; she clutched the purse and ran the dark alley she had mapped in advance for escape, ran with all her might and slid left, right, right, along a broad back street, down yet another alley. They were after her in the twilight of the maze, cursing and with swords gleaming bare.

It was no ordinary cutpursing. She had tripped something, indeed. She ran until her heart was nigh to bursting, took the desperate chance of a stack of firewood to scamper to a ledge and into the upper levels of the midtown maze.

She watched them then, she lying on her heaving belly and trying not to be heard breathing. They were someone's hired bravos for certain, scarred of countenance, with that touch of the garish that bespoke gutter origins.

"Common cutpurse," one said. That rankled. She had other skills.

"Someone has to have seen her," said another. "Money will talk, even in the Sink."

They went away. Gillian lay still, panting, opened the purse with trembling fingers.

A lead cylinder stamped with a seal; lead, and a

finger-long sealed parchment, and a paltry three silver coins.

Bile welled up in her throat. They had sworn to search for her even into the impenetrable Sink. She had stolen something terrible; she had ruined herself; and even the Sink could not hide her, not against money, and such men.

Jensy, she thought, sick at heart. If passersby had seen her strolling there earlier and described Jensy— their memories would be very keen, for gold. The marks on the loot were ducal seals, surely; lesser men did not use such things. Her breath shuddered through her throat. Kings and dukes. She had stolen lead and paper, and her death. She could not read, not a word—not even to know *what* she had in hand.

—and *Jensy!*

She swept the contents back into the purse, thrust it into her blouse and, dropping down again into the alley, ran.

II

The tinsel shrine was closed. Gillian's heart sank, and her vision blurred. Again to the alleys and behind, thence to a lower-story window with a red shutter. She reached up and rapped it a certain pattern with her knuckles.

It opened. Sophonisba's painted face stared down at her; a torrent of abuse poured sewer-fashion from the dewy lips, and Jensy's dirty-scarfed head bobbed up from below the whore's ample bosom.

"Come *on*," Gillian said, and Jensy scrambled, grimaced in pain, for Sophonisba had her by the hair.

"My cut," Sophonisba said.

Gillian swallowed air, her ears alert for pursuit.

She fished the two coppers from her purse, and Sophonisba spat on them. Heat flushed Gillian's face; the next thing in her hand was her razor.

Sophonisba paled and sniffed. "I know you got better, slink. The whole street's roused. Should I take such risks? If someone comes asking here, should I say lies?"

Trembling, blind with rage, Gillian took back the coppers. She brought out the purse, spilled the contents: lead cylinder, parchment, three coins. "Here. See? Trouble, trouble and no lot of money."

Sophonisba snatched at the coins. Gillian's deft fingers saved two, and the other things, which Sophonisba made no move at all to seize.

"Take your trouble," Sophonisba said. "And your brat. And keep away from here."

Jensy scrambled out over the sill, hit the alley cobbles on her slippered feet. Gillian did not stay to threaten. Sophonisba knew her—knew better than to spill to king's-men . . . or to leave Jensy on the street. Gillian clutched her sister's hand and pulled her along at a rate a twelve-year-old's strides could hardly match.

They walked, finally, in the dark of the blackest alleys and, warily, into the Sink itself. Gillian led the way to Threepenny Bridge and so to the Rat's Alley and the Bowel. They were *not* alone, but the shadows inspected them cautiously: the trouble that lurked here was accustomed to pull its victims into the warren, not to find them there; and one time that lurkers did come too close, she and Jensy played dodge in the alley. "Cheap flash," she spat, and: "Bit's Isle," marking herself of a rougher brotherhood than theirs. They were alone after.

After the Bowel came the Isle itself, and the

deepest part of the Sink. There was a door in the alley called Blindman's, where Genat had sat till someone knifed him. She dodged to it with Jensy in tow, this stout door inconspicuous among others, and pushed it open.

It let them in under Jochen's stairs, in the wine-smelling backside of the Rose. Gillian caught her breath then and pulled Jensy close within the shadows of the small understairs pantry. "Get Jochen," she bade Jensy then. Jensy skulked out into the hall and took off her scarf, stuffed that in her skirts and passed out of sight around the corner of the door and into the roister of the tavern.

In a little time she was back with fat Jochen in her wake, and Jochen mightily scowling.

"You're in trouble?" Jochen said. "Get out if you are."

"Want you to keep Jensy for me."

"Pay," Jochen said. "You got it?"

"How much?"

"How bad the trouble?"

"For her, none at all. Just keep her." Gillian turned her back—prudence, not modesty—to fish up the silver from her blouse, not revealing the purse. She held up one coin. "Two days' board and close room."

"You *are* in trouble."

"I want Nessim. Is he here?"

He always was by dark. Jochen snorted. "A cut of what's going."

"A cut if there's profit; a clear name if there's not; get Nessim."

Jochen went. "I don't want to be left," Jensy started to say, but Gillian rapped her ear and scowled so that Jensy swallowed it and looked frightened. Finally a muddled old man came muttering their way and Gillian snagged his sleeve. The reek of wine was strong; it was perpetual about Nessim Hath, excommunicate priest and minor dabbler in magics. He read, when he was sober enough to see the letters; that and occasionally effective magics—wards against rats, for one—made him a livelihood and kept his throat uncut.

"Upstairs," Gillian said, guiding sot and child up the well-worn boards to the loft and the private cells at the alleyside wall. Jensy snatched the taper at the head of the stairs and they went into that room, which had a window.

Nessim tottered to the cot and sat down while Jensy lit the stub of a candle. Gillian fished out her coppers, held them before Nessim's red-rimmed eyes and pressed them into the old priest's shaking hand.

"Read something?" Nessim asked.

Gillian pulled out the purse and knelt by the bedside while Jensy prudently closed the door. She produced the leaden cylinder and the parchment. "Old man," she said, "tell me what I've got here."

He gathered up the cylinder and brought his eyes closely to focus on it, frowning. His mouth acquired a tremor to match his hands, and he thrust it back at her. "I don't know this seal. Lose this thing in the canal. Be rid of it."

"You know it, old man."

"I don't." She did not take it from him, and he held it, trembling. "A false seal, a mask seal. Something some would know—and not outsiders. It's no good, Gillian."

"And if some would hunt a thief for it? It's good to someone."

Nessim stared at her. She valued Nessim, gave him

coppers when he was on one of his lower periods: he drank the money and was grateful. She cultivated him, one gentle rogue among the ungentle, who would not have failed at priesthood and at magics if he did not drink and love comforts; now he simply had the drink.

"Run," he said. "Get out of Korianth. Tonight."

"Penniless? This should be worth something, old man."

"Powerful men would use such a seal to mask what they do, who they are. Games of more than small stakes."

Gillian swallowed heavily. "You've played with seals before, old man; read me the parchment."

He took it in hand, laid the leaden cylinder in his lap, turned the parchment to all sides. Long and long he stared at it, finally opened his purse with much trembling of his hands, took out a tiny knife and cut the red threads wrapped round, pulled them from the wax and loosed it carefully with the blade.

"Huh," Jensy pouted. *"Anyone* could cut it." Gillian rapped her ear gently, bit her lip as Nessim canted the tiny parchment to the scant light. His lips mumbled, steadied, a thin line. When he opened his mouth they trembled again, and very carefully he drew out more red thread from his pouch, red wax such as scribes used. Gillian held her peace and kept Jensy's, not to disturb him in the ticklish process that saw new cords seated, the seal prepared—he motioned for the candle and she held it herself while he heated and replaced the seal most gingerly.

"No magics," he said then, handing it back. "No magics of mine near this thing. Or the other. Take them. Throw them both in the River."

"Answers, old man."

"Triptis. Promising—without naming names—twenty thousand in gold to the shrine of Triptis."

Gillian wrinkled her nose and took back parchment and cylinder. "Abhizite god," she said. "A dark one." The sum ran cold fingers over her skin. "Twenty thousand. That's—*gold*—twenty thousand. How much do rich men have to spend on temples, old thief?"

"Rich men's *lives* are bought for less."

The fingers went cold about the lead. Gillian swallowed, wishing Jensy had stayed downstairs in the pantry. She held up the lead cylinder. "Can you breach that seal, old man?"

"*Wouldn't.*"

"You tell me why."

"It's more than a lead seal on that. Adepts more than the likes of me; I know my level, woman; I know what not to touch, and you can take my advice. Get out of here. You've stolen something you can't trade in. They don't need to see you, do you understand me? This thing can be traced."

The hairs stirred to her nape. She sat staring at him. "Then throwing it in the River won't do it, either."

"They might give up then. Might. Gillian, you've put your head in the jaws this time."

"Rich men's lives," she muttered, clutching the objects in her hand. She slid them back into the purse and thrust it within her blouse. "I'll get rid of it. I'll find some way. I've paid Jochen to keep Jensy. See he does, or sour his beer."

"Gillian—"

"You don't want to know," she said. "I don't want either of you to know."

There was the window, the slanting ledge outside; she hugged Jensy, and old Nessim, and used it.

III

Alone, she traveled quickly, by warehouse roofs for the first part of her journey, where the riggings and masts of dockside webbed the night sky, by remembered ways across the canal. One monstrous old warehouse squatted athwart the canal like a misshapen dowager, a convenient crossing that avoided the bridges. Skirts hampered; she whipped off the wrap, leaving the knee breeches and woolen hose she wore beneath, the skirt rolled and bound to her waist with her belt. She had her dagger, her razor and the cant to mark her as trouble for ruffians—a lie: the nebulous brotherhood would hardly back her now, in her trouble. They disliked long looks from moneyed men, hired bullies and noise on dockside. If the noise continued about her, she might foreseeably meet with accident, to be found floating in a canal—to quiet the uproar and stop further attentions.

But such as she met did not know it and kept from her path or, sauntering and mocking, still shied from brotherhood cant. Some passwords were a cut throat to use without approval, and thieves out of the Sink taught interlopers bitter lessons.

She paused to rest at the Serpentine of midtown, crouched in the shadows, sweating and hard-breathing, dizzy with want of sleep and food. Her belly had passed the point of hurting. She thought of a side excursion—a bakery's back door, perhaps—but she did not dare the possible hue and cry added to what notoriety she already had. She gathered what strength she had and set out a second time, the way that led to the tinsel shrine and one house that would see its busiest hours in the dark.

Throw it in the canal: she dared not. Once it was gone from her, she had no more bargains left, nothing. As it was she had a secret valuable and fearful to someone. *There comes a time,* Genat had told her often enough, *when chances have to be taken—and taken wide.*

It was not Sophonisba's way.

Panting, she reached the red window, rapped at it; there was dim light inside and long delay—a male voice, a curse, some drunken converse. Gillian leaned against the wall outside and slowed her breathing, wishing by all the gods of Korianth (save one) that Sophonisba would make some haste. She rapped again finally, heart racing as her rashness raised a complaint within—male voice again. She pressed herself to the wall, heard the drunken voice diminish— Sophonisba's now, shrill, bidding someone out. A door opened and closed.

In a moment steps crossed the room and the shutter opened. Gillian showed herself cautiously, stared up into Sophonisba's white face. "Come on out here," Gillian said.

"Get out of here," Sophonisba hissed, with fear stark in her eyes. *"Out,* or I call the watch. There's *money* looking for you."

She would have closed the shutters, but Gillian had both hands on the ledge and vaulted up to perch on it; Gillian snatched and caught a loose handful of Sophonisba's unlaced shift. "Don't do that, Sophie. If you bring the watch, we'll both be sorry. You know me. I've got something I've got to get rid of. Get dressed."

"And lose a night's—"

"Yes. Lose your nose if you don't hurry about it." She brought out the razor, that small and wicked knife of which Sophonisba was most afraid. She sat polishing it on her knee while Sophonisba sorted into a flurry of skirts. Sophonisba paused once to look; she let the light catch the knife and Sophonisba made greater haste. "Fix your hair," Gillian said.

"Someone's going to come back here to check on me if I don't take my last fee front—"

"Then fix it on the way." Steps were headed toward the door. "Haste! Or there'll be bloodletting."

"Get down," Sophonisba groaned. "I'll get rid of her."

Gillian slipped within the room and closed the shutters, stood in the dark against the wall while Sophonisba cracked the door and handed the fee out, heard a gutter dialogue and Sophonisba pleading indisposition. She handed out more money finally, as if she were parting with her life's blood, and closed the door. She looked about with a pained expression. "You owe me, you owe me—"

"I'm carrying something dangerous," Gillian said. "It's being tracked, do you understand? Nessim doesn't like the smell of it."

"O gods."

"Just so. It's trouble, old friend. Priest trouble."

"Then take it to priests."

"Priests expect donations. I've the scent of *gold,* dear friend. It's rich men pass such things back and forth, about things they don't want authority to know about."

"Then throw it in a canal."

"Nessim's advice. But it doesn't take the smell off my hands or answer questions when the trackers catch me up—or *you,* now, old friend."

"What do you want?" Sophonisba moaned. "Gillian, please—"

"Do you know," she said softly, reasonably, "if we take this thing—*we*, dear friend—to the wrong party, to someone who isn't disposed to reward us, or someone who isn't powerful enough to protect us so effortlessly that protection costs him nothing—who would spend effort protecting a whore and a thief, eh, Sophie? But some there are in this city who shed gold like dogs shed hair, whose neighborhoods are so well protected others hesitate to meddle in them. Men of birth, Sophie. Men who might like to know who's paying vast sums of gold for favors in this city."

"Don't tell me these things."

"I'll warrant a whore hears a lot of things, Sophie. I'll warrant a whore knows a lot of ways and doors and windows in Korianth, who's where, who has secrets—"

"A whore is told a lot of lies. I can't help you."

"But you can, pretty Sophonisba." She held up the razor. "I daresay you know names and such—even in the king's own hall."

"*No!*"

"But the king's mad, they say; and who knows what a madman might do? What other names do you know?"

"I don't know *anyone*, I swear I don't."

"Don't swear; we've gods enough here. We improvise, then, you and I." She flung the shutter open. "Out, out with you."

Sophonisba was not adept at ledges. She settled herself on it and hesitated. Gillian thought of pushing her; then, fearing noise, took her hands and let her down gently, followed after with a soft thud. Sophon-

isba stood shivering and tying her laces, the latter un-
successfully.

"Come on," Gillian said.

"I don't walk the alleys," Sophonisba protested in
dread; Gillian pulled her along nonetheless, the back
ways of the Grand Serpentine.

They met trouble. It was inevitable. More than
once gangs of youths spotted Sophonisba, like dogs a
stray cat, and came too close for comfort. Once the
cant was not password enough, and they wanted more
proof: Gillian showed that she carried, knife-carved
in her shoulder, the brotherhood's initiation, and
drunk as they were, they had sense to give way for
that. It ruffled her pride. She jerked Sophonisba along
and said nothing, seething with anger and reckoning
she should have cut one. She could have done it and
gotten away; but not with Sophonisba.

Sophonisba snuffled quietly, her hand cold as ice.

They took to the main canalside at last, when they
must, which was at this hour decently deserted. It was
not a place Gillian had been often; she found her
way mostly by sense, knowing where the tall, domed
buildings should lie. She had seen them most days of
her life from the rooftops of the Sink.

The palaces of the great of Korianth were walled,
with gardens, and men to watch them. She saw seals
now and then that she knew, mythic beasts and
demon beasts snarling from the arches over such
places.

But one palace there was on the leftside hill, op-
posed to the great gold dome of the King's Palace, a
lonely abode well walled and guarded.

There were guards, gilt-armed guards, with plumes
and cloaks and more flash than ever the rufflers of
midtown dared sport. Gillian grinned to herself and

felt Sophonisba's hand in hers cold and limp from dread of such a place.

She marked with her eye where the guards stood, how they came and went and where the walls and accesses lay, where trees and bushes topped the walls inside and how the wall went to the very edge of the white marble building. The place was defended against armed men, against that sort of threat; against —the thought cooled her grin and her enthusiasm— guilded Assassins and free-lancers; a prince must worry for such things.

No. It was far from easy as it looked. Those easy ways could be set with traps; those places too un-guarded could become deadly. She looked for the ways less easy, traced again that too-close wall.

"Walk down the street," she told Sophonisba. "Now. Just walk down the street."

"You're mad."

"Go."

Sophonisba started off, pale figure in blue silks, a disheveled and unlaced figure of ample curves and confused mien. She walked quickly as her fear would urge her, beyond the corner and before the eyes of the guards at the gate.

Gillian stayed long enough to see the sentries' at-tention wander, then pelted to the wall and carefully, with delicate fingers and the balance Genat had taught, spidered her way up the brickwork.

Dogs barked the moment she flung an arm over. She cursed, ran the crest of the thin wall like a trained ape, made the building itself and crept along the masonry—*too much of ornament, my lord!*—as far as the upper terrace.

Over the rim and onto solid ground, panting.

Whatever had become of Sophonisba, she had served her purpose.

Gillian darted for a further terrace. Doors at the far end swung open suddenly; guards ran out in consternation. Gillian grinned at them, arms wide, like a player asking tribute; bowed.

They were not amused, thinking of their hides, surely. She looked up at a ring of pikes, cocked her head to one side and drew a conscious deep breath, making obvious what they should see; that it was no male intruder they had caught.

"Courier," she said, "for Prince Osric."

IV

He was not, either, amused.

She stood with a very superfluous pair of men-at-arms gripping her wrists so tightly that the blood left her hands and the bones were like to snap, and the king's bastard—and sole surviving son—fingered the pouch they had found in their search of her.

"Courier," he said.

They were not alone with the guards, he and she. A brocaded troop of courtiers and dandies loitered near, amongst the porphyry columns and on the steps of the higher floor. He dismissed them with a wave of his hand; several seemed to feel privileged and stayed.

"For whom," the prince asked, "are you a courier?"

"Couriers bring messages," she said. "I decided on my own to bring you this one. I thought you should have it."

"Who are you?"

"A free-lance assassin," she said, promoting herself, and setting Prince Orsic back a pace. The guards nearly crushed her wrists; they went beyond pain.

"Jisan," Osric said.

One of the three who had stayed walked forward, and Gillian's spine crawled; she knew the look of trouble, suspected the touch of another brotherhood, more disciplined than her own. "I was ambitious," she said at once. "I exaggerate."

"She is none of ours," said the Assassin. A dark man he was, unlike Osric, who was white-blond and thin; this Jisan was from southern climes and not at all flash, a drab shadow in brown and black beside Osric's glitter.

"Your name," said Osric.

"Gillian," she said; and recalling better manners and where she was: "—majesty."

"And how come by this?"

"A cutpurse . . . found this worthless. It fell in the street. But it's some lord's seal."

"*No* lord's seal. Do you read, guttersnipe?"

"Read, I?" The name rankled; she kept her face calm. "No, lord."

He whisked out a dagger and cut the cords, unfurled the parchment. A frown came at once to his face, deepened, and his pale eyes came suddenly up to hers. "Suppose that someone read it to you."

She sucked a thoughtful breath, weighed her life, and Jensy's. "A drunk clerk read it—for a kiss; said it was something he didn't want to know; and I think then—some great lord might want to know it; but which lord, think I? One lord might make good use and another bad, one be grateful and another not—might make rightest use of something dangerous—might be glad it came here in good loyal hands, and not where it was supposed to go; might take notice of a stir in the lowtown, bully boys looking for that cutpurse to cut throats, armed men and some of them not belonging hereabouts. King's wall's too high, majesty, so I came here."

"Whose bravos?" Jisan asked.

She blinked. "Wish I knew that; I'd like to know."

"You're that cutpurse," he said.

"If I were, would I say yes, and if I weren't, would I say yes? But I know that thing's better not in my hands and maybe better here than in the River. A trifle of reward, majesty, and there's no one closer mouthed than I am; a trifle more, majesty, and you've all my talents at hire: no one can outbid a prince, not for the likes of me; I know I'm safest to be bribed once and never again."

Osric's white-blue eyes rested on her a very long, very calculating moment. "You're easy to kill. Who would miss you?"

"No one, majesty. No one. But I'm eyes and ears and Korianthine—" Her eyes slid to the Assassin. "And I go places where *he* won't."

The Assassin smiled. His eyes did not. Guild man. He worked by hire and public license.

And sometimes without.

Osric applied his knife to the lead cylinder to gently cut it. "No," Gillian said nervously. And when he looked up, alarmed: "I would not," she said. "I have been advised—the thing has some ill luck attached."

"Disis," Osric called softly, and handed the cylinder into the hands of an older man, a scholarly man, whose courtier's dress was long out of mode. The man's long, lined face contracted at the touch of it in his hand.

"Well advised," that one said. "Silver and lead—a confining. I would be most careful of that seal, majesty; I would indeed."

The prince took the cylinder back, looked at it with a troubled mien, passed it back again. Carefully then he took the purse from his own belt, from beside his dagger. "Your home?" he asked of Gillian.

"Dockside," she said.

"All of it?"

She bit her lip. "Ask at the Anchor," she said, betraying a sometime haunt, but not Sophonisba's, not the Rose either. "All the Sink knows Gillian." And that was true.

"Let her go," Osric bade his guards. Gillian's arms dropped, relief and agony at once. He tossed the purse at her feet, while she was absorbed in her pain. "Come to the garden gate next time. Bring me word—and *names*."

She bent, gathered the purse with a swollen hand, stood again and gave a shy bow, her heart pounding with the swing of her fortunes. She received a disgusted wave of dismissal, and the guards at her right jerked her elbow and brought her down the hall, the whole troop of them to escort her to the door.

"My knives," she reminded them with a touch of smugness. They returned them and hastened her down the stairs. She did not gape at the splendors about her, but she saw them, every detail. In such a place twenty thousand in gold might be swallowed up. *Gillian* might be swallowed up, here and now or in the Sink, later. She knew. She reckoned it.

They took her through the garden, past handlers and quivering dogs the size of men, and there at the garden gate they let her go without the mauling she had expected. Princes' favor had power even out of princes' sight, then; from what she had heard of Osric, that was wise of them.

They pitched the little bundle of her skirt at her

feet, undone. She snatched that up and flung it jaun-
tily over her shoulder, and stalked off into the alleys
that were her element.

She had a touch of conscience for Sophonisba.
Likely Sophonisba had disentangled herself by now,
having lied her way with some small skill out of whatever predicament she had come to, appearing in the
high town: *forgive me, lord; this lord he brought me
here, he did, and turned me out, he did, and I'm lost,
truly, sir . . .* Sophonisba would wait till safe daylight and find her way home again, to nurse a grudge
that money would heal. And she . . .

Gillian was shaking when she finally stopped to
assess herself. Her wrists felt maimed, the joints of
her hands swollen. She crouched and slipped the
knives back where they belonged, earnestly wishing
she had had the cheek to ask for food as well. She
rolled the skirt and tied it in the accustomed bundle
at her belt. Lastly—for fear, lastly—she spilled the sack
into her cupped hand, spilled it back again quickly,
for the delight and the terror of the flood of gold that
glinted in the dim light. She thrust it down her
blouse, at once terrified to possess such a thing and
anxious until she could find herself in the Sink again,
where she had ratholes in plenty. This was not a
thing to walk the alleys with.

She sprang up and started moving, alone and free
again, and casting furtive and careful glances all
directions, most especially behind.

Priests and spells and temple business. Of a sudden
it began to sink into her mind precisely what services
she had agreed to, to turn spy; Triptis's priests
bought whore's babes, or any else that could be
stolen. That was a thief's trade beneath contempt; a
trade the brotherhood stamped out where it found it

obvious: grieving mothers were a noise, and a desperate one, bad for business. It was *that* kind of enemy she dealt with.

Find me names, the lord Osric had said, with an Assassin standing on one side and a magician on the other. Of a sudden she knew who the old magicker had been: Disis, the prince had called him; Aldisis, more than dabbler in magics—part and parcel of the prince's entourage of discontents, waiting on the mad king to pass the dark gates elsewhere. The prince had had brothers and a sister, and now he had none; now he had only to wait.

Aldisis the opener of paths. His ilk of lesser station sold ill wishes down by the Fish, and some of those worked; Aldisis had skills, it was whispered.

And Jisan cared for those Aldisis missed.

Find me names.

And what might my lord prince do with them? Gillian wondered, without much wondering; and with a sudden chill: *What but lives are worth twenty thousand gold? And what but high-born lives?*

She had agreed with no such intention; she had priest troubles and hunters on her trail, and she did not need to know their names, not from a great enough distance from Korianth. One desperate chance—to sell the deadly information and gamble it was not Osric himself, to gamble with the highest power she could reach and hope she reached above the plague spot in Korianth . . . for gold, to get her and Jensy out of reach and out of the city until the danger was past.

Dangerous thoughts nibbled at her resolve, the chance she had been looking for, three years on the street with Jensy—a chance not only of one purse of gold . . . but of others. She swore at herself for thinking on it, reminded herself what she was; but there was also what she might be. Double such a purse could support Jensy in a genteel order: learning and fine clothes and fine manners; freedom for herself, to eel herself back dockside and vanish into her own darknesses, gather money, and power . . . No strange cities for her, nothing but Korianth, where she knew her way, all the low and tangled ways that took a lifetime of living to learn of a city—no starting over elsewhere, to play whore and teach Jensy the like, to get their throats cut in Amisent or Kesirn, trespassing in another territory and another brotherhood.

She skipped along, the strength flooding back into her, the breath hissing regularly between her teeth. She found herself again in familiar territory, known alleys; found one of her narrowest boltholes and rid herself of the prince's purse, all but one coin, itself a bit of recklessness. After that she ran and paused, ran and paused, slick with sweat and light-headed with fortune and danger and hunger.

The Bowel took her in, and Blindman's—home territory indeed; her sore, slippered feet pattered over familiar cobbles; she loosed her skirt and whipped it about her, mopped her face with her scarf and knotted that about her waist, leaving her curls free. The door to the Rose was before her. She pushed it open.

And froze to the heart.

V

All the Rose was a shambles, the tables broken, a few survivors or gawkers milling about in a forlorn knot near the streetside door. There was chill in the air, a palpable chill, like a breath of ice. Fat Jochen lay stark on the floor by the counter, with all his skin gone gray and his clothes . . . faded, as if cobweb composed them.

"Gods," Gillian breathed, clutching at the luck piece she bore, easygoing Agdalia's. And in the next breath: "Jensy," she murmured, and ran for the stairs.

The door at the end of the narrow hall stood open, moonlight streaming into a darkened room from the open window. She stopped, drew her knife—clutched the tawdry charm, sick with dread. From her vantage point she saw the cot disheveled, the movement of a shadow within, like a lich robed in cobwebs.

"Jensy!" she shouted into that dark.

The wraith came into the doorway, staggered out, reached.

Nessim. She held her hand in time, only just, turned the blade and with hilt in hand gripped the old man's sticklike arms, seized on him with both hands, heedless of hurts. He stammered something. There was a silken crumbling in the cloth she held, like something moldered, centuries old. The skin on Nessim's poor face peeled in strips like a sun-baked hinterlander's.

"Gillian," he murmured. "They wanted you."

"Where's Jensy?"

He tried to tell her, pawed at the amulet he had worn; it was a crystal, cracked now, in a peeling hand. He waved the hand helplessly. "Took Jensy," he said. He was bald, even to the eyebrows. "I saved myself—saved myself—had no strength for mousekin. Gillian, run away."

"Who, blast you, Nessim!"

"Don't know. Don't know. But Triptis. Triptis's priests . . . ah, go, go, Gillian."

Tears made tracks down his seared cheeks. She thrust him back, anger and pity confounded in her. The advice was sound; they were without power, without patrons. Young girls disappeared often enough in the Sink without a ripple.

Rules changed. She thrust past him to the window and out it, onto the creaking shingles, to the eaves and down the edge to Blindman's. She hit the cobbles in a crouch and straightened.

They were looking for her. For her, not Jensy. And Nessim had survived to give her that message.

Triptis.

She slipped the knife into her belt and turned to go, stopped suddenly at the apparition that faced her in the alley.

"Gillian," the shadow said, unfolding upward out of the debris by Goat's Alley.

Her hand slipped behind her to the dagger; she set her back against solid brick and flicked a glance at shadows . . . others, at the crossing of Sparrow's. More around the corner, it was likely.

"Where is it?" the same chill voice asked.

"I sell things," she said. "Do you want it back? You have something I want."

"You can't get it back," the whisper said. "Now what shall we do?"

Her blood went colder still. They knew where she had been. She was followed; and no one slipped up on Gillian, no one.

Seals and seals, Nessim had said.

"Name your price," she said.

"You gained access to a prince," said the whisper. "You can do it again."

Osric, she thought. Her heart settled into a leaden, hurting rhythm. *It was Osric it was aimed at.*

"We also," said the whisper, "sell things. You want the child Jensy. The god has many children. He can spare one."

Triptis; it was beyond doubt; the serpent-god, swallowing the moon once monthly; the snake and the mouse. *Jensy!*

"I am reasonable," she said.

There was silence. If the shadow smiled, it was invisible. A hand extended, open, bearing a tiny silver circlet. "A gift you mustn't lose," the whisper said.

She took the chill ring, a serpent shape, slipped it onto her thumb, for that was all it would fit. The metal did not warm to her flesh but chilled the flesh about it.

A second shadow stepped forward, proffered another small object, a knife the twin of her own. "The blade will kill at a scratch," the second voice said. "Have care of it."

"Don't take off the ring," the first whispered.

"You could hire assassins," she said.

"We have," the whisper returned.

She stared at them. "Jensy comes back alive," she said. "To this door. No cheating."

"On either side."

"You've bid higher," she said. "What proof do you want?"

"Events will prove. Kill him."

Her lips trembled. "I haven't eaten in two days; I haven't slept—"

"Eat and sleep," the shadow hissed, "in what leisure you think you have. We trust you."

They melted backward, shadow into shadow, on all sides. The metal remained cold upon her finger. She carried it to her lips, unconscious reflex, thought with cold panic of poison, spat onto the cobbles again and again. She was shaking.

She turned, walked into the inn of the Rose past Jochen's body, past Nessim, who sat huddled on the bottom of the steps. She poured wine from the tap, gave a cup to Nessim, drank another herself, grimacing at the flavor. Bread on the sideboard had gone hard; she soaked it in the wine, but it had the flavor of ashes; cheeses had molded: she sliced off the rind with a knife from the board and ate. Jochen lay staring at the ceiling. Passersby thrust in their heads and gaped at a madwoman who ate such tainted things; another, hungrier than the rest, came in to join the pillage, and an old woman followed.

"Go, run," Nessim muttered, rising with great difficulty to tug at her arm, and the others shied from him in horror; it was a look of leprosy.

"Too late," she said. "Go away yourself, old man. Find a hole to hide in. I'll get Jensy back."

It hurt the old man; she had not meant it so. He shook his head and walked away, muttering sorrowfully of Jensy. She left, then, by the alleyway, which was more familiar to her than the street. She had food in her belly, however tainted; she had eaten worse.

She walked, stripped the skirt aside and limped along, feeling the cobbles through the holes that had worn now in her slippers. She tucked the skirt in a seam of itself, hung it about her shoulder, walked with more persistence than strength down Blindman's.

Something stirred behind her; she spun, surprised nothing, her nape prickling. A rat, perhaps; the alleys were infested this close to the docks. Perhaps it was not. She went, hearing that something behind her from time to time and never able to surprise it.

She began to run, took to the straight ways, the ways that no thief liked to use, broke into the streets and raced breathlessly toward the Serpentine, that great canal along which all the streets of the city had their beginnings. Breath failed her finally and she slowed, dodged late walkers and kept going. If one of the walkers was that one who followed her . . . she could not tell.

The midtown gave way to the high; she retraced ways she had passed twice this night, with faltering steps, her breath loud in her own ears. It was late, even for prowlers. She met few but stumbled across one drunk or dead in the way, leapt the fallen form and fled with the short-range speed of one of the city's wary cats, dodged to this course and that and came out again in the same alley from which she and Sophonisba had spied out the palace.

The garden gate, Prince Osric had instructed her. The ring burned cold upon her finger.

She walked into the open, to the very guards who had let her out not so very long before.

VI

The prince was abed. The fact afforded his guards no little consternation—the suspicion of a message urgent enough to make waking him advisable; the suspicion of dangerous wrath if it was not. Gillian, for her part, sat still, wool-hosed ankles crossed, hands folded, a vast fear churning at her belly. They had taken the ring. It had parted from her against all the advice of him who had given it to her; and it was not pleasing them that concerned her, but Jensy.

They had handled it and had it now, but if it was cold to them. they had not said, had not reacted. She suspected it was not. It was hers, for her.

Master Aldisis came. He said nothing, only stared at her, and she at him; him she feared most of all, his sight, his perception. His influence. She had nothing left, not the ring, not the blades, not the single gold coin. The scholar, in his night robe, observed her and walked away. She sat, the heat of exertion long since fled, with her feet and hands cold and finally numb.

"Mistress Gillian," a voice mocked her.

She looked up sharply, saw Jisan standing by a porphyry column. He bowed as to a lady. She sat still, staring at him as warily as at Aldisis.

"A merry chase, mistress Gillian."

Alarm might have touched her eyes. It surprised her, that it had been he.

"Call the lord prince," the Assassin said, and a guard went.

"Who is your contract?" she asked.

He smiled. "Guildmaster might answer," he said. "Go ask."

Patently she could not. She sat still, fixed as under a serpent's gaze. Her blades were in the guards' hands, one more knife than there had been. They suspected something amiss, as it was their business to suspect all things and all persons; Jisan knew. She stared into his eyes.

"What game are you playing?" he asked her plainly.

"I've no doubt you've asked about."

"There's some disturbance down in lowtown. A tavern with a sudden . . . unwholesomeness in it. Dead men. Would you know about that, mistress Gillian?"

"I carry messages," she said.

His dark eyes flickered. She thought of the serpent-god and the mouse. She kept her hands neatly folded, her feet still. This was a man who killed. Who perhaps enjoyed his work. She thought that he might.

A curse rang out above, echoing in the high beams of the ceiling. Osric. She heard every god in the court pantheon blasphemed and turned her head to stare straight before her, smoothed her breeches, a nervousness—stood at the last moment, remembering the due of royalty, even in night dress.

Called from some night's pleasure? she wondered. In that case he might be doubly wrathful; but he was cold as ever, thin face, thin mouth set, white-blue eyes as void of the ordinary. She could not imagine the man engaged in so human a pastime. Maybe he never did, she thought, the wild irrelevance of exhaustion. Maybe that was the source of his disposition.

"They sent me back," she said directly, "to kill you."

Not many people surely had shocked Osric; she had succeeded. The prince bit his lips, drew a breath, thrust his thin hands in the belt of his velvet robe. "Jisan?" he asked.

"There are dead men," the Assassin said, "at dockside."

"Honesty," Osric murmured, looking on her, a mocking tone.

"Lord," she said, at the edge of her nerves. "Your enemies have my sister. They promise to kill her if I don't carry out their plans."

"And you think so little of your sister, and so much of the gold?"

Her breath nigh strangled her; she swallowed air and kept her voice even. "I know that they will kill her and me whichever I do; tell me the name of your enemies, lord prince, that you didn't tell me the first time you sent me out of here with master Jisan behind me. *Give me names,* lord prince, and I'll hunt your enemies for my own reasons, and kill them or not as you like."

"You should already know one name, thief."

"A god's name? Aye, but gods are hard to hunt, lord prince." Her voice thinned; she could not help it. "Lend me master Aldisis's company instead of master Jisan's, and there's some hope. But go I will; and kill me priests if you haven't any better names."

Osric's cold, pale eyes ran her up and down, flicked to Jisan, back again. "For gold, good thief?"

"For my *sister,* lord prince. Pay me another time."

"Then why come here?"

"Because they'd know." She slid a look toward the guards, shifted weight anxiously. "A ring; they gave me a ring to wear, and they took it."

"Aldisis!" the prince called. The mage came, from some eavesdropping vantage among the columns or from some side room.

An anxious guard proffered the serpent ring, but Aldisis would not touch it; waved it away. "Hold it awhile more," Aldisis said; and to Osric: "They would know where that is. And whether she held it."

"My sister," Gillian said in anguish. "Lord, give it back to me. I came because they'd know if not; and to find out their names. Give me their names. It's almost morning."

"I might help you," said Osric. "Perhaps I might die and delight them with a rumor."

"Lord," she murmured, dazed.

"My enemies will stay close together," he said. "The temple—or a certain lord Brisin's palace . . .

likely the temple; Brisin fears retaliation; the god shelters him. Master Aldisis could explain such things. You're a bodkin at best, mistress thief. But you may prick a few of them; and should you do better, that would delight me. Look to your reputation, thief?"

"Rumor," she said.

"Chaos," muttered Aldisis.

"You advise me against this?" Osric asked.

"No," said Aldisis. "Toward it."

"You mustn't walk out the front gate this time," Osric said, "mistress thief, if you want a rumor."

"Give me what's mine," she said. "I'll clear your walls, lord, and give them my heels; and they'll not take me."

Osric made a sign with his hand; the guards brought her her knives, her purse and her ring, the while Osric retired to a bench, seated himself, with grim stares regarded them all. "I am dead," he said languidly. "I shall be for some few hours. Report it so and ring the bells. Today should be interesting."

Gillian slid the ring onto her finger; it was cold as ever.

"*Go!*" Osric whispered, and she turned and sped from the room, for the doors and the terrace she knew.

Night opened before her; she ran, skimmed the wall with the dogs barking, swung down with the guards at the gate shouting alarm—confused, and not doing their best. She hit the cobbles afoot as they raced after her, and their armor slowed them; she sprinted for known shadows and zigged and zagged through the maze.

She stopped finally, held a hand to a throbbing side

and fetched up against a wall, rolled on a shoulder to look back and find pursuit absent.

Then the bells began out of the dark—mournful bells, tolling out a lie that must run through all of Korianth: the death of a prince.

She walked, staggering with exhaustion, wanting sleep desperately; but the hours that she might sleep were hours of Jensy's life. She was aware finally that she had cut her foot on something; she noted first the pain and then that she left a small spot of blood behind when she walked. It was far from killing her; she kept moving.

It was midtown now. She went more surely, having taken a second wind.

And all the while the bells tolled, brazen and grim, and lights burned in shuttered windows where all should be dark, people wakened to the rumor of a death.

The whole city must believe the lie, she thought, from the Sink to the throne, the mad monarch himself believed that Osric had died; and should there not be general search after a thief who had killed a prince?

She shivered, staggering, reckoning that she ran ahead of the wave of rumor: that by dawn the name of herself and Jensy would be bruited across the Sink, and there would be no more safety.

And behind the doors, she reckoned, rumor prepared itself, folk yet too frightened to come out of doors—never wise for honest folk in Korianth.

When daylight should come . . . it would run wild—mad Seithan to rule with no hope of succession, an opportunity for the kings of other cities, of up-coast and upriver, dukes and powerful men in Kori-anth, all to reach out hands for the power Seithan could not long hold, the tottering for which all had been waiting for more than two years ...

This kind of rumor waited, to be flung wide at a thief's request. This kind of madness waited to be let loose in the city, in which all the enemies might surface, rumors in which a throne might fall, throats be cut, the whole city break into riot ...

A prince might die indeed then, in disorder so general.

Or . . . a sudden and deeper foreboding possessed her . . . a king might.

A noise in one place, a snatch in the other; thief's game in the market. She had played it often enough, she with Jensy.

Not for concern for her and her troubles that Osric risked so greatly . . . but for *Osric's* sake, no other.

She quickened her pace, swallowing down the sickness that threatened her; somehow to get clear of this, to get away in this shaking of powers before two mites were crushed by an unheeding footstep.

She began, with the last of her strength, to run.

VII

The watch was out in force, armed men with lanterns, lights and shadows rippling off the stone of cobbles and of walls like the stuff of the Muranthine Hell, and the bells still tolling, the first tramp of soldiers' feet from off the high streets, canalward.

Gillian sped, not the only shadow that judged the neighborhood of the watch and the soldiers unhealthy; rufflers and footpads were hieing themselves to cover apace, with the approach of trouble and of dawn. She skirted the canals that branched off the Serpentine, took to the alleys again and paused in the familiar alley off Agdalia's Shrine, gasping for breath in the flare of lanterns. A door slammed on the street: Agdalia's was taking precautions. Upper windows closed. The trouble had flowed thus far, and folk who did not wish to involve themselves tried to signify so by staying invisible.

The red-shuttered room was closed and dark; Sophonisba had not returned . . . had found some safe nook for herself with the bells going, hiding in fear, knowing where her partner had gone, perhaps witness to the hue and cry after. *Terrified,* Gillian reckoned, and did not blame her.

Gillian caught her breath and took to that street, forested with pillars, that was called the Street of the Gods. Here too the lanterns of the watch showed in the distance, and far away, dimly visible against the sky . . . the palace of the king upon the other hill of the fold in which Korianth nestled, the gods and the king in close association.

From god to god she passed, up that street like an ascent of fancy, from the bare respectability of little cults like Agdalia's to the more opulent temples of gods more fearsome and more powerful. Watch passed; she retreated at once, hovered in the shadow of the smooth columns of a Korianthine god, Ablis of the Goldworkers, one of the 52,000 gods of Korianth. He had no patronage for her, might, in fact, resent a thief; she hovered fearfully, waiting for ill luck; but perhaps she was otherwise marked. She shuddered, fingering that serpent ring upon her thumb, and walked further in the shadow of the columns.

It was not the greatest temple nor the most conspicuous in this section, that of Triptis. Dull black-green by day, it seemed all black in this last hour of night, the twisted columns like stone smoke, writhing up to a plain portico, without window or ornament. She caught her breath, peered into the dark that surrounded a door that might be open or closed; she was not sure.

Nor was she alone. A prickling urged at her nape, a sense of something that lived and breathed nearby; she whipped out the poisoned blade and turned.

A shadow moved, tottered toward her. "Gillian," it said, held out a hand, beseeching.

"Nessim," she murmured, caught the peeling hand with her left, steadied the old man. He recoiled from her touch.

"You've something of them about you," he said.

"What are you doing here?" she hissed at him. "Old man, go back—get out of here."

"I came for mousekin," he said. "I came to try, Gillian."

The voice trembled. It was, for Nessim, terribly brave.

"You would die," she said. "You're not in their class, Nessim."

"Are you?" he asked with a sudden straightening, a memory, perhaps, of better years. "You'd do what? *What* would you do?"

"You stay out," she said, and started to leave; he caught her hand, caught the hand with the poisoned knife and the ring. His fingers clamped.

"No," he said. "No. Be rid of this."

She stopped, looked at his shadowed, peeling face. "They threatened Jensy's life."

"They know you're here. You understand that? With this, they know. Give it to me."

"Aldisis saw it and returned it to me. *Aldisis* himself, old man. Is your advice better?"

"My reasons are friendlier."

A chill went over her. She stared into the old man's eyes. "What should I do?"

"Give it here. Hand it to me. I will contain it for you . . . long enough. They won't know, do you understand me? I'll do that much."

"You can't light a candle, old trickster."

"Can," he said. "Reedlight's easier. I never work more than I have to."

She hesitated, saw the fear in the old man's eyes. A friend, one friend. She nodded, sheathed the knife and slipped off the ring. He took it into his hands and sank down in the shadows with it clasped before his lips, the muscles of his arms shaking as if he strained against something vastly powerful.

And the cold was gone from her hand.

She turned, ran, fled across the street and scrambled up the stonework of the paler temple of the Elder Mother, the Serpent Triptis's near neighbor . . . up, madly, for the windowless temple had to derive its light from some source; and a temple that honored the night surely looked upon it somewhere.

She reached the crest, the domed summit of the Mother, set foot from pale marble onto the darker roof of the Serpent, shuddering, as if the very stone were alive and threatening, able to feel her presence.

To steal from a god, to snatch a life from his jaws . . .

She spun and ran to the rear of the temple, where a well lay open to the sky, where the very holy of the temple looked up at its god, which was night. *That* was the way in she had chosen. The sanctuary, she realized with a sickness of fear, thought of Jensy and took it nonetheless, swung onto the inside rim and looked down, with a second impulse of panic as she saw how far down it was, a far, far drop.

Voices hailed within, echoing off the columns,

shortening what time she had; somewhere voices droned hymns or some fell chant.

She let go, plummeted, hit the slick stones and tried to take the shock by rolling . . . sprawled, dazed, on cold stone, sick from the impact and paralyzed.

She heard shouts, outcries, struggled up on a numbed arm and a sprained wrist, trying to gain her feet. It was indeed the sanctuary; pillars of some green stone showed in the golden light of lamps, pillars carved like twisting serpents, even to the scales, writhing toward the ceiling and knotting in folds across it. The two greatest met above the altar, devouring a golden sun, between their fanged jaws, above her.

"Jensy," she muttered, thinking on Nessim and his hands straining about that thing that they had given her.

She scrambled for the shadows, for safety if there was any safety in this lair of demons.

A man-shaped shadow appeared in that circle of night above the altar; she stopped, shrank back further amongst the columns as it hung and dropped as she had.

Jisan. Who else would have followed her, dark of habit and streetwise? He hit the pavings hardly better than she, came up and staggered, felt of the silver-hilted knife at his belt; she shrank back and back, pace by pace, her slippered feet soundless.

And suddenly the chanting was coming this way, up hidden stairs, lights flaring among the columns; they hymned Night, devourer of light, in their madness beseeched the day not to come—forever Dark, they prayed in their mad hymn. The words crept louder and louder among the columns, and Jisan lingered, dazed.

"Hsst!" Gillian whispered; he caught the sound, seemed to focus on it, fled the other way, amongst the columns on the far side of the hall.

And now the worshippers were within the sanctuary, the lights making the serpent columns writhe and twist into green-scaled life, accompanied by shadows. They bore with them a slight, tinseled form that wept and struggled. Jensy, crying! she never would. Gillian reached for the poisoned blade, her heart risen into her throat. Of a sudden the hopelessness of her attempt came down upon her, for they never would keep their word, never, and there was nowhere to hide: old Nessim could not hold forever, keeping their eyes blind to her.

Or they knew already that they had been betrayed.

She walked out among them. "We have a bargain!" she shouted, interrupting the hymn, throwing things into silence. "I kept mine. Keep yours."

Jensy struggled and bit, and one of them hit her. The blow rang loud in the silence, and Jensy went limp.

One of them stood forward. "He is dead?" that one asked. "The bargain is kept?"

"What else are the bells?" she asked.

There was silence. Distantly the brazen tones were still pealing across the city. It was near to dawn; stars were fewer in the opening above the altar. Triptis's hours were passing.

"Give her back," Gillian said, feeling the sweat run down her sides, her pulse hammering in her smallest veins. "You'll hear no more of us."

A cowl went back, showing a fat face she had seen in processions. No priest, not with that gaudy dress beneath; Duke Brisin, Osric had named one of his enemies; she thought it might be.

And they were not going to honor their word.

Someone cried out; a deep crash rolled through the halls; there was the tread of armored men, sudden looks of alarm and a milling among the priests like a broken hive. Jensy fell, dropped; and Gillian froze with the ringing rush of armored men coming at her back, the swing of lanterns that sent the serpents the more frenziedly twisting about the hall. "Stop them," someone was shouting.

She moved, slashed a priest, who screamed and hurled himself into the others who tried to stop her. Jensy was moving, scrambling for dark with an eel's instinct, rolling away faster than Gillian could help her.

"Jisan!" Gillian shouted to the Assassin, hoping against hope for an ally; and suddenly the hall was ringed with armed men, and herself with a poisoned bodkin, and a dazed, gilt child, huddled together against a black wall of priests.

Some priests tried to flee; the drawn steel of the soldiers prevented; and some died, shrieking. Others were herded back before the altar.

"Lord," Gillian said nervously, casting about among them for the face she hoped to see; and he was there, Prince Osric, in the guise of a common soldier; and Aldisis by him; but he had no eyes for a thief.

"*Father*," Osric hailed the fat man, hurled an object at his feet, a leaden cylinder.

The king recoiled pace by pace, his face white and trembling, shaking convulsively so that the fat quivered upon it. The soldiers' blades remained leveled toward him, and Gillian seized Jensy's naked shoulder and pulled her back, trying for quiet retreat out of this place of murders, away from father and son, mad king who dabbled in mad gods and plotted murders.

"Murderer," Seithan stammered, the froth gathering at his lips. "Killed my legitimate sons . . . every one; killed me, but I didn't die . . . kin-killer. Kin-killing bastard . . . I have loyal subjects left; you'll not reign."

"You've tried *me* for years, honored father, majesty. *Where's my mother?*"

The king gave a sickly and hateful laugh.

There was movement in the dark, where no priest was . . . a figure seeking deeper obscurity; Gillian took her own cue and started to move.

A priest's weapon whipped up, a knife poised to hurl; she cried warning . . . and suddenly chaos, soldiers closed in a ring of bright weapons, priests dying in a froth of blood, and the king . . .

The cries were stilled. Gillian hugged Jensy against her in the shadows, seeing through the forest of snakes the sprawled bodies, the bloody-handed soldiers, Osric—king in Korianth.

King! the soldiers hailed him, that made the air shudder; he gave them orders, that sent them hastening from the slaughter here.

"The *palace!*" he shouted, urging them on to riot that would see throats cut by the hundreds in Korianth.

A moment he paused, sword in hand, looked into the shadows, for Jensy glittered, and it was not so easy to hide. For a moment a thief found the courage to look a prince in the eye, wondering, desperately, whether two such motes of dust as they might not be swept away. Whether he feared a thief's gossip, or cared.

The soldiers had stopped about him, a warlike knot of armor and plumes and swords.

"Get moving!" he ordered them, and swept them away with him, running in their haste to further murders.

Against her, Jensy gave a quiet shiver, and thin arms went round her waist. Gillian tore at a bit of the tinsel, angered by the tawdry ornament. Such men cheated even the gods.

A step sounded near her. She turned, dagger in hand, faced the shadow that was Jisan. A knife gleamed in his hand.

He let the knife hand fall to his side.

"Whose are you?" she asked. He tilted his head toward the door, where the prince had gone, now king.

"Was," he said. "Be clever and run far, Gillian thief; or lie low and long. There comes a time princes don't like to remember the favors they bought. Do you think King Osric will want to reward an assassin? Or a thief?"

"You leave first," she said. "I don't want you at my back."

"I've been there," he reminded her, "for some number of hours."

She hugged Jensy the tighter. "Go," she said. "Get out of my way."

He went; she watched him walk into the beginning day of the doorway, a darkness out of darkness, and down the steps.

"You all right?" she asked of Jensy.

"Knew I would be," Jensy said with little-girl nastiness; but her lips shook. And suddenly her eyes widened, staring beyond.

Gillian looked, where something like a rope of darkness twisted among the columns, above the blood that spattered the altar; a trick of the wind and the lamps, perhaps. But it crossed the sky, where the stars paled to day, and moved against the ceiling. Her right hand was suddenly cold.

She snatched Jensy's arm and ran, weaving in and out of the columns the way Jisan had gone, out, out into the day, where an old man huddled on the steps, rocking to and fro and moaning.

"Nessim!" she cried. He rose and cast something that whipped away even as he collapsed in a knot of tatters and misery. A serpent-shape writhed across the cobbles in the beginning of day . . .

. . . and shriveled, a dry stick.

She clutched Jensy's hand and ran to him, her knees shaking under her, bent down and raised the dry old frame by the arms, expecting death; but a blistered face gazed back at her with a fanatic's look of triumph. Nessim's thin hand reached for Jensy, touched her face.

"All right, mousekin?"

"Old man," Gillian muttered, perceiving something she had found only in Jensy; he would have, she vowed, whatever comfort gold could buy, food, and a bed to sleep in. A mage; he was that. And a man.

Gold, she thought suddenly, recalling the coin in her purse; and the purse she had buried off across the canals.

And one who had dogged her tracks most of the night.

She spat an oath by another god and sprang up, blind with rage.

"Take her to the Wyvern," she bade Nessim and started off without a backward glance, reckoning ways she knew that an Assassin might not, reckoning on throat-cutting, on revenge in a dozen colors.

She took to the alleys and began to run by alleys a big man could never use, cracks and crevices and ledges and canal verges.

And made it. She worked into the dark, dislodged the stone, took back the purse and climbed catwise to the ledges, to lurk and watch.

He was not far behind, to work his big frame into the narrow space that took hers so easily, to work loose the self-same stone.

Upon her rooftop perch she stood, gave a low whistle . . . shook out a pair of golden coins and dropped them ringing at his feet, a grand generosity, like the prince's.

"For your trouble," she bade him, and was away.

Parting Gifts

by Diane Duane

I have elsewhere wondered out loud (well, in print, anyway) why it is that so many of the best writers of fantasy happen to be women. To this question I have found no easy answer, but it certainly is as true as it is remarkable: think of Ursula K. LeGuin, Evangeline Walton, C. J. Cherryh, Tanith Lee, Grail Undwin, Patricia A. McKillip, and you will realize what I mean.

To this distinguished and talented company Diane Duane now belongs. She took her place among these fine writers with a single novel, her first, the stunning *Door Into Fire,* which Dell published a few years ago. At the time I thought it was the best new fantasy novel of the year, and nothing has happened since to change my mind about Diane Duane or her extraordinary talent.

The new story that follows only adds fresh luster to her name. It has a depth of characterization, a resonance of emotional content that are, quite simply, beautiful.

Let us all hope it is only the first of many more . . .

PARTING GIFTS

Every Dragon has its lair, every bird its nest; the
Shadow has only our hearts. . . . But we may
as easily evict It as charge rent.

Darthene Prosectics, 21

Outside her dream it was winter, and night. But Sirronde wandered beyond the gates of dream, straying a
long while among the golden landscapes of long-dead
summers, until at last she came to the forges of evening. She stopped by the smithy door and looked into
the smoky, dim-lit, lightning-smelling place, where in
a pit banked deep with sunset fires a young woman
was forging souls.

As Sirronde watched the woman reached into the
pit, not with tongs but with her bare hand. She
plucked out one soul that burned at white heat and
began to beat it out on a cloud-gray anvil with a
hammer wrought of thunder. A great shower of blue
sparks went up as she worked the soul into the shape
she needed. Some minutes passed before the woman
glanced up at Sirronde. When she did, breathing
hard, she smiled; but the smile was abstracted and
brief. "I have a job for you," she said.

Sirronde looked more carefully at the woman, and
the sudden calm realization of dream came over her.
This was not just any village smith in worn clothes
and a stained leather apron. The braided hair held
out of the young woman's way with a leather band

was darker than the ancient night before the stars were made; beneath the smooth, sweaty, heat-reddened brow, eyes blue as the blue Flame of Power gazed at Sirronde with a regard affectionate, and immeasurably powerful, and not quite sane. Sirronde bowed slightly, a careful, awed courtesy, for the Goddess in Her Maiden aspect is as mad as one must be to constantly create in a universe where one's creations are quickly marred by death. "Lady and Queen," Sirronde said, "after fifty winters spent in Your service, I thought my questing days were over."

"You still have the Fire I gave you," the Maiden said, picking up the soul She had been working on and thrusting it deep into the pit of sunset embers again.

"That's so. But at my age I'm not as good a channel for it as I used to be. . . ."

"I know," the Maiden said. She wiped Her brow and gestured at the pit; the sunset fires blazed up burning white. "I need you to take a message for Me."

"Your servant," said Sirronde, bowing again.

The Maiden was watching the fires of the forge pit with a critical eye. "The day after tomorrow, the Moon is dark," She said, "and that day, about noontime, it eclipses the Sun as well. And that night of new Moon is Opening Night. . . ."

Sirronde's dream-calm began to give way to nervous foreboding. On Opening Night, the longest night of the year, the boundaries between worlds grew thin, and unquiet spirits walked abroad. Moondark, the most perilous time of any month, would make matters worse, lending the evil things strength. But an eclipse as well—this would be a day of triple dark, and on such a day all the powers of darkness are given into the hand of the Shadow. The Goddess's old enemy would have the strength to do what It had tried again and again to do—destroy Her world, and the creations It hated most: humankind. . . .

"Tomorrow morning," the Maiden said, "go south. On foot."

"South?" Sirronde was incredulous. "In *this* weather?"

The Maiden glanced at Sirronde as She took the white-hot soul out of the forge pit and laid it on the anvil again. Her look was mild.

"Sorry, my Lady," Sirronde said. "Say on."

The Maiden picked up Her hammer again. "Go south until you see what needs to be done. That's all."

"Uh—can't You tell me a little more? You *do* know everything—"

"Yes," the Maiden said wearily, keeping Her eyes on Her work as She started hammering again, "I do."

Sirronde breathed out, both worried and intrigued, and tried one last time. "Will I be going alone?"

At that the Maiden paused and looked up, that absent, gentle look again, and Sirronde's heart ached briefly with love for the contrasts of Her—the serene, divine beauty; the stubborn, human determination to create faster than the death She'd accidentally let into Her world could destroy. "Mother," the Maiden said, "have you ever?"

"Daughter, now that You mention it, no. You've always been with me."

The Maiden nodded. "Go well, then," She said, and began hammering hard again, so that sparks flew thick as She smote the soul into shape on the anvil—

—and Sirronde woke up to a chill pale light inside her little house. Waking took a few moments; the vividness of dreaming true had always made mere physical reality seem rather thin afterward. She got out of bed with a blanket around her and went quickly across the hard dirt floor to the thick-glazed front window. On the small square of glass a delicate hand had etched fern feathers of frost to go with the new snowfall that lay outside. The roofs of the scattering of houses that made up Marrish village were thatched thick with it, and the fields were carpeted deep; whiteness stretched unbroken southward to the skirts of the mountains. Over everything lay a molten winter dawn, the east streaked with clouds iron gray below and blazing white above, as if in the fields of the morning Someone worked late at the forge.

Sirronde swore at her stiff joints, got dressed, found her haversack and started packing.

Marrish had one street, and even in cold weather most family fights seemed to take place in the middle of it. This one was no exception. "Mother, you're too *old* for this!" Sirronde's daughter Andric was shouting, while her husband Torve muttered agreement behind her. *Of course I am,* Sirronde thought, but wouldn't say it. She reflected with rueful humor on how this scene must look to the neighbors peering through their windows; tall fair sharp-faced Andric waving her arms and yelling down at her little silver-haired sharp-faced mother—both of them bundled in furs like bears, one of them a bear on snowshoes with a pack and skis strapped to her back, and her old blackthorn Rod sheathed at her side. "I may be old, dear, but I'm a Rodmistress," Sirronde said. "When the Goddess calls, I go, and I do what She tells me with the Power She gave me."

"But, Mother, at the bottom of the year? In the

middle of the Dreadnights, on the eve of Opening Night almost, you're going out into open country unprotected—"

Sirronde felt about stiffly for her Rod and drew it, then reached down inside her and called the Power up. The Fire came, rippling and flowing around the Rod that conducted it, spilling down onto the dirty ice of the street in a flamefall of brilliant blue. "Tell me I'm unprotected," Sirronde said dryly, while under the pooling Fire the ice melted and grass began to grow. She did her best not to show that the small wreaking was causing her strain.

"Yes, Mother, but—"

Sirronde sighed. *You're working too hard, can't some younger Rodmistress do it, you've earned a rest, let the Goddess ask someone else. . . .* The argument was years old and would get a couple hours older if she let it. She had never been able to get Andric to understand how difficult it was to say no to the Goddess, Who never asked for help unless She needed it. "Andi," Sirronde said, "if I'm not back before New Year's, take an extra drink from the First Cup for me. And milk the cow while I'm gone, will you?" Then off she went, past her daughter and her son-in-love, past the staring neighbors. *Where's that crazy lady going this time?* she heard one of them thinking. Sirronde chuckled; probably because of the general annoyance of being rousted out of her comfortable home into the cold, her underhearing was sharp this morning. *Lady grant it stays that way—I may need it.* She walked off the end of the village's single street into the fields, heading southward toward the places where no one lived, toward the southern edge of the maps of Darthen, the Highpeaks.

She struck the snowy road leading southeast to

Orsvier and Hard Shielings, scuffing along less briskly than she wished—her joints, full of the stiffening-ague of age, were twinging in protest at being made to move so early in the day. These days not even her Fire could do much about the old familiar pain, but she didn't dwell on that just now. *She never did tell me what the message was,* Sirronde thought. *I wish I knew what I was supposed to do. . . .* In her younger days she had eagerly sought out the Shadow, facing It down in many forms: earthquake and flood, forest fire and plague, monsters, demons, sometimes men—but never before in a situation where It had so many of the advantages. The foreboding feeling of the dream crept over her again as she thought of the lovely face averted from her, the tired voice with so little to say. *And why me? Why now, when I'm long past my prime, when it's all I can do to call up enough Fire to cure dried-up cows and melt ice? Why has She chosen a weapon that will probably break in Her hand? What's going to be asked of me?*

No answers came and Sirronde kept walking, gazing up at the mountain wall, gray and white and shadow-blue, that reared up before her a third of the way to the zenith. The mountains of the Highpeaks' Erchámë range were old friends, innocent, savage, much beloved. They had killed men, but Sirronde still called them by name and thought them beautiful. Erchámë, Dikhála with her two peaks, red-shouldered Sespe, Rodochroun, low-hunched Blackmount, Aglaurë, Wíren—*Two days' walk will bring me to the feet of them easily—the Shadow's country, on the Shadow's night. And then what? Do I stand there at the edge of the world and yell insults until It hears me?*

She stopped in an aspen dell for nunch, brushing

off a boulder to sit on, and ate a cold meal of trail-cake and spiced wine among the slim white trunks and branches, listening to the hiss and rattle of the last few yellow shreds of leaf as the south wind worried them off the trees. The dappled cloud cover of the morning was giving way to heavier stuff, a silver-gray overcast pregnant with storm. "You might keep it from snowing, at least," Sirronde said reproachfully to the sky. The sky, indifferent, grew darker.

"Oh, well," Sirronde said, and got up, stretching. Hard Shielings was five miles down the road; she would make it there by the time darkness fell and have a hot dinner at the Tartaret and Block. . . . She picked up her staff and turned toward the road, and a motion off to one side caught her attention.

From beside the base of a triple-trunked aspen, a small blot of darkness took a clumsy-delicate step toward her and paused. Sirronde stared. It was a kitten, a bedraggled gray-and-black tabby kitten with wild, wide eyes, and bumps under its fur, visibly ribs. It looked at Sirronde, silent for a second, and then opened its mouth as if to meow or speak, but no sound came out. It made no other move.

Sirronde thought immediately of two things—of the chicken breast in her food wallet, which she had been saving for tomorrow, and of the terrible pride of cats, even the very young ones. She nodded the kitten courtesy, sat carefully back down on the boulder and unslung her wallet. "I hadn't thought to meet with company so far from town," she said, getting out the chicken breast. "Doubtless you've already eaten, but perhaps you'd consider taking traveler's hospitality with me, just for the form of things. . . ."

She waited. The kitten stared at Sirronde, blinking, and finally came slowly toward her, floundering through the drifted snow with what dignity it could manage. It jumped up on the boulder, looked hard at her again, then crouched down and began to bolt the pieces of chicken she had already shredded for it, almost choking in its haste. Sirronde nibbled an occasional bit of the meat, just for the form of things, and looked at her guest with concern. *Four months old, or maybe five. But so thin! Did he go astray from a wild litter? Or maybe he's from Hard Shielings, and got lost—*

She waited, and the kitten finished his chicken, then sat up and washed himself most carefully before looking up at Sirronde again out of big green-golden eyes. "Thank you," he said in a small, dry, calm voice.

"You're welcome. I'm heading for the Tartaret at the Shielings, to stay the night; would you care to come with me?"

"All right," the kitten said, and climbed up Sirronde's arm to settle in her hood.

"Off we go, then." She packed up her wallet again, picked up her staff and made for the road.

The kitten said nothing for the rest of the day, except to grumble a bit when the snow began toward nightfall. It crawled inside Sirronde's coat while she did on her skis and raced the snowstorm down to the lighted windows of Hard Shielings town in its little vale.

The Tartaret and Block was the largest building in the thirty-house village, being both inn and town hall as well as home of the innkeeper's great-family—three marriages and various grandparents, children, grandchildren, cousins, aunts, uncles and hangers-on. Sirronde was spotted in the inn yard by several of the children as she was taking off her skis. By the time

she got them racked and was heading for the door,
Poole the innkeeper was there, talking, hugging her
and helping her out of her furs, all at once. He was a
tall, angular man, built narrow and strong, balding
on top but with a radiant smile that was the envy of
people with more hair. "I *told* my wives," he was saying, "I told them, you watch, even if we didn't send, I
bet Sirronde'll show up anyway—"

"You were right as usual," she said, reaching into
her coat for the kitten. "What happened? Your still
break down again?"

Poole grimaced. "The last batch of starfire came
out tasting like hellfire instead. If you'd have a look at
it—"

"I'd better. I have to drink the stuff, don't I?" She
let him draw her into the inn's common room, full of
children shouting at some game, adults talking and
laughing, warm fireglow from three hearths. "The
still first," she said, handing Poole the kitten and her
coat, "then supper and beer for me. And bring a
mouse for my friend."

"We're out of mice," Poole said, looking down be-
mused at the kitten. "The roast beef is good,
though."

"Fine. Make him milk the cow for you," Sirronde
called to the kitten as Poole carried him away.

Sirronde made her way back to the kitchen and
there spent most of an hour using the Fire to clean
scale out of the still's copper tubing while surrounded
by an audience of children demanding that she summon up the Goddess, make it snow more, bring Dai's
dead rat back to life, make the stew pot fall on
Tathë's mother, do a *real* magic! "This *is* real
magic," Sirronde said sedately, peering up into the
still's innards, "and it *is* snowing more." There was

an immediate rush for the windows, followed by noisy celebration and praise of Sirronde's powers. As Sirronde got up and wiped the sweat of exertion off her face, she threw a glance at the ceiling, in the general direction of the creator of snowstorms and frosty artwork on windowpanes. *After this bit of work, I doubt I could start it snowing even with the weather the way it is. Thanks for getting me off the spot!*

Sirronde went back out to the common room after being handed a plate with more beef and white beans on it than she could have eaten in a week. She found the kitten lolling on the hearth, licking itself luxuriously after a surfeit of the same beef. Sirronde sat down at a nearby table, and Poole came by with a couple of pots of beer and sat down to keep her company. He chatted with aimless amiability about local business and local gossip, and Sirronde listened with half an ear, as she knew he meant her to, while she looked around the room at Poole's family and the inn's guests. *Not many outsiders here tonight. Well, it's unlucky to journey during the Dreadnights, and even people safe at home are nervous till the New Year comes. Though they do get noisier, livelier, as if they're trying to distract themselves from the long darkness, the cold at the bottom of the year. . . .* That *one's certainly being lively enough*—She found herself looking across the room at a young man ensconced in an armchair by the furthest hearth. Curly-haired and fair he was, with an animated, graceful manner and oddly vague blue eyes. He was talking with many smiles and gestures to one of the local farmers, telling a story perhaps; *this big!* he seemed to be saying, as he stretched arms out and bounced in his chair to emphasize a point. He was a pleasant and amusing sight, but in the back of Sirronde's head a

silent jangling had begun, her Rodmistress's instinct
for something slightly off, something slightly odd.
"Poole," she said abruptly, interrupting her friend in
the middle of an anecdote about someone's brood
sow, "who's that blondish fellow in the corner there?
The one who can't stop smiling."

"Oh, Tav." Poole chuckled. "He came in from
Orsvier a couple nights ago—he's a traveler, he says. I
get the feeling he doesn't quite know where he's going next. But he's certainly been some interesting
places, to hear him talk. . . ."

"I'll be back," she said, patting Poole's arm as she
got up. There was an empty chair by that far hearth,
in the chimney corner, behind Tav's and just to one
side. She slipped into it unnoticed with her beer and
sat drinking and listening.

The young man didn't have much of a traveler's
look about him—he was slim and spare and looked as
if he could be broken between two hands like an ar-
row shaft—but he was a fine storyteller, voluble and
clever, with a talent for small details.

"Tell about the Holding of the Éorlhowe!" one
young girl listening said, and Tav recounted the tale
as if he had been with the Dragons that day two
thousand years before. One could clearly see the returned Dark creeping like a blight across the Middle
Kingdoms, hear the desperate last song of the Dragons clouded about the Howe, the equally desperate
cry of M'athwinn of the Worldfinder's line as she ar-
rowed into the deadly Dark for the sake of her still-
shelled hatchlings. "Tell Bluepeak!" someone else
said, and Tav told it as if he had fought there himself
under Lion or Eagle and seen the Transformation in
which men sacrificed their mortality to become gods.

Sirronde barely noticed the wind moaning in the

chimney or the kitten's jump into her lap; she was
fascinated, and still troubled by that warning jangle
that wouldn't give her peace. Tav told whatever tale
was demanded of him, easily. He remembered Raela
and Béorgan and the Five Who Loved as if he had
journeyed with them to the Lost Mere or the Morrowfane or Dragons' Onolí. "But where have you
been yourself?" said the young girl, and Tav smiled
and told them, no less volubly. Then it was that Sirronde began to understand what had been alarming
her undermind, for Tav spoke of hunting Fyrd and
other minor demons on the plains of Steldin; of climbing Mount Adíně high enough to see the Skybridge,
and Glasscastle at its end; of taking ship from North
Arlen and glimpsing the Isles of the North from a
moonlit deck, hearing the singing that comes out over
the Sea on summer nights. The tales covered a great
deal of journeying into unlikely and perilous places—
more, perhaps, than so young a man could manage.
Again Tav spoke easily and with animation, but the
laughs and looks of his listeners were becoming hollow, those of people who would like to believe a story
but can't quite.

Sirronde sat still as the tales grew more and more
fantastic, and one by one Tav's listeners began to slip
away, smiling, still hollowly. At last the one remaining farmer excused himself because of the lateness of
the hour and went away. Tav sat alone, unmoving.
Slowly his face slackened, turned blank and weary, a
look Sirronde doubted he meant anyone to see. After
a time he reached down and rested one hand against
the hilt of a long straightsword that leaned sheathed
against his chair—an absent gesture, not affectionate
but propitiatory, as if encouraging the sword to lie
quiet. He took a long drink of beer.

"That's a fine sword you have there," Sirronde said, very quietly. Startled, Tav almost dropped his beerpot. He glanced around and saw her, and the smile leaped back onto his face as if she had frightened it there.

"Thank you," he said in a light, pleasant tenor. "Would you like to see it?" Sirronde nodded, and courteously, with care, Tav drew about a span's worth of steel from the scabbard and handed the whole business to Sirronde.

She tried to keep her eyes from going too unfocused as she called up the Fire from within her and ran it invisibly up and down the blade. *Oh dear . . . as I thought. This blade has never killed anything. It's hardly ever been drawn—and it's been out of the forge for seven or eight years. So about ninetenths of the stories he's been telling about himself are—* She handed the sword back. "Tav, your name is?"

He nodded. "If I might ask . . ."

"Sirronde," she said, and leaned across to touch hands with him. His glance lighted on her sheathed Rod, about which blue tongues of the Flame wound lazily, and his eyes widened.

"You live here, lady?" Tav said.

"Up in Marrish."

"What brings you out at this time of year, in this weather?"

She was wondering how to begin her answer when the night spoke for her. The wind outside, already gusting uneasily, grew in the space of a few breaths to alarming wildness. Down that wind from high above came blowing a frightening storm of voices—men and women crying out in awful anguish, tortured screams of loss and rage and pain, mixed with agonized yap-

pings and snarlings and a great rush of wingbeats.
The blast and the terrible cries stooped from the
heights to hurtle over the roofs of Hard Shielings and
shake the inn. Shutters clapped, shingles tore away,
the front door rattled frantically between its jambs.
All the lamps and candles flickered, their flames
crouching low, and one fire flattened and drowned in
a sudden wash of cold air down its flue. Tav sat frozen-
faced, only his eyes alive with fear. Sirronde stared at
the kitten, who stared back; they both knew what they
heard. *This is no simple little task I've been sent on,*
Sirronde thought in horror. *The* Hunt *is up! Even if I
were young and in my prime I couldn't—*

The screaming and howling went on and on; the
wind buffeted the inn with unseen blows. No one
moved. At last a horn snarled somewhere above, and
slowly the horrible cries began to fade, tumbling
away on the wind. Finally the wind itself gusted
down to a last few gasps of exhaustion and died. A
deathly silence remained, broken shortly by the sound
of crying children, frightened parents hushing them,
many people getting up as quietly as they could and
going hurriedly to bed.

Sirronde swallowed to get her voice working again.
She was afraid, but something else was working in
her, too. *After one dreams true, there's rarely such a
thing as a chance meeting. There's some reason this
boy-man has come to my attention.* "*That* brings me
out," she said as steadily as she could. "Since you're a
stranger in these parts, you may not know what that
outcry was." She knew he did—the tale was famous—
but she wanted to see Tav's reaction. "The Shadow—"

Tav's mouth went tight and he drew an aroint-sign
with one hand, but Sirronde didn't echo it. There
was no use her trying to avoid the Dark One's notice.

"—the Shadow takes many forms, but in the mountain country in wintertime. It rides as the Hunter, the Master of the Wild Hunt. In that form He hunts down human souls, and those He catches, those who have let His part of them grow too strong, those souls He keeps. You heard them. They ride with Him forever, in torment, unable to rest—dead, but so bound to Him that they can't pass the Door into Starlight. I'm on quest for the Lady, Tav. The Shadow will do the world a mischief on Opening Night, if He can—and since He's riding as Hunter just now, it's in that form I must seek Him. And confront Him, try to stop Him. . . ."

She swallowed again. It was hard to say so casually something she had just realized herself.

Tav, across from her, looked exquisitely uneasy. When he spoke his face worked as if the upcoming words were what he had to say, not what he wanted to. "Must you do this alone?"

Sirronde shrugged. "Company wasn't forbidden me. But it seems foolish. Anyone who goes up against the Shadow is courting death. Or likely something worse."

"Well . . . Perhaps, if it pleased you . . . I might go with you." The words came out in a rush. "Two are safer than one, in this weather, and the south country has other dangers than, than just that . . . I'm sure you could use a swordsman. . . ."

"I certainly could," said Sirronde. Then, *No, no, no!* she thought fiercely. *Take this poor frightened child with his tall tales into the grasp of the Master of Lies?* "But this is life-or-death danger, Tav. I can't let you—"

"Certainly you can."

"No, I—" She stopped again. *Will I be going alone?*

her memory said, and *Have you ever?* came the answer. *Is She sending me help? An odd sort—but if She'll use a flawed weapon like me, who am I to scruple about another?* "Very well," Sirronde said, and Tav's face went slack with surprise. "If you're sure . . ."

"Yes, of course," Tav said, and *No, what have you gotten yourself into!* yelled his undermind, loudly enough for Sirronde to hear. She ignored the clamor and her own desire to order him to stay here, and looked down at the kitten. "What about you?" she said.

He glanced at the ceiling. "That was just the One Who kills for sport," he said, his small voice scornful. "I'll go with you."

Reluctant, Sirronde nodded. "First light in the morning, then, we leave. You have skis?" she said to Tav. "Good. You're *sure* about this now? You say you've handled Fyrd and demons and such, but this game is bigger—"

"I'll be there," Tav said, calm with terror.

Sirronde nodded and got up to go to bed, being careful not to start shuddering until she was up the stairs and out of sight. *Mad, I'm mad. Of course, so is She. I just hope one of us knows what we're doing. . . .*

They set out into a morning illuminated by that peculiar omnidirectional sheen of dawn over open snowy country. Not much forest remained this close to the great peaks; the dells of the undulating country sheltered occasional stands of fir or white pine, their branches weighed down or breaking under snow. Tav chose to be their pathfinder through this country, and Sirronde noted gratefully through the morning and afternoon that he was good at it, as well as good on his skis. He was considerate of her need for a pace slower than his best, but sometimes he would shoot ahead, as if looking at Sirronde made him nervous. When she caught up again, his face always wore that smile, bright, defensive, with meaning sheathed in it like a knife. *Probably,* she thought, *he thinks I'm reading his mind . . . as if I have the strength to do that while skiing all out! Or else he's having regrets.* The kitten, huddled in her hood, was holding its silence almost obstinately. *And what's going to happen to this one, I don't know. Why a four-month-old kitten would choose to head into the heart of winter on what it must know is a fool's errand where we're probably all going to get—*

The boulder seemed to jump right up under her skis, and Sirronde couldn't avoid it in time. She went flying sideways and splatted into the snow. Just before she hit, the kitten jumped ship and came down splayed beside her like a small furry hand. She sat up groggily. The kitten threw a deadly look at her and started washing furiously.

Tav whooshed up beside them, stopping in a shower of snow. "Looks like we found that river we have to cross," he said. "Are you all right?"

Sirronde reached Tav a hand, and he helped her up. "Nothing broken," she said, brushing herself off. "But my friend here got a bit ruffled—"

Tav groaned. Or at first Sirronde thought he did, but then realized that he was staring at the river, where the ice had suddenly begun groaning tremendously, cracking thunderously, heaving upward. "Tav, don't look!" she shouted, and for safety's sake hooked one ski out from under him so he sprawled facedown in the snow. She drew her Rod and hurriedly shook the Fire through it, down it, out, careless of the pain so sudden an activation was causing her. Blue Flame poured down like water to the snow and pooled there. The kitten, startled, prudently leaped to hide behind Tav. In the river, foot-thick ice slabs cracked and slid ponderously over one another as something pale and shiny started to bulge up from underneath them. Sirronde whipped the Rod once around her head, flinging Fire in a circle around herself and Tav and the kitten. She closed the circle just as the white basilisk's head broke surface and its eyes fixed full on them.

Sirronde stood straight, holding her Rod at the ready. All around them, where the basilisk's glance fell, she could hear snow crackling as it instantly crusted over. Where the smoke of her breath drifted outside the circle, it fell suddenly to the snow in a glitter of frost crystals. Muted shattering sounds came from a lone fir behind them, now completely glazed in thick ice and breaking under its weight.

Tav sat up, spitting snow. "Can I look?"

"You'll throw up," Sirronde said. Tav looked, then turned his face away and began to cough. The basilisk's huge lizardish body wasn't so bad, scaled above and plated below in a dirty, slick, pitted white like new brine-ice. But its pallid face was that of a monstrous child who has died in pain, and its eyes were frozen to milky marbles by the power that blasted through them. The thing's jaw munched and mumbled horribly, as if in senile anticipation of a meal or memory of the last one. "Die," the basilisk said in a thick cold voice, drooling icicles that cracked and fell as it spoke.

"No indeed," Sirronde said, desperately trying to ignore the sound of Tav being ill. If she should succumb to her own nausea and lose control of the Fire, the basilisk's power could strike them all three to ice. Even now she was having a hard time keeping the circle firm; she hadn't needed to call up this much Fire for anything in years.

"Die!" the basilisk said again, and stared harder, rearing itself up on the riverbank on crooked front limbs. Where it stepped the snow froze solid on the instant, and all around them Sirronde could feel the air go still with a new cold, one that burned at her controlling mind. Her thinking started to numb. Completing one thought and starting another was an effort like walking into an icy wind. Not even the Flame could—

Alarm shocked through Sirronde and brought her fully aware just a second before her own conviction that the Fire was useless would have pulled it in and left them all unprotected. She poured the Flame out harder, till the Rod in her hand shone like a star and the snow blazed blue all around with Fire that forced the thought-cold back.

"Die!" the basilisk said again, striking in with a third attack, a different cold. *You will die alone and unloved,* Sirronde's own mind said to her in chilly certainty. She had never wed, had always lived alone; the dim freezing anguish took root too readily. *No arms to hold you, no heart to hold your secrets safe, alone forever—*

The burning of her tears and the more terrible burning of the cold breaking through her circle came together. Enraged and terrified, Sirronde lifted her Rod and slashed the air in front of her, striking the basilisk's power aside with a long whip of Flame that cracked across its face. Wincing and blinking, the basilisk ducked back, cowed now that its best effort had failed. "Go back to your lair," Sirronde said, gasping, "and tell your Master when you see It that we'll die when our Lady pleases, no sooner. Meantime I have defeated you here, and by right of Power I bind you in your lair for seven years' time, not to come out by day or night or twilight, by dusk or dawn. Now go!" She lashed at it again, and the basilisk tried to shy out of range; but the Fire found its mark, coiled like a collar and sank into the frigid flesh, setting the binding deep. Snarling with rage but impotent now, the basilisk turned and lumbered back into the riverbed, burrowed down among the shattered ice cakes and was gone.

Tav sat up weakly, scrubbing at his face with snow. When she saw he was all right, Sirronde put out her circle, staggered away several yards and was sick herself. *Too old for this, too old, I* told *You!* she cried out silently, bent double with more than mere nausea. She had done no wreaking this large for years, and her nerves, overloaded by the sudden intense Fireflow, were roasting her with phantom pains. But after a while the agony passed, leaving Sirronde confused and disturbed by the odd exhilaration she felt and wondering whether this was how Poole's still had felt after she reamed the scale out of it. She got up and went back to her companions, who were both staring at her—the kitten with calm approval, Tav with unease and fear. "Come on," Sirronde said, "we've still got a long way to go, and that was meant to slow us up. I'd rather it didn't. Are you all right now?"

"Slow us up?"

Sirronde bent with some difficulty to check the binding on one of her skis. "Tav, that was sent from upriver, from the mountains, to meet us here. If there were a basilisk's lair anywhere around here, I'd know about it. That's my business. This was a test to see what kind of power we're bringing to our meeting with its Master—"

Tav gulped. "He—It *knows* we're . . ."

He trailed off into a dry-mouthed silence. "He," Sirronde said. "It takes male form as the Hunter. Of course He knows. The Shadow's in you as much as the Goddess is: He's Her child, He partakes of Her nature. What you know, He knows. We're fighting gods here, Tav. If you want to turn back . . ."

He stared at her shakily for a few moments and made no answer except to ski off eastward along the broken watercourse, looking for a place to cross.

Sirronde bent down to pick up the kitten. "How are *you?*"

"Hungry."

"We'll stop in a while."

The kitten curled itself up in her hood, unconcerned. All the rest of the day Tav skied hard, seeming to have lost his concern for Sirronde's old age after seeing what she did to the basilisk. Or maybe something else was on his mind, for he skied like a man running from something that pursues him rather than one hurrying into fear to get it over with.

In late afternoon they ran into wild snow, fluffy unpacked stuff that blew stinging on the gusting wind and slowed them much more effectively than the basilisk had. Finally they stopped for dinner in a narrow coomb between two hills running east and west, taking what cold comfort they could find with their backs to three close-clumped firs. Out of sight over snowy rises to the west, the declining Sun lay wrapped in a bank of cottony silver cirrus. Tav and Sirronde sat on rocks and ate, watching a small colony of bouncemice who had burrowed up through the snow to get seeds from the last pinecones dropped by the trees. The mice were fearless of people, and any number of white-flagged tails were leaping about the copse after their owners. Sirronde glanced at the kitten, who was watching them with interest but no enjoyment. "Hunting looks good around here," she said. "Why not go fetch some dinner?"

The kitten stared at one mouse as it vanished down a hole. "I don't hunt," he said in a tone of voice calculated to make anyone believe he had no desire to do so, ever. But Sirronde's underhearing was abnormally alive after the brush with the basilisk, so that she clearly heard a great thorny burden of fear and longing under the words. *Not that he doesn't hunt. He doesn't know how—or doesn't dare—or both.* Curious, she sought briefly behind the fear and caught a few swift murky images, complex and obscure as feline imageries tended to be, but fairly intelligible. First the sight of something twitching, then the image bobbled wildly with the kitten's playful pounce. But delight fled as the tantalizing something turned abruptly into a great menacing shape that leaped at her; *too big! too big!*—the dog, its teeth tearing her, anguish, intolerable, *no*—

Sirronde shuddered, taking some pains to turn the gesture into a shrug. "Well, I'm full for the moment," she said, putting her dinner of trailcake aside. "Care for an exercise?"

"Exercise . . ." For the first time the kitten sounded unsure.

Sirronde unsheathed her Rod and closed her eyes for a moment, searching for the memory she needed. "This kind," she said, and called up the Fire, first running it through the Rod to focus it, then back through her mind to the pattern she had wrought for Andric's amusement when she was very small. *It's been a long time, I don't know if I can*—but memory proved stronger than her misgivings, and the Fire stronger than both. She fell through its blueness, momentarily blinded, a short fall ending in a frightening crash and the sound of a small heart that raced. Terrible sensations of compactness and dense fur devoured her. Then they weren't terrible anymore but normal. She looked up at the kitten and Tav from the mouse body, blinking jet-bead eyes, and would have laughed at the look on Tav's face if she could have remembered how.

"You, uh," he said.

(I used to be pretty good at shapechange,) she said to him with the speech of the mind, keeping to herself her surprise at how good she still was. (Come on, my friend. Come hunt.)

The kitten stared at her, not moving except for his tail, which twitched. "I don't want to hurt you—"

(You probably will, the first couple of times, but that's what practice is for. Soon enough you'll learn to kill a mouse so fast it won't know it's dead till it's past the last Door.)

The kitten looked skeptical and tucked himself into a small rounded shape on the boulder. "I'm not interested," he said.

(As you like. But don't blame me when all the other cats tease you for eating grass like an ox. . . .) She bounced out of her pile of cast-off clothes and began leaping about in the snow, testing the spring built into the body and reveling in it, meanwhile taking care not to look at the kitten at all. The attack she was expecting took about three minutes to occur, and it was clumsy. The kitten went for the white flag at the tail's end, doubtless what the Goddess had designed the flag for. With her tail still in the kitten's mouth, Sirronde did something she had once seen a desperate bouncer do to a wolf that was trying to catch it alive—she twisted around and leaped straight at the kitten's face. Shocked, he dropped her tail, and she jumped away, making the noisy chittering that passes for laughter among bouncers. (I've maligned the whole race of oxen! Even a cow could do better than *that*—)

No cat likes to be laughed at, especially by a mouse. The kitten spent the next half hour learning that mere energetic kittenish rage may be good for catching string and leaves, but for live game, skill is necessary. When his teeth finally met at the back of Sirronde's neck and he flipped her over to begin kicking her insides out, (Good!) she said. In utter surprise at the praise, he dropped her again. (Bite the throat first, the next time,) she said. (I'm going to get back in my own shape now.)

The kitten, too worked up to just stop, scuttled off through the snow and vanished under the fir trees. (Turn your back, would you, Tav?) she said, taking human form again and dressing very hurriedly.

When she sat down and started gnawing at her trailcake again, Tav looked over at Sirronde with great discomfort. "That basilisk this afternoon—"

"Ugly, wasn't it. My appetite's off too."

"That's not what I meant."

She kept quiet and went on eating.

"I . . . haven't really had that much experience with this . . . this kind of thing. . . ." His voice came hard, and Tav squirmed. Sirronde restrained herself from squirming in sympathy and said nothing.

"I didn't even draw on it; I could've done that much—"

"To an ice basilisk? You'd have made a pretty statue with your sword in your hand. Heroic." She kept eating, refusing to see what he was driving at until he came right out and said it.

There was a long pause. "Dammit, Sirronde," Tav said at last in a voice rich with self-hatred, "I've never drawn on *anything!*" He gasped after the last word, like someone struggling for air at the end of a race, and turned his face away.

"I know," Sirronde said.

Incredulous, Tav stared at her. "But you didn't . . ."

She went on with her eating.

He looked away again, spending a few moments gazing at the western sky, where the clouds had begun to show golden undersides. "I would've told you the truth if you'd asked me," he said finally, low and shamed.

Sirronde nodded. "But should people have to go around asking each other if they're telling the truth? Why the lies, Tav?"

Another long silence fell. Then Tav stammered one by one through several false starts, veering away from new lies each time, though not by much. Sirronde sighed; only the knowledge that she knew his weakness was keeping him honest. "I'm . . . oh Dark. I'm alone. And I'm scared. And I found out awhile back that if you seem like more than you are, people let you be."

"They certainly do. . . . But, Tav, you weren't always alone. Your family—"

"I might as well have been alone," Tav said, bitter. For that moment his mind was unveiled, and Sirronde got a glimpse of a hard-faced father who intimidated his son into telling the truth about wrongs done and then beat him for truth told—or so it seemed to the son. *No wonder he lies,* Sirronde thought. *For so long it was the only way to keep the pain from happening.* "You ran away, then."

"I even stole his sword when I left," Tav said with the weary air of a surrendered criminal confessing everything, not caring anymore about penalties. "Not that I have the slightest idea how to use it. But then neither did he . . ."

"I know."

Sirronde went back to finishing her dinner. Tav stared at her, anger and loathing and confusion chasing one another across his face as he awaited condemnation, scorn, punishment. Sirronde said nothing.

"I suppose you'll get rid of me now and go back to the Shielings for a real swordsman," Tav said at last.

Sirronde looked at him calmly. "I knew what I was getting when you offered to travel with me. And besides, there's no time to go back. Tomorrow the Sun eclipses, and tomorrow night is Opening Night. We go forward. Oh dear—" This last was for the kitten, which reappeared around the bole of one of the fir trees, proudly carrying in its mouth the torn-off tail of one of the bouncemice. Tav glanced off to one side, ostensibly to admire the reddening sunset, and wisely didn't laugh. "Not much meat on that," Sirronde said, "but not bad for a beginner. Eat up; we have to make a few more miles before we stop for the night. And next time, remember, go for the throat."

By the time they set out again the Sun was almost gone. It set swiftly, as if in a hurry to get out of the sky. The burning clouds went out, their fire quenched in dusk; the stars shone through them only fitfully, and the Moon, so close to its dark, was in hiding. The prospect southward leveled out into a long, rising plateau reaching up to the feet of the mountains. Sirronde and Tav went on over the deep snow without pause, trying to make use of the twilight before the night went completely black. But the wind was in their faces, and they barely made the few miles Sirronde wanted before the uphill course exhausted them.

"The snow's well packed here," Sirronde gasped. "We can make a shelter before we get stiff. Get that sword out and we'll cut blocks."

They worked in haste in the dark, like confused burglars bricking up a wall instead of breaking through it, bumping into each other and laughing under their breaths. But Sirronde lost her laughter as the wind began to rise. The wind itself she had expected, but the voices she could faintly hear crying down it were arriving too soon. The worst fate a traveler could face was about to come upon them. Caught out in the middle of nowhere, far from any protecting hearth or threshold, armed only with Fire. And not even the Fire could—

Sirronde swore. "Let that go, Tav," she said, and he turned to her in confusion from the gap he was sealing up in the snow wall. "We're about to have company. If you've got to speak, speak fair and be polite, but unless you've got something really good to say, try to keep quiet. . . ." She drew her Rod and kindled it bright.

"What's the—" Once again the night answered one of Tav's questions. Down the wailing wind came a savage and exultant howling, first one voice alone, then many more as the quarry was sighted and the chase begun. Under the voices, the horn that heralds death growled deep, calling the other riders to the hunt. Tav stood motionless, ashen, the sword shaking in his hand.

The Hunt came about them like blown leaves, roaring down from the black sky on the back of the bitter south wind. The riders were many, fifty or a hundred or two hundred shapes made indistinct by darkness, mounted on steeds twisted like the basilisk, but winged and horribly fleet. Most ringed them round above, treading air; many came to ground and surrounded Tav and Sirronde and the kitten there, though not too closely. They seemed reluctant to get too close to her Rod, perhaps because its light found no reflection in their eyes and cast no shadows behind them. Just at the edge of the circle of blue light the riders milled, shouting, laughing terribly, brandishing vague weapons, spurring their steeds till they screamed. The steeds were frightful creatures, parodies of living beasts, but no more terrible than the empty-eyed dead who rode them: men and women whose humanity was forced out of their faces by the darkness to which they had relinquished themselves. Hounds of all sorts and a few hunting cats ran with them, for the beasts of those taken by the Hunt follow their masters faithfully into torment, coursing new game with them and sharing their pain, though not fully understanding it. In the middle of the whirlwind of dark wings and anguish, Sirronde stood erect with Tav and the kitten, the Rod blazing in her hand, and waited. After a short eternity of screaming, the airborne hunters began to beat frantically to one side and the other. Those on the ground ceased their threats and waving of phantom spears to look up, fearful, adoring and hating.

The Hunter came to ground in a rush of wind and darkness, and paced leisurely over to where the three stood. His mount, a huge, winged black tiger reined with iron chains and bitted with the thighbone of a man, fretted at the bit and glared hungrily at Sirronde, but she ignored it. On its back loomed the Shadow in the shape of a great dark man in huntsman's dress, lean and powerful and menacing but inhumanly handsome, wearing a young face with treacherously gentle eyes in it. He was consciously radiating malice, watching Sirronde with open contempt to see what she would do.

I can be contemptuous too, Sirronde thought. *It'll probably amuse Him.* "So, dark Lord," she said as casually as she might have to a neighbor met on the street in the morning, "what are You hunting tonight?"

There was feverish, unpleasant mirth among the riders. "The usual," said the Shadow, in a voice that sounded like a shark's smile, as He leaned on His saddlebow and gazed down at Sirronde. "But the sport is poor. The game won't run."

Sirronde allowed a shade of amusement to show on her face. "What a shame."

"Indeed. I might ask why you've taken your aching bones so far from human habitations at this dangerous time of year. . . ."

"I am on errantry," Sirronde said, "and You know Who for." The riders muttered among themselves. A faint vertical line of frown indented itself between the Hunter's eyes, turning that young face less young, more perilous. "Tonight, though," Sirronde said, as if undaunted, "I'm in no great hurry. I would bid You to dinner, but having neither house nor hold here, nor food to feed so many guests, perhaps You'll take the intent for the deed...."

He laughed, and all the riders laughed with Him, a fearful sound. "Human creatures rarely offer Me hospitality so readily," the Shadow said. "I shall return the favor. Come guest with Me tomorrow eve, Sirronde. I have a small feast preparing."

"Certainly, dark Lord, we shall be honored. Of course we shall demand full guestright from You, and parting gifts suitable to our rank...."

"Demand?" the Hunter said, soft-voiced. His eyes on Sirronde were gentle no longer; they pierced like black ice. The dead all around smiled anticipatory smiles.

Sirronde swallowed. "In the Name of the First Loved," she said, "yes, I so demand."

The Shadow froze silent. "In that Name," He said at last, slow and reluctant and angry, "in that Name, very well. And well for you that you invoked it. Not that parting gifts should be expensive . . . for whatever rank an old woman, a young liar and a half-starved mouse might possess...."

The kitten, crouching in Sirronde's hood and peering nervously over her shoulder, began to bristle, but said nothing. Tav beside her was still as a hare that has stumbled into a hounds' parliament. "Doubtless the expense will be small," Sirronde said, straining to sound offhand. "Where are we feasting, Lord?"

"Blackmount," the Hunter said, "at midnight. I trust you will be prompt."

"We'll be there."

The Shadow hauled back on His reins. The tiger reared back, spreading its wings and fighting the air with its claws, as its rider unsheathed the pale blade that always runs blood and saluted Sirronde with it.

She stood straight and returned the salute with her
Rod, a quick insolent up-and-down gesture that left
a lingering trail of Fire on the air between them. The
light of it caught darkly in the Shadow's eyes. He
looked away as if pained by it and spurred the tiger.
Up it went in a cold blast of wind, and the rest of the
Hunt whirled after, crying louder than storm, beating away southward toward the desolate Peaks.

Sirronde waited until they were out of sight and
hearing, then sat down in the snow and let her teeth
begin to chatter. In her hood the kitten was washing
frantically. " 'Just the One Who hunts for sport,' eh?"
she said to him. "Are you all right?"

The kitten paused, fixing her with a dark, oblique
look. "Being alone again would be worse," he said,
and went back to his washing.

She had no answer for that. Behind her, Tav still
had not moved. "He—He," Tav said, and his voice
got stuck in his throat. "He could just have *taken*
us—"

"No, He couldn't." Sirronde hid her face in her
hands. There was no escaping the terror of the
Shadow, though it might be briefly postponed. "He
can't touch those on the Goddess's errantry unless
they give themselves over to Him willingly."

"And you did! If we're His guests, then He can—"
Tav sat down too, more an involuntary reaction than
otherwise. "Oh, dear Mother of Everything—"

"It's the only way," Sirronde said, unsure which of
them she was reassuring. "There's no way to win
against *that* one except on His terms. On His ground,
a victory will be complete."

Tav exploded. "Are you kidding? You know the
stories as well as I do! Béorgan, Earn and Héalhra at
Bluepeak, Bron who fought all the way through an

army of demons with his bare hands so he'd have virgin steel to use on Him—what good did it do any of them? You either die of meddling with Him, or if you happen by some wild chance to kill Him, He doesn't *stay* dead, He just comes back after a while!" Tav snorted. " 'Victory!' "

"Of course you can't kill Him for good. The best we can do is slow Him down. Not even the Goddess can do better until this world dies and She makes a new one. But for now, slowing Him down until the next time is enough. So, yes, 'victory.' We have to do what we can, Tav!"

"And what about defeat?"

"I hope you're a good rider," Sirronde said more quietly. "Eternity is a long time to be in the saddle."

". . . He was the Goddess's son, and She gave Him the First Loved to share Himself with, forever . . . but jealousy came upon Him, and He slew the Loved." Sirronde paused between strokes of her ski poles to wipe tears out of her eyes; it was a windy morning. "Think past the legend, Tav. He killed His loved, but His love lives on—if there's a worse torment than that, I can't think of it. Since then He goes about the worlds venting his rage on everything that still lives and loves, on all the Goddess's works. He blames Her for everything. Had the Maiden not let death into the world, so He thinks, none of this would have happened. . . ."

Tav, skiing beside her, shook his head. "He really believes that?"

"It's the lie He tells Himself to make eternity bearable. And so He's become the Master of Lies, of all the untruths we tell ourselves. Beware what you see and hear at the feasting, Tav. He'll tell your own lies back to you; they're the ones you're most likely to believe. . . ."

They came to the top of another rise and paused for breath. "There you are," Sirronde said. "Nine miles, maybe ten." The kitten poked his head up out of her hood to look with them at the southern vista. The eclipse was well along toward totality, and the snowfields slanting up to the skirts of the mountains wore a yellowish taint under the strange, dull, brassy day. Erchámë and the other great peaks reared halfway up the sky like the walls of the world, but right now height was their only splendor; despite new cloaks of snow they looked dull and dingy. Between Erchámë's great north-reaching spurs crouched Blackmount, low and craggy, a blunted pyramid shape like an ancient burial mound. Its dark stone wore only a sheath of melt-ice, and the dimmed sunlight shone from it harshly, a dark-hearted, hurting brightness.

"Some place for a feast," Tav said. "I don't know what we can possibly do that'll keep Him there till dawn—"

"Exploit our guestright. He has to let us eat undisturbed . . . tell our tales without being interrupted. Past that—" Sirronde shrugged. "Amuse Him. Provoke Him. Occupy Him with something He can't ignore. We'll have to judge the situation, and improvise. . . ."

"Sirronde," Tav said, quiet and worried. "I told you, I'm no hero."

Far away, silent, a soft-looking sheet-mass of white bulged away from the west side of the Erchámë massif and slid lazily downward. A breath later the faint, ruinous mutter of the avalanche drifted to them through the glassy air. "Afraid of failing?" Sirronde said. "Haven't learned anything from all those stories you know, have you, Tav? No one will beat you if you mess this up. There may be no one *left*."

Tav looked over his shoulder, back the way they had come, and wouldn't meet Sirronde's gaze. "What the—" he said.

She looked where he did. Sweeping upslope from the northwest, long parallel bands of shadowlike waves of a tide of darkness were running at them over the dull-lit snowy lowlands. Above them the sky was deepening suddenly into twilight, an abnormal and uncanny violet-blue, threatening as a storm. Tav glanced toward the Sun. "Don't," Sirronde said quickly. "When the Shadow has enough power to put out the Lady's light, the sight can strike you blind. Come on. . . ."

She pushed off the top of the rise, poling hard. Tav came after. One by one the brightest stars of summer came out, still and strange above the snow; and finally, against the cold, black-violet sky, the pearly brilliance of the Sun's revealed soul flared and struggled from behind the darkness that had eaten the light. Tav and Sirronde raced to the next shallow rise, over it and down, not looking back, and in broad noon the night followed them.

They came under Blackmount shortly before midnight and saw they were expected. Above the Mount, balefires flickered; murky, reddish lights like strayed auroras, twisting and wrinkling about the scarps and steeples of the mountain.

"Well, Tav?" Sirronde said as they took their skis off. "Last chance to turn back."

"And leave a kitten and a lady old enough to be my mother alone at the back of nowhere on Opening

Night, sitting on the Shadow's doorstep waiting to get killed? I may be a coward, but I'm not a dastard."

"You're no coward, Tav. Watch your lies," Sirronde said with hidden satisfaction. "If you lie under His roof, you're His forever."

"Mmnh. What about you?"

"You mean, how do I feel?" She glanced up at the Mount and shivered. "Tired . . . scared. And burnt out. I've used too much Fire in the past couple days. Still—" She unsheathed her Rod, wondering at the brightness of the Fire wreathing about it. It had been years since she'd seen it burn so fiercely. *And I thought I was getting old. Is this all I needed—a large wreaking or two, a dose of fear to fan the Flame back to the old heat? Why didn't I do this sooner instead of taking the loss for granted, instead of settling into cleaning stills and curing dried-up cows?*

"We'd better get going," Tav said. "We're going to be late for dinner."

Blackmount reached down the slope toward the travelers with two long, craggy arms of stone. Where the arms met at the mountain's root, they made a rude, dark archway, unillumined by the balefires that seethed and poured like fog elsewhere on the mountain. Toward the blind stone of the archway Sirronde and Tav walked, side by side, the kitten peering out of Sirronde's hood as usual. As they got closer they began to hear voices—those of the Wild Hunt's doomed riders, singing in crooked harmonies, talking in bitter accents, all muffled as if sealed in stone. Likewise muffled came the sounds of furious feasting; plates and goblets clattered, and warped musicians played agonized instruments out of tune.

Right up to the rough, unbroken mountain face Tav and Sirronde went, and there they waited, but nothing happened. No one came to greet them or show them a way in.

"Doorward!" Sirronde shouted. The noise of feasting only got louder.

"Doorward!"

No response, and the racket within the Mount grew incredible, as if giants feasted there—or someone who preferred that the dinner guests remain seemingly unnoticed outside and thus forfeit their souls for breaking a commitment to the Shadow.

"All right," Sirronde said, "He wants me to use up some Power, fine. . . ." She raised her Rod and called up the Fire, recklessly demanding more even than she had used on the basilisk. Too obedient, it blasted up through her in harrowing intensity, and Sirronde slashed at the wall, her pain coiling with the Fire into a blazing lash that cracked against the stone with a deafening clap like thunder. Black rock exploded inward as if lightning stricken. Sirronde stood gasping a moment, aware of sudden silence and many hate-filled eyes staring from inside the Mount, as Tav moved to hand her across the threshold in courtly fashion.

Within the hollow Mount the Hunt sat feasting and carousing at many stone tables, the feasters and their food and drink lit in ghastly yellow-green or bloody red by balefires writhing from sconces and candlesticks and clinging to the walls. "Good evening," Sirronde said loudly. "Rude, locking the dinner guests out in the cold like that. Perhaps the host will add to the rudeness by sending some lackey to escort us to our places?"

The unwholesome laughter of the lost went up as a stately figure stepped toward them from a high table at the Mount's heart. It was the Shadow, not in the

rough garb of the Master of the Hunt, but darkly re-
splendent in sable and midnight velvet and black
dragonhide sapphires, wearing a crown of obsidian
and jet steel. "Your places are prepared," He said,
and led them to the center table, seating them on either side of Him. No king's table could have been
better laid; it was crowded with rich dishes and
bright wines, and the plate was solid diamond. "To
you, my guests," the Shadow said, raising a goblet of
glass and iron to pledge them.

Sirronde's glance crossed with Tav's as they lifted
their cups to return the courtesy. "Libation first," Sirronde said. "To Our Lady of the Dark Moon, present
though unseen . . ." She poured out first drops on
the floor, a quick splash, and then peered down at the
abruptly smoking puddle. "Dear me," she said, "the
wine seems to be dissolving the flagstones. Dark Lord,
does Your hospitality include serving Your guests
venom and man's-flesh?" For at her invocation the
fair seeming had fallen away from the dishes and de-
canters on the table. Tav and the kitten, who had
crept out of Sirronde's hood to sit by him, were studi-
ously avoiding looking at them. "I had thought better
of You. What need to stoop to trickery, Lord? You
have us safe enough; we came in willingly." And inside Sirronde, hope stirred. *Can it be He's afraid?*

The Shadow gazed at Sirronde, unsmiling, a look
worse than drawn steel. "I see I'll have to stand on
particulars," Sirronde said. "In our case guestright
must be construed to mean food and drink that are
safe for us, and diversions that won't secretly imperil
our souls. I say *secretly—*" She paused while the
Shadow's face smoothed as He considered the
loophole, the potential entertainment she was offering. "And by the way, You must keep time running

the same in the Mount as it is outside. No use our walking out at the feast's end to find that a hundred years have passed and our loved ones are all dead—"

A flicker of anger stirred in the dark eyes. "You are importunate, Sirronde. And too knowledgeable for your own good."

"I am careful, dark Lord. One who has the Power and ignores legends is usually destined to become one. Now then, our food?"

The Shadow clapped His hands, and some of the Hunt came and went as servitors, clearing the table and bringing new dishes. The new food was good, and hot, and Tav and Sirronde fell to eagerly. The kitten absconded with a breast of pheasant from Tav's plate and sat crunching it on the damask tablecloth, favoring the Shadow all the time it ate with the contemptuously friendly glare of a cat who knows it's in front of someone who hates cats. Sirronde's heart rose at the sight. *He is afraid of us. The little one there* knows. *Maybe—just maybe . . .*

Dinner took awhile; Tav and Sirronde were leisurely about eating. When the dishes were removed at last, the Shadow leaned back in His chair with a cup of the black mead spoken of in old lore, the kind brewed from heart's-blood and honey. "Perhaps now our guests will entertain us with tales," He said, courteous and mocking.

"I'll do that," Tav said, so suddenly that he seemed to startle himself with his own words.

Sirronde swallowed, nervous for his sake as the room fell silent to hear. Then she swallowed again, nervous for a different reason; for Tav leaned back as calm as if he were sitting in the Tartaret and Block and began telling the old story of Jarrin's Debt, of the young actor who tricked the Shadow out of overturning the world in fire and storm a thousand years before. He told it well, so that it seemed Jarrin's voice and not Tav's that rang out: "I wager I could act a role so well, not even You could make me break character!"—and so he had, acting death the best way, by dying for real and leaving the outraged Shadow oathbound to keep His word. No stirring went through the hall under the Mount when Tav was done, and the Shadow was gazing at him with that drawn-steel look; but Tav went on as if unheeding, even smiling a bit. He told the tale of Béorgan, who opened the Morrowfane Gate and entered the Otherworlds to slay the Shadow in vengeance for her mother's death; he told of Raela Way-Opener, who met the Shadow at the Door into Starlight when He tried to close it against the souls of the dead, and who cast Him seven worlds away, so that it took Him seven years to find His way back. He told of Ferrigan and her traveling companion the Pooka, who met the Shadow as Torturer; he told of Earn and Héalhra, who met Him as the Gnorn. He told of Enra and Ostig and Bron, and many others, and Tav's voice grew hoarse, but he told on and on, despite the Shadow's steadily blackening looks. Every tale he told had their host at the heart of it, and in every tale, He failed. Tav would not stop, even when his voice had worn down to a whisper; but in the middle of the tale about the thief who stole the Shadow's crown, it gave out completely. No amount of wine drinking would restore it, and Tav looked desperately over at Sirronde. *I tried,* the look said.

She could do little more than smile sad pride at him, for he had used up a great deal of time. Sirronde turned then to the Shadow, daring those dark and wrathful eyes.

"And what have you to say for yourself?" the Shadow said, His voice tightly controlled.

"I thought perhaps I would inquire what Your plans are for after the feast," Sirronde said.

A terrible smile crossed His face, showing a mere tithe of the anger to which Tav's genteel taunting had provoked Him. "Fire and storm were the limit of My agreement with Jarrin," He said. "I never said anything about water. I think tomorrow morning these mountains will be the shore of the Sea, and the Middle Kingdoms will be its bottom."

"Not this time," Sirronde said, and swallowed hard, recognizing in her words the message the Goddess had wished delivered. "We will stop You."

"Certainly you will try," the Shadow said, that smile growing more terrible. "You challenge Me?"

"We challenge You."

"Then as challenged I have the right to determine the style of combat." He sounded peremptory now, His earlier leisure gone. *It must be getting near dawn,* Sirronde thought. "I will offer the two of you three combats. Three times you must meet Me, and three times defeat Me, and if you do that, then I will let the world be—for a while. One defeat, of either of you, and you are all Mine. Even the mouse here." He smiled at the kitten, who sat up straight and stared back, disdaining to bristle this time.

"That's hardly fair," Sirronde said.

"The heroes of whom your young friend told didn't say that sort of thing," the Shadow said. "But they were great powers, and you are not, so I suppose it's understandable. Do you accept?"

Sirronde looked over at Tav.

"Yes," he whispered.

"Let it begin, then," she said.

The Shadow rose. Tables and chairs and all but a few balefires vanished. Sirronde and Tav and the kitten were alone in the midst of a great darkness. Not an empty one: the balefire flickers picked out here a glassy eye, there the hilt of a bloodied weapon, among those of the Hunt who stood circled round to watch.

"You will be first, Sirronde," said their host's voice, huge in the darkness.

"Very well," she said, and almost jumped at the feel of a touch from behind. But it was Tav's hand on her shoulder, gripping, saying what his voice couldn't. "Thanks," she whispered, and drew her Rod, kindling it.

Its light was answered from across the circle of the dead. Another light, blue also, slowly dawned and began to flow about a pair of great hands. The light spread, and Sirronde's throat constricted, for it was the Fire. But not hot white at its heart, as her Flame was. The vivid blueness shaded to an eye-hurting black, the core of a malign Fire that sucked light instead of giving it. *She gave Him the Flame, too, at the beginning of things,* Sirronde thought, fighting her panic, *life's Power, the power most like Her own. But this is what He wields now, what His hatred has made of it—* The silence became oppressive, dreadful, as the deathly Firelight grew. Her foe stood cloaked in it, clothed in it, beautiful of form but burning with malice. His blaze of darkness, His sheer scorn of her puny light, smote Sirronde to the heart. She staggered back a step, raising her Rod and kindling it brighter, pushing the Fire through it past the pain the effort caused her, past her terror.

"You are old, Sirronde," the voice said, the voice of earthquake and avalanche, irresistible. "And you laid

the Power aside except for little wreakings a long
time ago—for what? To spare yourself, to postpone
your burnout and live a little longer?" Mockery rang
in the Shadow's voice. Sirronde went cold inside, for
sometimes to suit His own purposes, the Dark One
will tell the truth. *Did I—is that why—*

"Of course it is," her enemy said, "and now your
age is all the weapon I need against you. You are far
spent already. If you summon up enough Flame to
resist Me now, you will burn out and die of the exertion."

The figure with its polluted Fire was coming slowly
nearer. Terror fed Sirronde's Flame brighter, her
Rod blazed too fiercely for her eyes to bear—but she
could not slow the Shadow's advance or pierce the
darkness of the midnight Fire she could feel sucking
at both her Flame's light and her life.

"Don't waste your time in struggle," said the approaching enemy. "If you defy Me, Sirronde, My vengeance will follow you far. Don't think I would not
bar your way through the Door into Starlight. I have
done it before, and stopping Me took greater power
than anything you have." He drew closer, calm and
sure and terrible.

*He's right, He's right, if I keep this up much long-
er I'll—* Sirronde's heart twisted inside her, or was
twisted by the enfeebling blackness His dark Fire
wove about it. Who was she to pit herself against the
force behind blight and plague, against Whom not
even the Goddess would prevail until time's end?
"Give this over," the reasonable voice said, "and I
will grant you a clean death and a quick passage . . ."

She fell to her knees, and the figure wreathed in
blue-black flames paused, turning to Tav. "See, your
friend is wise," He said, as Sirronde desperately

fumbled down past her agony and her fear for the
life-fire she had been hoarding away from herself and
the Goddess, the energy meant to keep her alive for
the rest of her years. She freed it all at once. It erupt-
ed through her and out of her, burning, lifted the
Rod she had no strength to lift, and leapt like a lev-
in bolt across the hall, blasting the dark Flame out as
one brushfire burns out another, knocking its source
off His feet. The crash of His fall echoed under the
Mount like thunder, and the shadowless dead stood
aghast. Burning blue in her own Fire, helpless, Sirronde fell over sideways and got ready to die.

Tav was pulling at her, trying to sit her up, as
across the hall the Shadow stood up, taller and more
terrible yet. "It's all right, I'm just dying, pay attention to Him!" she said in a thread of voice, all she
had left. Her Rod would not stop burning. By its
light she saw Tav straighten up with something in his
eyes she had never seen yet: rage.

"Well," he croaked, "is it my turn?"

The black-blue Fire flared up again, writhed and
twisted around its master, then died down. "It is,"
said another voice, a different voice from the
Shadow's—higher, weaker, but no less daunting. Where
the Shadow had been now stood a smallish man with
hair the color of iron and pale, narrow eyes, his stance
and his hard, blunt face those of someone whose chief
delight looked to be punishment. "Tav, *what did you
do with my sword?*"

Tav went rigid as his father approached. Sirronde
lay in terror, as much of it as it's possible to feel
when one already has one's own death to worry
about. For Tav put his hand to his side and found
the sword tangible, but suddenly invisible, an invitation to the lie. His father was walking closer, with the

old purposeful walk that had a beating at the end of it. The enemy's malevolent power wound through the air, making it seem as though one might more successfully stand up to a tidal wave than to this man.

"Where is it!" yelled the harsh, hateful voice, promising awful pain if Tav didn't satisfy its owner somehow. This was not a mount in the Highpeaks, this was the house in Orsvier, late at night, with no help anywhere, *why bother trying to explain, you know what'll happen, don't make it worse, tell him you don't know, tell him the neighbor borrowed it, tell him—* Tav stood trembling. His father walked up to him and shouted right in his face. *"Where is it? ? ! !"*

"Ruh, ruh, right here," Tav whispered, putting his hands to his side and lifting away something he could feel but couldn't see. His father looked down at his offering hands, seeing nothing. "I—I stole it," Tav whispered, choking with the effort of the admission. "Here."

His father stared. "What are you trying to pull!" he said, low and enraged, and struck Tav a vicious backhanded blow in the face. Tav barely started to duck aside, to run—but the slight motion turned him toward where Sirronde lay in her fading Fire. In midmotion he did the impossible, the sacrilegious, the offense that meant death. He hit his father back, spearing him hard in the gut with the hilt of the sheathed and invisible sword.

The cry of wild fury that followed sent Tav reeling back as if from another blow. He sprawled beside Sirronde as the Hunt fled the Mount in terror, as the Shadow crashed to the floor and fell out of shape. Sirronde's Rod still burned, but its light would not illumine the terrifying blaze of darkness about their

foe as He drew a last shape about Himself and rose
again.

Slowly He paced toward them, and they watched in
exhausted fear, powerless to prevent Him, Sirronde
bracing herself up on her forearms and holding on to
life by main force, Tav half-blinded by running
blood, his face broken by the blow he'd been struck,
the kitten crouching as small as it could between
them. The form the Shadow wore now was twice the
size of the tiger He had ridden as Master of the Hunt,
and blacker, burning with a frightening unlight that
forced the eyes away like the Sun. The Palug Cat
stalked them, the merciless Shadow of the feline
kind—a slow, leisurely, sharp-fanged darkness moving
inexorably through gloom that grew as Sirronde's
Fire flickered low.

"Third time will pay for all," the silken, wicked
cat's voice said. "I hope you three dined well, for be
assured, I shall. And after I'm through with you,
there's still time to do My business." The Cat
laughed. "Sooner or later I knew She would miscalcu-
late, I knew She would send Me a fool or a weakling
or a failure on My night. . . ."

Sirronde tried to lever herself up straighter. It
didn't work.

Tav stared at the sword he was clutching, visible
now. "It's never been used. I guess this is its last
chance," he whispered, and drew it.

The Cat laughed again at the sight of it faintly
gleaming. "Don't bother, child," He said, ten feet
away now, five feet away, "I'm much faster than you
in this form," and He crouched for the last spring,
hindquarters twitching slightly, and with no warning
whatsoever the kitten sprang straight for the Cat's
face, and "Tav! *Virgin steel!*" Sirronde cried. The

Shadow pulled His head back, startled, the kitten fell down and leaped again, this time for the huge barrel of a throat; the Cat reared up yowling and clawed the kitten away, flinging it halfway across the hollow Mount, and as He came down on all fours again, Tav was waiting for Him, bracing the stolen sword point up against the floor. The Shadow crashed onto the point of the sword and stabbed Himself to the heart.

His horrible scream of shock and thwarted rage left them all deaf for many moments. When it faded, Tav and Sirronde found themselves alone in the darkening hall, and ominous rumblings were coming from the roof. "Come on," Tav gasped, picking up the blackened sword that lay beside him and sheathing it, then grabbing Sirronde and half-carrying, half-dragging her to the door.

"The kitten!" she whispered, but even as she spoke, he scooped it up off the floor, and the three of them made for the entrance. Outside, the first dawn of the new year was toying with the horizon—a faint light that seemed like full day after the smothering darkness of the Mount. Tav and Sirronde staggered down to the snowfield at Blackmount's feet and fell there, covering their heads as the roof of the Mount fell crashing in.

When the last stones stopped rolling, Tav tried to get Sirronde to sit up. "Come on, come on!" he said, weeping, and Sirronde squinted up at him with affectionate annoyance. "For pity's sake, Tav, I'm *dying*, may I please do it lying down??!"

He laid her down again with her head in his lap, and was a long time finding words. Finally, through his tears, he said, "We never did get our parting gifts."

"No?" Sirronde said, blinking, having trouble focusing or speaking. (This is better,) she said with the voice of the mind, but the thought still came feebly. (I seem to have gotten back something I lost a long time ago—or gave up. Whichever. What about you?)

Tav shook his head. "I don't know—" He gulped, and reluctantly, over the space of a few breaths, began to accept the gift. "Maybe—maybe the truth—a little of it. At least, a story of my own to tell . . . But Sirronde—no one will believe me!"

(Since it really happened, does it matter?)

"No." He wiped at his eyes. "We killed Him," he said wonderingly to the kitten, who was lying on his knee, dazed and bruised but otherwise unhurt. "*We* killed Him! Fools and weaklings and failures—" He shook his head again, and Sirronde found the breath for a last laugh. (None of those,) she said. (But we didn't know what we had . . . and so neither did He. . . .)

"But what does it *matter?*" Tav said, the tears running down. "He won't stay dead!"

(Neither will we,) Sirronde said silently, (and there'll be a world for us to come back to, full of the children of those who didn't die tonight. That's worth something. . . . Where will you go now, Tav?)

He stared at the sword lying in the snow beside him. "Home, I think." The words came halting and fearful, but they had resolve at their roots. "I have someone to . . . to tell a few truths to, maybe . . . and a sword to give back. After that—I'm tired of this running around, running away. I think I'll settle down somewhere and farm, and let other people be the stories. I'd sooner just tell them. . . ."

(Go up to Marrish,) Sirronde said, closing her eyes,

(and find my daughter Andric, and tell her I told you to milk my cow and mind my house till I get back.)

"Sirronde..."

She fell silent. The kitten got up stiffly, stretched and reached out with a black-padded paw to gently touch Sirronde's cheek. She smiled. (The throat,) she said. (Right for the throat. Not bad for a beginner....)

She did not speak again. Tav and the kitten, listening for her failing thought, saw ever so briefly what she saw—darkness and a Door without lintels or posts; beginnings and endings on this side, on the other the unnumbered stars. Sirronde let go her hold, remotely feeling the last of her Fire burst forth, shattering the unneeded Rod as her soul broke the bonds that held it. She stepped forward, taking the gift with her into the new life.

In the forges of evening, the Maiden struck away a tear, set aside for a while the new-tempered soul She had been working, and laid a fresh one in the fire....

A Dealing with Demons
by Craig Shaw Gardner

One of the things I like best about fantasy per se, and
Sword & Sorcery in particular, is its use of magicians.
They are almost always more interesting than the
heroes (especially those of the brawny barbarian
type, like Howard's Conan and John Jakes's Brak and
my own Thongor). Think of Merlyn in *The Once
and Future King*, Dr. Vandermast in Eddison's
Mistress of Mistresses, Meliboë the Enchanter in
Fletcher Pratt's *The Well of the Unicorn*, or Gandalf
himself in *The Lord of the Rings* and you will see
what I mean.

To this exclusive guild let us now add the remarkable Ebenezum. I first made his acquaintance in a
story Craig Shaw Gardner had in Ted White's *Fantastic* and promptly snapped it up for the next volume
of my *Year's Best Fantasy* anthologies.

If you have not yet had the pleasure of his company, then I invite you to meet Ebenezum in the
story that follows ...

A DEALING WITH DEMONS

I

Every sorcerer should explore as much of the world as he can, for travel is enlightening. There are certain circumstances, such as a major spell gone awry or an influential customer enraged at the size of your fee, in which travel becomes more enlightening still.

—from *The Teachings of Ebenezum,*
Volume 5

We were forced, at last, to leave our cottage and go seek outside assistance. My master realized he could not cure his own affliction—the first time, I think, that the wizard had to face up to such a circumstance. So we traveled to find another mage of sufficient skill and cunning to cure my master's sorcerous malady, though we might have to travel to far Vushta, the city of a thousand forbidden delights, before we found another as great as Ebenezum.

Still, ever since the wizard had contracted the malady that caused him to sneeze uncontrollably in the presence of magic, life had been something of a problem. The affliction had occurred shortly after my master encountered a certain powerful demon from the seventh Netherhell. Ebenezum banished the creature in the end, surely the most fearsome he had ever faced, but his victory was not without its cost. From his moment of triumph onward, should he be confronted by sorcery in any form whatsoever, Ebenezum sneezed.

I believe Ebenezum had coped better than many would have in similar circumstances, still managing to ply his trade in small ways, mostly through the use of his wits rather than spells. But, then, Ebenezum had always told me that nine-tenths of magic was in the imagination.

Now, however, I was worried.

Ebenezum walked before me along the closest thing we could find to a path in these overgrown woods. Every few paces he would pause, so that I, burdened with a pack stuffed the arcane and heavy paraphernalia, could catch up with his wizardly strides. He, as usual, carried nothing, preferring, as he often said, to keep his hands free for quick conjuring and his mind free for the thoughts of a mage.

But all was not right with my master. I saw it in his walk—the same long strides he always took, but something was missing—the calm placing of one foot in front of another, knowing that whatever lay in one's path, a wizard could handle it. He walked too swiftly now, anxious to be done with what I imagined he thought the most unsavory of tasks: asking another wizard for aid. It threatened to affect his whole bearing. For the first time in my long apprenticeship I feared for my master.

The wizard stopped mid-path to gaze at the thick growth about us. "I will admit I'm worried, Wunt." He scratched at the thick, white hair beneath his sorcerer's cap. "My maps and guidebooks indicated this was a lively area, with much commerce and no dearth of farms and friendly inns. That is the prime reason I took this route, for though we have cash from our recent exploits, a little more wouldn't hurt in the least."

The wizard stared out into the dark wood, his bushy eyebrows knit in concern. "Frankly, I wonder now about the effectiveness of certain other preparations I made for our journey. You never know what you'll encounter when traveling."

There was a great crashing of underbrush to one side of the trail. Branches were rent asunder; leaves rustled and tore away; small forest creatures cried in fright.

"Doom!" cried someone from within the thicket. Something large fell between my master and myself. Ebenezum sneezed. There was sorcery in the air!

"Doom!" the voice cried again, and the dark brown object that had fallen between us rose again into the air. It was a tremendous club, I realized, for attached to the end nearest the thicket was a large hand, in turn attached to an arm that disappeared into the heavy greenery. Ebenezum fell back a few paces along the path and blew his nose on a wizardly sleeve, ready to conjure despite his affliction.

The club rose and fell repeatedly to crush the underbrush. A man appeared in the cleared space. He was enormous—well over six feet in height, with a great bronze helmet topped by ornamental wings that made him look even taller. And he was almost as wide as he was tall, his stomach covered by armor of the same dull bronze.

He stepped out to block our path. "Doom!" his deep voice intoned once more. Ebenezum sneezed.

There was no helping it. I dropped my pack and grabbed my stout oak staff in both hands. The armored man took a step toward the helplessly sneezing wizard.

"Back, villain!" I cried in a voice rather higher than I would have liked. Waving the staff above my head, I rushed the fiend.

"Doom!" the warrior intoned again. His barbed club met my staff in midair, shearing the sturdy oak in two.

"Doom!" The fiend swung once more. I ducked to avoid the blow and slipped on a pile of crushed leaves and vines littered beneath my feet. My left foot shot from under me, then my right. I fell into a bronze-plated belly.

"Doo-oof!" the warrior cried as he fell. His helmet struck the base of a tree, and he cried no more.

"Quick, Wunt!" Ebenezum gasped. "The club!"

He tossed a sack at my shoulder. I pushed myself off the armored belly and managed to fit the cloth around the heavy weapon. The wizard let out a long sigh and blew his nose.

"Enchanted."

So it was the club, and not the warrior, that had caused my master's sneezing attack. I regarded our now-prone opponent with some curiosity. The warrior groaned.

"Quick, Wunt!" Ebenezum called. "Quit dawdling and tie the fellow up. I have a feeling we have more to learn from our rotund assailant than first meets the eye."

The big man opened his eyes as I tightened the final knot on his wrists. "What? I'm still alive? Why haven't you killed and eaten me, like demons usually do?"

"What?" Ebenezum stared down at him, his eyes filled with wizardly rage. "Do we look like demons?"

The huge man paused. "Now that you mention it, not all that much. But you must be demons! It is my doom to always confront demons, my fate to fight them everywhere I turn, lest I be drawn into the Netherhells myself!" A strange light seemed to come into the large man's eyes, or perhaps it was only the quivering of his massive cheeks. "You could be demons in disguise! Perhaps you wish to torture me—slowly, exquisitely—with a cruelty known only to the Netherhells! Well, let's get it over with!"

Ebenezum stared at the quivering warrior for a long moment, pushing his fingers through his great, white beard. "I think the best torture would be to leave you talking to yourself. Wunt, if you'll shoulder your pack again?"

"Wait!" the stout man cried. "Perhaps I was hasty. You don't act like demons, either. And the way you felled me—lucky blow to the stomach! You must be human! No demon could be that clumsy!

"Come, good fellows, I shall make amends!" He tugged at his hands, bound behind him. "But someone's tied me up!"

I assured him it had only been a precaution. We thought he might be dangerous.

"Dangerous?" That look came into his eyes again, or perhaps it was the way his helmet fell to his eyebrows. "Of course I'm dangerous! I am the dread Hendrek of Melifox!"

He paused expectantly.

"You haven't heard of me?" he asked after neither of us responded. "Hendrek, who wrested the enchanted war club Headbasher from the demon Brax, with the promise that it would be mine forever? The cursed Headbasher, which drinks the memories of men? Yet I cannot rid myself of it, for the power it gives me! I need the club, despite its dread secret."

His sunken eyes turned to the sack that held his

weapon. "The demon did not inform me of the terms!" The warrior began to shake. "No man can truly own Headbasher! He can only rent it! Twice a week, sometimes more, I am confronted by demons making demands. I must slay them or do their fearsome bidding! For Brax did not tell me when I won the club, I won it on the installment plan!" He quivered uncontrollably, his armor clanking against his corpulent form.

"Installment plan?" mused Ebenezum, his interest suddenly aroused. "I had not thought the accountants of the Netherhells so clever."

"Aye, clever and more than that! Poor warrior that I am, I despaired of ever finding anyone to save me from this curse till I heard a song from a passing minstrel about the deeds of a great magician, Ebenezer!"

"Ebenezum," my master corrected.

"You've heard of him?" A cloud seemed to pass from before Hendrek's eyes. "Where can I find him? I am penniless, on the edge of madness! He's my last hope!"

I glanced at the wizard. Didn't the warrior realize?

"But he's—"

Ebenezum silenced me with a finger across his lips. "Penniless, did you say? You realize a wizard of his stature must charge dearly for his services. Of course, there is always barter—"

"But of course!" Hendrek cried. "You're a magician, too! Perhaps you can help me find him. I ask not only for myself, but for a noble cause—a curse that threatens the entire kingdom, emanating from the very treasury of Melifox!"

"Treasury?" Ebenezum stood silent for a long moment, then smiled broadly for the first time since we began our journey. "Look no farther, good Hendrek.

I am Ebenezum, the wizard of whom you speak. Come, we will free your treasury of whatever curse has befallen it."

"And my doom?"

My master waved a hand in sorcerous dismissal. "Of course, of course. Wunt, untie the gentleman."

I did as I was told. Hendrek pushed himself erect and lumbered over to his club.

"Leave that in the sack, would you?" Ebenezum called. "Just a sorcerous precaution."

Hendrek nodded and tied the sack to his belt.

I reshouldered my pack and walked over to my master. He seemed to have the situation well in hand. Perhaps my concern had been misplaced.

"What need have you to worry?" I asked in a low voice. "Minstrels still sing your praises."

"Aye," Ebenezum whispered back. "Minstrels will sing anyone's praises for the right fee."

II

A professional sorcerer must espouse a strict code of ethics; a position that is not as limiting as it first appears. Most things are still possible within these ethical restrictions, so long as the sorcerer takes every precaution that, whatever he may do, he does not get caught doing it.

—from *The Teaching of Ebenezum,*
Volume 9

The warrior Hendrek led us through the thick underbrush, which, if anything, became more impassable with every step. The late-afternoon sun threw long shadows across our paths, making it difficult to see exactly where you placed your feet, which made the going slower still.

As we stumbled through the darkening wood, Hendrek related the story of the curse of Krenk, capital city of the kingdom of Melifox, and how demons roamed the city, making it unsafe for human habitation, and how the land all around the capital grew wild and frightening, like the woods we passed through now. How Krenk had two resident wizards, neither of whom had been able to lift the curse, so that as a last resort Hendrek had struck a bargain for an enchanted weapon, but had failed to read the infernally small print. But then their ruler, the wise and kind Urfoo the Brave, heard a song from a passing minstrel about a great wizard from the forest country. Hendrek had been sent to find that wizard, at any cost!

"Any cost?" Ebenezum echoed. His step had regained the calm dignity I was more familiar with, not even faltering in the bramble patch we were now traversing.

"Well," Hendrek replied, "Urfoo has been known to exaggerate slightly on occasion. I'm sure, though, that as you're the last hope of the kingdom, he'll—"

Hendrek stopped talking and stared before him. We had reached a solid wall of vegetation, stretching as far as the eye could see and a dozen feet above our heads. "This wasn't here before," Hendrek muttered. He reached out a hand to touch the dense green wall. A vine snaked out and encircled his wrist.

Ebenezum sneezed.

"Doom!" Hendrek screamed and pulled his great club Headbasher from the sack at his belt.

Ebenezum sneezed uncontrollably.

Hendrek's club slashed at the vine, but the greenery bent with the blow. The whole wall was alive now, a dozen vines and creepers waving through the air. They reached for Hendrek's massive form; his swinging club pushed them back. Ebenezum hid his head within his voluminous robes. Muffled sneezing emerged from the folds.

Something grabbed my ankle; a brown vine, even thicker than those that threatened Hendrek, winding up my leg toward my thigh. I panicked, tried to leap away but only succeeded in losing my footing. The vine dragged me toward the unnatural wall.

Hendrek was there before me, slashing in the midst of the gathered green. His strokes were weaker than before, and he no longer cried out. Vines encircled his form, and it was only the matter of a moment before he was lost to the leafage.

I yanked again at the creeper that held me captive. It still held fast, but I caught a glimpse of my master behind me as I was dragged the last few feet to the wall.

The vines crept all about the wizard but were only now pushing at his sorcerous robes, as if the animate vegetation somehow sensed that Ebenezum was a greater threat than either Hendrek or myself. A gnarled tendril crept toward the wizard's sleeve, groped toward his exposed hand.

Ebenezum flung the robes away from his face and made three complex passes in the air, uttering a dozen syllables before he sneezed again. The tendril at his sleeve grew brown and withered, dissolving into dust.

My leg was free! I kicked the dead vine away and stood. Ebenezum blew his nose heartily on his sleeve. Hendrek had collapsed in what had been the vegetable wall. Leaves crackled beneath him as he gasped in air.

"Doom," Hendrek groaned as I helped him to his feet. " 'Tis the work of demons, set on extracting vengeance on me for nonpayment!"

Ebenezum shook his head. "Nonsense. 'Twas nothing more than sorcery. A simple vegetable-aggression spell, emanating from Krenk, I imagine." He started down the newly cleared path. "Time to be off, lads. Someone, it appears, is expecting us."

I gathered up my gear as quickly as possible and trotted after Ebenezum. Hendrek took up the rear, muttering even more darkly than before. I saw what looked like a city before us on a distant hill, its high walls etched against the sunset sky.

We reached the walls some time after nightfall. Hendrek pounded on the great oak gate. There was no response.

"They fear demons," Hendrek said in a low voice. Rather more loudly, he called: "Ho! Let us in! Visitors of Importance to the Township of Krenk!"

"Says who?" A head clad in an ornate silver helmet appeared at the top of the wall.

"Hendrek!" the warrior intoned.

"Who?" the head replied.

"The dread Hendrek, famed in song and story!"

"The dread who?"

The warrior's hand clutched convulsively at the sack that held the club. "Hendrek, famed in song and story, who wrested the doomed club Headbasher—"

"Oh, Hendrek!" the head exclaimed. "That large fellow that King Urfoo the Brave sent off on a mission the other day!"

"Aye! So open the gates! Don't you recognize me?"

"You do bear a passing resemblance. But one can't

be too careful these days. You look like Hendrek, but you might be two or three demons, huddled close together."

"Doom!" Hendrek cried. "I must get through the gate, to bring the wizard Ebenezum and his assistant before the king!"

"Ebenedum?" The head's voice rose in excitement. "The one the minstrels sing about?"

"Ebene*zum*," my master corrected.

"Yes!" Hendrek roared back. "So let us in. There are demons about!"

"My problem exactly," the head replied. "The two others could be demons, too. With the three huddled together to masquerade as Hendrek, that would make five demons I'd be letting through the gate. One can't be too careful these days, you know."

Hendrek threw his great winged helmet to the ground. "Do you expect us to stand around here all night?"

"Not necessarily. You could come back first thing in the morni—" The head's suggestion was cut short when it was swallowed whole by some large green thing that glowed in the darkness.

"Demons!" Hendrek cried. "Doom!" He pulled his war club from the sack. Ebenezum sneezed violently. Meanwhile, up on the parapet, a second thing had joined the first. This one glowed bright pink.

What appeared to be an eye floating above the circular green glow turned to regard the pink thing, while the eye above the pink turned to look at the green. Something dropped from the middle of the green mass and writhed its way toward us down the wall. A similar tentacle came from the pink creature to grab the green appendage and pull it back up the wall. Both orbs grew brighter, with a whistling sound that rose and rose; then both vanished with a flash and a sound like thunder.

The door to the city opened silently before us.

The wizard turned away from Hendrek and blew his nose.

"Interesting city you have here," Ebenezum said as he led the way.

There was something waiting for us inside. Something about four and a half feet high, its skin a sickly yellow. It wore a strange suit of alternate blue and green squares, as if someone had painted a chessboard across the material. A piece of red cloth was tied in a bow around its neck. There were horns on its head and a smile on its lips.

"Hendrek!" the thing cried. "Good to see you again!"

"Doom," the warrior replied as he freed his club from the sack. Ebenezum stepped away and held his robes to his nose.

"Just checking on my investment, Henny. How do you like your new war club?"

"Spawn of the Netherhells! Headbasher will never be yours again!"

"Who said we wanted it? Headbasher is yours—for a dozen easy payments! And nothing that costly. A few souls of second-rate princes, the downfall of a minor kingdom, a barely enchanted jewel or two. Then the wondrous weapon is truly yours!"

The creature deftly dodged the swinging war club. Cobblestones flew where the club hit the street.

"And what a weapon it is!" the demon continued. "The finest war club to ever grace our showroom! Did I say used? Let's call it previously owned. This cream puff of a weapon sat in the arsenal of an aged king, who only used it on Sunday to bash in the heads of convicted felons. Thus its colorful name and its beautiful condition. Take it from me, Smilin' Brax—" The demon fell to the pavement as Headbasher whizzed overhead. "—there isn't a finer used club on the market today. As I was saying just the other day to my lovely—*urk*—"

The demon stopped talking when I hit it on the head. I had managed to sneak up behind the creature as it babbled and knocked it with a rather large cobblestone. The creature's blue and green checked knees buckled under the blow.

"Easy terms!" it gasped.

Hendrek quickly followed with a blow from Headbasher. The demon ducked, but it was still groggy from the first blow. The club caught its shoulder.

"Easy payments!" the thing groaned.

Hendrek's club came down square on the sickly yellow head. The demon's smile faltered. "This may be—the last time—we make this special offer!" The creature groaned again and vanished.

Hendrek wiped the yellow ichor off Headbasher with a shabby sleeve. "This is my doom," he whispered hoarsely. "To be forever pursued by Smiling Brax, with his demands for Headbasher, which no man can own but can only rent!" That strange light seemed to come into his eyes again, though perhaps it was only the reflection of the moon on the cobblestones.

Ebenezum stepped from the shadows. "It doesn't seem as bad as all that—uh, put that club back in the sack, would you? That's a good mercenary; mustn't take any chances." He blew his nose. "The two of you defeated the demon tidily."

My master pulled his beard reflectively. "As I see it, the effectiveness of any curse depends on how the

cursed looks at it. Watching the proceedings very
carefully, with a wizard's trained eye, mind you, I can
state categorically that once we disenchant the
treasury, you'll have nothing to worry about."

A weight seemed to lift from Hendrek's brow.
"Really?"

"You may depend on it." Ebenezum brushed at his
robes. "Incidentally, does good King Urfoo really consider us his last hope for rescuing his gold?"

III

A wizard who wants to build his reputation
rapidly should locate in a rural rather than an
urban setting. Magic seems more majestic when
set against the broad vistas of the countryside.
Townspeople, on the other hand, are so used to
the action of certain tradespeople and govern-
ment officials in their midst that the average con-
jurer's trick pales in comparison.

—from *The Teachings of Ebenezum*,
Volume 10

Hendrek led us through the silent, winding streets
of Krenk to the castle of King Urfoo. Having grown
up in the duchy of Gurnish, in and around Wizard's
Woods, Krenk was the largest town I had ever seen,
with walls and a gate, as many as five hundred buildings, even paved streets! But I saw nothing else as we
walked. Where were the taverns at which we could
stop and exchange pleasantries with the natives?
Where were the town's attractive young women? How
could I be prepared when we finally arrived in

Vushta, the city of a million forbidden delights, if every town we came to was as dead as this?

There was a scream in the distance. Hendrek froze, but the scream was followed by a woman's laughter. At least someone was enjoying herself, I supposed. Was the whole town so afraid of demons?

We came to an open space, in the middle of which was a building twice as grand and five times as large as anything around it. There was a guard standing in front of the place's huge door, the first human (not counting the head) we'd seen since entering Krenk.

"Halt!" the guard cried as we walked into the courtyard before him. "And be recognized!"

Hendrek kept on moving. "Important business with King Urfoo!" he replied.

The guard unsheathed his sword. "Identify yourself, under penalty of death!"

"Doom!" the immense warrior moaned. "Don't you recognize Hendrek, back from an important mission for the king?"

The guard squinted in the darkness. "Don't I recognize who? I didn't quite catch the name."

"The dread Hendrek, here with the wizard Ebenezum!"

"Ebenezus? The one they all sing about?" The guard bowed in my master's direction. "I'm honored, sir, to meet a wizard of your stature."

The guard turned back to Hendrek, who was quite close to the door by now. "Now, what did you say your name was again? I can't let just anybody through this door. You can't be too careful these days, you know."

"Doom!" Hendrek cried, and with a speed amazing in one so large, pulled his club from its restraining sack and bashed the guard atop the head.

"Urk," the guard replied. "Who are you? Who am I? Who cares?" The guard fell on his face.

"Headbasher, the club that drinks the memories of men. He will recover anon but will remember none of this, or anything else, for that matter." Hendrek resheathed his club. "Come, we have business with Urfoo." He kicked the door aside and stormed into the castle.

I glanced at my master. He stroked his mustache for a moment, then nodded and said: "The treasury." We followed Hendrek inside.

We walked down a long hall. Sputtering torchlight made our shadows dance against huge tapestries that covered the walls. A breeze from somewhere blew against my coat to make me feel far colder than I had outside. This, I realized, was the castle with the curse.

Two guards waited before a door hung with curtains at the far end of the hall. Hendrek bashed them both before either could say a word.

Hendrek kicked this door open as well.

"Who?" a voice screamed from the shadow of a very large chair on a raised platform in the room's center.

"Hendrek," the warrior replied.

"Who's that?" A head sporting a crown peered over the arm of the great chair. "Oh, yes, that portly fellow we sent off last week. What news, what?"

"I've brought Ebenezum."

There was a great rustling as people rose from their hiding places around the room. "Nebeneezum?" someone said from behind a chair. "Ebenezix?" came a voice from behind a pillar.

"Ebenezum," my master replied.

"Ebenezum!" a chorus of voices responded as a good two dozen people stepped from behind marble columns, tapestries and suits of armor to stare at my master.

"*The* Ebenezum? The one they sing about?" King Urfoo sat up straight in his throne and smiled. "Hendrek, you shall be justly rewarded!" The smile fell. "Once we take the curse off the treasury, of course."

"Doom," Hendrek replied.

King Urfoo directed us to sit on cushioned chairs before him, then paused to look cautiously at the room's shadow-hung corners. Nothing stirred. The ruler coughed and spoke. "Best get down to business, what? One can't be too careful these days."

"My thoughts exactly, good king." Ebenezum rose from his seat and approached the throne. "I understand there's a cursed treasury involved? There's no time to waste."

"Exactly!" Urfoo glanced nervously at the rafters overhead. "My money involved, too. Lovely money. No time to waste. I'd best introduce you now to my sorcerous advisers."

Ebenezum stopped his forward momentum. "Advisers?"

"Yes, yes, the two court wizards. They can fill you in on the details of the curse." Urfoo tugged a cord by his side.

"I generally work alone." My master pulled at his beard. "But when there's a cursed treasury involved, I suppose one can adjust."

A door opened behind the king and two robed figures emerged, one male, one female. "No time to waste!" the king exclaimed. "May I introduce you to your colleagues, Granach and Vizolea?"

The newcomers stood at either side of Urfoo's throne, and the three wizards regarded each other in silence for an instant. Then Vizolea smiled and bowed to my master. She was a tall, handsome woman of middle years, almost my height, red hair spiced with gray, strong green eyes, white teeth showing in an attractive smile.

Ebenezum returned the gesture with a flourish.

Granach, an older man dressed in gray, nodded to my master in turn, something on his face half-smile, half-grimace.

"The problem," King Urfoo said, "is demons, of course." He cringed on the word "demons," as if he expected one of them to strike him down for mentioning their existence. "We're beset with them. They're everywhere! But mostly," he pointed a quivering hand toward the ceiling, "they're in the tower that holds the treasury!"

He lowered his hand and took a deep breath.

"Doom," Hendrek interjected.

"But perhaps," the king continued, "my court wizards can give you a better idea of the sorcerous fine points." He glanced quickly to either side.

"Certainly, my lord," Granach said quickly behind his half-grimace. "Although none of this would have been necessary if we had used the Spell of the Golden Star."

Urfoo sat bolt upright. "No! That spell would cost me half my funds! There has to be a better way. Doesn't there?"

Ebenezum stroked his mustache. "Most assuredly. If the other wizards are willing to discuss the situation with me, I'm sure we can come to some solution."

"Nothing's better than the Golden Star!" Granach snapped.

"Half my gold!" the king cried. He added in a whisper: "Perhaps you should all—uh—inspect the tower?"

Granach and Vizolea exchanged glances.

"Very good, my lord," Vizolea replied. "Do you wish to accompany us now?"

"Accompany you?" Urfoo's complexion grew paler still. "Is that completely necessary?"

Vizolea nodded, a sad smile on her face. "For the hundredth time, yes. It states directly in the sorcerer's charter that a member of the royal family must accompany all magicians on visits to the treasury."

"Signed right there," Granach added. "At the bottom of the page. In blood."

Urfoo pushed his crown back to mop his brow. "Oh dear. How could that have happened?"

"If you'll excuse me for mentioning it, my lord," Vizolea said with downturned eyes, "'twas you who stipulated the terms of the pact."

The king swallowed. "There is no time to waste. I must accompany you."

Granach and Vizolea nodded. "There's no helping it, without the Golden Star," Granach added.

"And so you shall!" My master's voice broke through the tension around the throne. "We shall inspect the treasury first thing in the morning!"

Urfoo, who had been sinking slowly in his throne, sat up again and smiled. "Morning?"

Ebenezum nodded. "My 'prentice and I have just completed a long journey. How much better to confront a curse during the light of day with a clear head!"

"Morning!" Urfoo the Brave shouted. He smiled at the court-appointed wizards. "You are dismissed until breakfast. Ebenezum, I can tell you are a wizard of rare perception. I shall have my serving girls make your beds and serve you dinner. And in the morning you will end the curse!"

I sat up straight myself. Serving girls? Perhaps there was something of interest in the township of Krenk after all.

"We must plan, Wunt," my master said when we were at last alone. "We only have till morning."

I turned from arranging the pile of cushions and skins that I was to sleep on. My master sat on the large bed they had provided him, head in hands, one on either side of his beard.

"I did not expect wizards." He threw his cap on the bed then and stood. "But the accomplished mage must be prepared for every eventuality. It is of utmost importance, especially concerning the size of our fee, that no one learn of my unfortunate malady."

The sorcerer paced across the room. "I shall instruct you on certain items that have been stored in your pack. We must keep up appearances. And the business with that warrior's enchanted club has given me an idea. We'll best my affliction yet."

There was a knock on the door.

"I was expecting that," Ebenezum said. "See which one it is."

I opened the door to find Granach. He shuffled into the room, still wearing his grimace smile.

"Excuse me for interrupting at so late an hour," the gray-clad wizard began, "but I did not feel earlier that I had the opportunity to welcome you properly."

"Indeed," Ebenezum replied, raising one bushy eyebrow.

"And I thought there were certain things you should be informed of. Before we actually visit the tower, that is."

"Indeed?" Both eyebrows rose this time.

"Yes. First a quick word of advice about our patron, King Urfoo the Brave. It is fortunate for him that Krenkians prefer epithets added early during a ruler's reign, for since he gave up chasm jumping at the age of sixteen, Urfoo has spent all his time in his treasury tower, counting his gold. Note that I didn't mention spending. Just counting. If you were anticipating a large return for your services, you might as well leave now. Our ruler should rather be called Urfoo the Stingy. The payment won't be worth the risk!"

"Indeed." Ebenezum stroked his beard.

Granach coughed. "Now that you know, I expect you'll be on your way."

My master tugged the creases of his sleeves into place and looked up at the other magician. "Indeed, no. A traveling magician, unfortunately, cannot pick and choose his tasks in the same way a town mage might. He has to accept what clients come his way and hope that what small payment he might receive will be enough to take him farther on his journey."

The toothy grimace disappeared completely from Granach's face. "You have been warned," he snarled from between tight lips. "The payment you will receive will in no way compensate for the danger you will face!"

Ebenezum smiled and walked to the door. "Indeed," he said as he opened it. "See you at breakfast?"

The other magician slithered out. Ebenezum closed the door behind him. "Now I'm sure there's money to be made here," he remarked. "But to business. I shall instruct you as to the proper volume and page number for three simple exorcism spells. I wonder, frankly, if we'll even need them."

He pulled one of the notebooks he was constantly

writing in from his pocket and began to tear out pages. "In the meantime I will prepare my temporary remedy.

"The idea came from Hendrek's enchanted club." He tore the pages into strips. "When Hendrek's club is in the open air, I sneeze. However, when the club is in the sack, my nose is unaffected. It can no longer sense the club's sorcerous aroma. Therefore, if I stop my nasal sensitivity to things sorcerous, I should stop my sneezing!" He rolled the first of the strips into a tight cylinder. "But how to accomplish this, short of standing in the rain till I catch cold?"

He held the cylinder aloft so I could get a good look at it, then stuffed it up his nose.

There was another knock on the door.

"High time," Ebenezum said, pulling the cylinder back out. "See who it is this time, Wunt."

It was Vizolea. She had changed from her stiff wizard's robes into a flowing gown with a low neckline. Her deep green eyes looked into mine, and she smiled.

"Wuntvor, isn't it?"

"Yes," I whispered.

"I would like to talk to your master, Ebenezum." I stepped back to let her enter the room. "I've always wanted to meet a wizard of your skill."

"Indeed?" my master replied.

She turned back to me, touched my shoulder with one long-fingered hand. "Wuntvor? Do you think you could leave your master and me alone for a while?"

I glanced at the mage. He nodded rapidly.

"Let me tell you about the Golden Star," Vizolea said as I closed the door behind me.

I stood in the hallway outside our room for a moment, stunned. I had a feeling from Vizolea's manner that she wanted to do more than talk. With my master? I had been known in recent months to keep company with a number of young ladies in my home district, but somehow Ebenezum had always seemed to be above that sort of thing.

But I was still only an apprentice, unaware of the nuances of a true sorcerer's life. I sat heavily, wondering how I would get to sleep on the hallway's cold stone floor, and wishing, for just a moment, that a serving maid of my very own might wander by and make my situation more comfortable.

She wanted to leave.

Wait! I cried. I'm a sorcerer's apprentice. When will you get another chance to dally with anyone half as interesting?

She wouldn't listen. She drifted farther and farther away. I ran after her, trying to shorten the distance. It was no use. She was oblivious to me. I grabbed at her low-cut serving gown, pushed the tray from her hands, begged her to give me a single word.

"Doom," she said in a voice far too low.

I awoke to see Hendrek's face, lit by torchlight.

"Beware, Wuntvor! 'Tis not safe to sleep in these halls! Demons roam them in the wee hours!" He leaned closer to me, his overstuffed cheeks aquiver, and whispered: "You moaned so in your sleep, at first I thought you were a demon, too!"

I saw then he held Headbasher in his free hand. "Some nights I cannot sleep, I fear the demons so. 'Tis strange, though. Tonight I've seen nary a one. Grab onto my club!" He helped me to my feet. "What brings you to moans in the hallway?"

I explained my dreams of serving maids.

"Aye!" Hendrek replied. "This place is full of

haunted dreams. This cursed palace was built by Urfoo's doomed grandfather—some called him Vorterk the Cunning, others called him Mingo the Mad. Still others called him Eldrag the Offensive, not to mention those few who referred to him as Greeshbar the Dancer. But those are other stories. I speak now of the haunted corridors Vorterk built. Sound will sometimes carry along them for vast distances, seemingly from a direction opposite to where it actually originates. Hush, now!"

I didn't mention that it was he who did all the talking, for there was indeed a voice in the distance, screaming something over and over. I strained to hear.

It sounded like "Kill Ebenezum! Kill Ebenezum! Kill Ebenezum!"

"Doom!" Hendrek rumbled. I took a step in the direction of the screams. Hendrek grabbed my coat in his enormous fist and dragged me the other way through the maze of corridors. He paused at each intersection for a fraction of a moment, waiting for the screams to tell him which way to turn. Sometimes it seemed we turned toward the sounds, other times away. I became lost in no time at all.

But the voices became clearer. There were two of them, and the one no longer shouted. Both were agitated, though.

"I don't think so."

"But we have to!"

"You want to move too fast!"

"You don't want to move at all! We'll have to wait for years before we get that treasury!"

"If I let you handle it, it will slip through our fingers! We should enlist Ebenezum!"

"No! How could we trust him? Ebenezum must die!"

"Perhaps I should join Ebenezum and do away with you!"

Hendrek stopped suddenly and I walked into him. His armor banged against my knee.

"There's someone out there!"

A door flung open just before us. I froze, waiting for the owners of the voices to emerge.

Something else came out instead.

"Doom," Hendrek muttered when he saw it crawl our way. It looked like a spider, except that it was as large as me and had a dozen legs rather than eight. It was also bright red.

Hendrek swung the club above his head. Head-basher looked far smaller than it had before.

The creature hissed and jumped across the hall. Something else followed it out of the room. Large and green, the newcomer looked somewhat like a huge, bloated toad with fangs. It jumped next to the spider-thing and growled in our direction.

"Doom, doom," Hendrek wheezed. I considered running, but Hendrek's bulk blocked my only escape route.

The bloated toad leapt in front of the almost-spider. Its fangs seemed to smile. Then the red many-legged thing scuttled over it in our direction. The toad growled and pushed past the dozen legs, but four legs wrapped around the toad and flipped it over. The almost-spider moved in front.

Then the toad-thing jumped straight on top of the many-legged red thing. The almost-spider hissed, the toad-thing growled. Legs interlocked; they rolled. Soon we could see nothing but flashing feet and dripping fangs.

Both disappeared in a cloud of brown, foul-smelling smoke.

"Doom," Hendrek muttered.

Another door opened behind us.

"Don't you think it was time you were in bed?"

It was Ebenezum.

I started to explain what had happened, but he motioned me to silence. "You need your sleep. We've a big day tomorrow." He nodded at Hendrek. "We'll see you in the morning."

The warrior looked once more at the spot where the creatures had disappeared. "Doom," he replied, and walked down the hall.

"Not if I can help it," Ebenezum said as he closed the door.

IV

Never trust another sorcerer is a saying unfortunately all too common among magical practitioners. Actually there are many instances in which one can easily trust a fellow magician, such as cases in which no money is involved or when the other mage is operating at such a distance that his spells can't possibly affect you.

—from *The Teachings of Ebenezum*,
Volume 14

No one ate when we met for breakfast. I sat quietly, running the three short spells I had memorized over and over in my head. My master was quieter than usual, too, being careful not to dislodge the thin rolls of paper that packed his nose. Vizolea and Granach glared at each other from opposite sides of the table, while Hendrek muttered and the king quivered.

Ebenezum cleared his throat and spoke with the lower half of his face. "We must inspect the tower." His voice sounded strangely hollow.

"The tower?" Urfoo whispered. "Well, yes, there's no time to lose." He swallowed. "The tower."

Ebenezum stood. The rest followed. "Hendrek," my master instructed, "lead the way."

The mage strode over to the king. "As we go on our inspection, Your Majesty, I should like to discuss the matter of our fee."

"Fee?" Urfoo quivered. "But there's no time to lose! The treasury is cursed!"

Vizolea was by my master's side. "Are you sure you really wish to inspect the tower? There may be things there you really don't want to see." Her hand brushed his shoulder. "You do remember our conversation last night?"

"Indeed." Ebenezum tugged his mustache meaningfully. "I have a feeling there are things about this treasury that will surprise all of us."

"Doom!" came from the front of the line as the procession moved from the throne room.

"Do I really have to come along?" came from the end.

"The charter," Granach replied.

"Perhaps we *are* being a bit hasty." The king wiped his brow with an ornate lace sleeve. "What say we postpone this, to better consider our options?"

"Postpone?" Granach exclaimed. He and Vizolea looked at each other. "Well, if we must."

They turned and started back for the great hall.

"If you postpone this," Ebenezum said as he caught

the eye of the king, "King Urfoo may never see his money again."

"Never?" The king positively shook. "Money? Never? Money? Nevermoney?" He took a deep breath. "No time to lose! To the tower!"

We climbed a narrow flight of stairs to a large landing and another thick oak door.

"The treasury," Hendrek intoned.

"Your Majesty. The incantation, if you would," Granach remarked.

Urfoo huddled in the rear corner of the landing, eyes shut tight, and screamed:

> Give me an O! O!
> Give me a P! P!
> Give me an E! E!
> Give me an N! N!
> What's that spell?
> Open! Open! Open!

The door made a popping noise and did as it was bidden. No sound came from within.

"Go ahead," Urfoo called. "I'll just wait out here."

Ebenezum strode into the treasury.

The room was not large, but it was not particularly small, either. And it was full—of orange boxes and stacks of gold, fantastic jewelry and unmarked sacks, piled waist high at least, shoulder height near the walls.

We waded into the midst of it.

"Doom," Hendrek murmured. "So where are the demons?"

An unearthly scream came from the landing. Urfoo entered, pursued by the spider.

"The Spider of Spudora!" my master cried. He held his nose.

"Granach!" Vizolea exclaimed. "We didn't talk about this!"

"Your Majesty!" Granach shouted. "There is only one hope! The Golden Star, performed by me!"

"No you don't!" Vizolea recited a few quick words beneath her breath. "If anyone recites the Golden Star, it will be me!"

The toad-thing hopped into the room.

"The Toad of Togoth!" my master said.

"Quick, Urfoo!" Granach cried. "Give me leave to perform the spell before it's too late!"

A red claw snapped out of a pile of jewels.

"The Crab of Crunz!" my master informed me.

"Not the crab!" Vizolea shrieked. "This time, Granach, you've gone too far! Bring on the Lice of Liftiana!"

Granach stepped aside to avoid the panting Urfoo, now pursued by the almost-spider, the bloated toad, and a grinning crustacean.

"Oh, no, you don't!" he cried. "Bring forth the Bats of Billilappa!"

The air was getting heavy with insects and wings.

"That won't stop me! I summon the Rats of Ruggoth!"

"So? See how you handle the Mice of Myrgoll!"

"You asked for it! I bring forth the dread Cows of Cuddotha!"

My master flung his hands in the air. "Stop this now! You'll cause a sorcerous overload!"

The air shimmered as the room was filled with a chorus of moos. A sickly yellow form solidified before us.

"Ah, good Hendrek!" smiling Brax exclaimed.

"How good to see you again. We of the demon per-
suasion like to check out areas of extreme sorcerous
activity; see if we can do a little business, as it were.
And boy, is there business here! Perhaps some of you
folks would like to purchase an enchanted blade or
two, before some of my folks arrive?"

"Doom," Hendrek muttered.

Urfoo ran past. "All right! All right! I'll think
about the Golden Star!" A blue cow with bloodshot
eyes galloped after him.

"The Lion of Lygthorpedia!"

"The Grouse of Grimola!"

"Stop it! Stop it! It's too much!" Ebenezum pulled
back his sleeves, ready to conjure.

"How about you, lad?" Brax said to me. "I've got
this nifty enchanted dagger, always goes straight for
the heart. Makes a dandy letter opener, too. I'm prac-
tically giving it away. Just sign on this line down
here."

"The Tiger of Tabatta!"

"The Trout of Tamboul!"

"Too much!" Ebenezum shouted and sneezed the
most profound sneeze I had ever seen. Paper show-
ered over the newly materialized devil trout, while
the force of the blow knocked Ebenezum back against
a pile of jewels.

He didn't move. He was out cold.

"Doom," Hendrek intoned.

"Then again," Brax said, looking around the room,
"maybe I'd better sell you an ax."

"The Antelope of Arasapora!"

Someone had to stop this! It was up to me. I had to
use the exorcism spells!

"Sneebly Gravich Etoa Shrudu—" I began.

"The Elephant of Erasia!"

Wait a second. Was it "Sneebly Gravich Etoa" or "Etoa Gravich Sneebly"? I decided to try it the other way, too.

"All right! You force my hand! The Whale of Wakkanor!"

There was an explosion in the center of the room. Instead of a materialized whale, there was a lightless hole.

Ebenezum stirred on his bed of jewels.

Brax looked over his shoulder as the black void grew. "Drat. This would have to happen now, right on the edge of a sale. Oh, well, see you in the Netherhells!" The demon disappeared.

It was suddenly quiet in the room. The two other magicians had stopped conjuring, and all the demon creatures, crabs and cows, tigers and trout, had turned to watch the expanding hole.

Ebenezum opened his eyes. "A vortex!" he cried. "Quick, we can still close it if we work together!"

A wind rose, sucked into the hole. The creatures of the Netherhells, bats and rats, mice and lice, were drawn into the dark.

Granach and Vizolea both gestured wildly into the void.

"Together!" Ebenezum cried. "We must work together!" Then he began to sneeze. He pulled his robes to his nose, stepped back from the vortex. It was no use. He doubled over, lost to his malady.

The darkness was taking the jewels now, and the sacks of gold. And I could feel the wind pulling me. Granach screamed at it, and was drawn in. Vizolea cried against it, then she was gone. The blackness reached out for Hendrek and the king, my master and me.

Ebenezum flung his robes away, shouted a few

words into the increasing gale. A bar of gold skidded by me and was swallowed. Ebenezum made a pass, and the vortex shrank. He gestured again, and the vortex grew smaller still, about the size of a man.

Then Ebenezum sneezed again.

"Doom!" Hendrek cried. King Urfoo, wide-eyed, was skidding across the floor to the void.

The warrior and I pushed against the wind to his aid. Jewels scattered beneath our feet and were lost. I pushed a chest toward the gaping maw, hoping to plug a part of it, but it was sucked straight through.

"My gold!" Urfoo cried as he rolled for the hole. I snagged a foot, Hendrek grasped the other. I struggled for footing on the loose jewels, which were moving beneath my feet. I slipped and fell into the warrior.

"Doo—oof!" he cried and lost his balance, back into the hole.

The wind stopped. Hendrek stood, half here and half somewhere else. His girth had plugged the vortex.

Ebenezum blew his nose. "That's better." He recited a few incantations, sneezed once more and the hole sealed up as we pulled Hendrek free.

My master then gave a brief explanation to the king, who sat glassy-eyed on the now-bare floor of the treasury. How his wizards had tried to cheat him of half the treasury by inventing a curse when they couldn't get the money any other way, thanks to the sorcerous charter that called for a member of the royal family to open the door. How he had discovered this plot, and how he should be amply rewarded for saving the king's money.

"Money?" King Urfoo the Brave whispered as he looked around the room, perhaps a dozen jewels and gold pieces left where once there was a room of plenty. "Money! You've taken my money! Guards! Kill them! They've taken my money! Urk!"

Hendrek hit him on top of the head.

"They've—what? Where am I? Oh, hello." The king lost consciousness.

"Doom," Hendrek murmured. "Headbasher does its hellish job again."

My master suggested it might be a good time to travel.

V

A wizard's robes are his badge of office, and one should always wear them proudly, unless one is not proud at that moment of being a wizard. In that case an artisan's frock, a monk's cowl or a dancer's veil are probably preferable, at least until the wizard reaches a friendlier clime.

—from *The Teachings of Ebenezum,*
Volume 17

We had to wait for some hours in the pouring rain before we could get a ride away from Krenk. Ebenezum had thought it best, in case of pursuit, to cover his wizardly robes with a more neutral cloth of brown, and passing wagons were reticent to pick up three characters as motley-looking as we were, especially with one the size of Hendrek.

"Perhaps," Ebenezum suggested with a pull on his beard, "we would have better luck if we separated."

"Doom!" Hendrek shivered and clutched at the bag that held Headbasher. "But what of my curse?"

"Hendrek." The wizard put a comradely hand on

the large warrior's shoulder." I can guarantee you'll see nothing of Brax for quite some time. The severity of that vortex was such that it shook through at least three levels of the Netherhells. Take it from an expert; their transportation lines won't even be cleared for months!"

"Then," rumbled Hendrek, "I'm freed of Brax and his kind?"

"For the time being. Only a temporary remedy, I'm afraid. I have a certain affliction"—he paused, looking Hendrek straight in the eye—"also temporary, I assure you, that keeps me from effecting a more permanent cure. However, I shall give you the names of certain sorcerous specialists in Vushta, who should be able to help you immediately." My master wrote three names on a page of his notebook and gave them to the warrior.

Hendrek thrust the piece of parchment in Headbasher's bag, then bowed low to my master. "Thank you, great wizard. To Vushta, then." His head seemed to quake with emotion, but perhaps it was only the rain pouring upon his helmet.

"We're bound to Vushta ourselves, eventually," I added. "Perhaps we'll meet again."

"Who knows what the fates will?" said Hendrek as he turned away. "Doom."

He was soon lost in the heavy downpour.

Once the warrior was gone, I looked again to my master. He stood tall in the soaking rain, every inch a wizard despite his disguise. If any doubts had assailed Ebenezum on our arrival in Krenk, his actions in the subsequent events seemed to have erased them from his mind. He was Ebenezum, the finest wizard in all the forest country. And in Krenk as well!

Finally I could bear it no longer; I asked my master what he knew about the plot against King Urfoo.

" 'Tis simple enough," Ebenezum replied. "Urfoo had the wealth that the wizards wanted but couldn't get to, because of the charm on the door, so they devised the Spell of the Golden Star, through which, by their definition, Urfoo would have to release half the gold from the charmed tower in order for the spell to work. I don't blame them, in a way. According to Vizolea, the king hadn't gotten around to paying them in all the years they were in his service. Unfortunately, they got greedy and didn't work in unison, and you saw what happened. They even considered working the Golden Star spell three ways; at least Vizolea suggested as much, although"—my master coughed—"I usually don't engage in such activities."

He looked up and down the deserted road, then reached in his damp coat to pull out a bar of gold. "Good. I was afraid I'd lost it in our flight. I have so many layers of clothing on, I could no longer feel it."

I gaped as he hid the gold again. "How did you get that? The floor of the treasury was stripped."

"The floor was." The wizard nodded. "The inside of my robes was not. A wizard has to plan ahead, Wunt. Sorcerers are expected to maintain a certain standard of living."

I shook my head. I should never have doubted my master for a moment.

A covered cart pulled over to the side of the road.

"Need a ride?" the driver called. We clambered into the back.

" 'Tis a dismal night," the driver continued. "I'll sing you a song to lift your spirits. That's what I am—a traveling minstrel!"

Ebenezum looked out from his hood in alarm, then averted his face so that it would be lost in shadow.

"Let's see, what would be appropriate?" The minstrel tugged the reins of his mule. "Ah! Just the thing for a night straight from the Netherhells. I'll sing you a song about the bravest wizard around; fellow from the forest country up Gurnish way—um—Neebednuzum, I think he's called. Now, this ditty's a little long, but I think you'll be struck by the fellow's bravery."

Ebenezum had fallen asleep by the third verse.

The Dry Season

by Tanith Lee

Tanith is another of Don Wollheim's more recent literary discoveries, and quite a gal she is, too. Her first novel, *The Birthgrave,* impressed the geehoozis out of me, and she simply continued to impress and entertain me with novel after novel, such as *Volkavaar,* which had another of those marvelous magicians in it such as I was discussing in the preface to the last story.

This new yarn is exemplary of her brilliant talents: crisp, vivid, written with color and verve yet also with economy of phrase and an infallible taste, it is a stunning performance by one of the best of the living writers in our field.

THE DRY SEASON

I

It was high summer when he came to Thraistum. There had been something of a ride, fifty miles of it, at a parade walk. The column of men and horses had marched its inexorable way through the opaque light of afternoon, the yellow dust going up like powdered biscuit. And along with the dust, the column carried its own weary clanking, the rumble of feet and wheels, the bitter reek of hot metal, raw leather stink and sweat stink. The baked clay road looked close to catching fire; the poplars at the roadside wafted an unslaked parchment smell. The kind of ride where you wanted water, not wine, at the end of it.

And Thraistum looked as if it had never seen water in all its days. The terra-cotta walls, flame-ringed by fields of tindery grain, the wretched red dwellings packed like cells in a hive. The fortress, built from rufus stone.

And he himself, Marsus Seteva, scorched bronze, shut in the armor of gilded iron, the lion's-blood cloak, thirty years old, and all his life a burning, of years, of hopes, of thought, of quietness. Never alone. Yet alone. Buckled into an iron shell and lost in a desert. His whole life, maybe, had been a ride like this ride to Thraistum. Predetermined, slow, without surprise. Without water.

"Does it never rain in this godforsaken place?" he asked the adjutant riding beside him.

"Oh, yes, sir," said the adjutant, who was afraid of him, launching into a travelogue of the region. Which gods obtained where. When the harvest was. How the rain never fell till Novemia.

Of course, there was water in the water bottles, warm gritty slosh tasting of leather.

The other water, the waters of life, like that same tepid filthy stuff? Plenty of wine, naturally. Smoky taverns, red whores, smart army orgies, decorous dinners, wine and women cooled by snow, melted, the shade of furnaces. But no water. Not before. Not now.

And then.

Water.

The somber papery trees had gathered themselves about a well. At the well a girl drawing up a vessel by a rope.

Her arms were white, and her neck, amazingly white in the sun-glare. Her hair was loosely knotted on her head. Fine hair, the color of—

Of water.

No color, in fact, just sheen, burnish, reflection. And texture—it looked like spun silk. No. Spun water.

Back along the line a couple of men called to the girl at the well. Scorpius's voice came next, yammering them into muteness and awarding god knew what penalty for breach of discipline, marching as they were into Thraistum, the velvet-sheathed ax blade of Remusa in this far-flung province.

But the girl seemed not to hear. She unbound the rope. She walked away from the well quietly, the vessel on her shoulder. The young girls here carried jars that way. The right shoulder. It meant they were virgin. He waited for the adjutant to tell him so, but the adjutant was silent.

Seteva turned his head slightly to watch her go down the slope carrying the virgin vessel. The poplar umbra splashed off her body like a wave. Suddenly she too turned and gazed straight at him, as if she felt his stare (the covert, leering stare, more likely, of half the column behind him). But she seemed to be look-ing at him. She had a strange expression. Almost of shock, but as if the shock had not yet reached her eyes, her lips, her physical surface. Her face was like the face of some alien creature, from another plane of existence. As though he had never seen a human face before.

So he recognized her. Infallibly. And equally infallibly, he, the leader of the column, was pushed onward by the column. Remorselessly on to the distant, redly bleeding town.

His oasis slid away. There had been no time to drink.

"I saw a girl I fancied, when I was riding in," he said idly over the sour wine to Cailo. "What are the local taboos like?"

"Variable. Where did you see her?"

"On the hill. By a well."

"There are always girls by wells," Cailo said, a bizarre apposition; but perhaps all he had intended was the domestic reference. "However, as it's the hill well . . . There's a temple precinct a quarter of a mile down from the road. She'd probably be one of the girls from there."

Seteva smiled. The smile was arid. He was glad, and sickened. He'd been recalling only how she had carried the vessel, on the right shoulder.

"No," Cailo said, catching the smile, "the temple girls here aren't that kind. That's Tynt you're thinking of, and Eshtira, in the south. All sorts there. Girls on their backs, boys on their faces. Fun all round. But here. Didn't they tell you at Mareuna?"

"They didn't tell me much. One major god. Puberty rites for males. Monogamy. And—what is it?—the doves are sacred to the temple, so don't let the men take slingshots at them, despite descending guano."

Cailo nodded.

"There's more. There's the sacrifice."

"Sacrifice?" Seteva repeated softly. He tried to go on grinning—doves spotting the valor of Remusa—but he saw flames curling out of a well.

"In five days' time. To make the rain come end-of-season."

"You mean an ox, or do these barbarians use horses?"

"Worse. I mean a girl. A temple girl, a virgin."

The fire ran into his mouth and through his belly.

"That's needlessly primitive, isn't it?" he said calmly. "Under Remusan rule, surely it gets stopped?"

"Hardly that. Come now, Marsus. You should know. The only thing that gets stopped under Remusan rule is failure to pay taxes. And insurrection. Remusa will tolerate anything else. Why not? Let the children play with their toys, as long as they're good children. And the Thraistians are models. Docile, friendly, courteous, hardworking. No problems here in twenty years. Their religion is the least we can let them have in return, if it keeps them so sweet. Come, it's not much to remember. Don't shoot the doves or shaft the temple girls. Sacrifice day is a festival. You'll probably be entertained by it. The town goes wild at sundown."

"And the girl? How do they choose? The shortest grass stem?"

"Not quite. It's an honor for her, actually, Marsus. That's how they see it. Die like this, and she's sure of her place in paradise. The same thing applies to their men who die in battle. Luckily they don't go in for battles anymore. That sort of incentive makes men hell to fight, hell to kill. Fanatics. I'd rather combat wolves."

"When?" Seteva asked.

"When what? Oh, that. The girl—they choose her today, near sunset. Probably about the time you brought your men into the fort. They'd have been doing it then."

Seteva drank the last mouthful of liquid bitumen called wine.

He knew they had chosen the girl. Her life was going to be poured away on their altar, for their god.

It didn't matter.

Some slut.

Some dirty, foreign slut. Possibly a whore, for all the ritual chat. Virgin—what was that anymore? They'd sew them up again in half the markets of the world for two silver Remusan capitas.

Stupid slut.

"Have some more wine," said Cailo.

In the dark, crickets, and through the slit of window the dry stars flickered in the brazen black of the sky.

Soaked in heat, too parched even to sweat, he lay on his back on the straight hard pallet, thinking of fountains, lakes, oceans. Water.

Cailo rode out in the morning with his six hundred, going west to Mareuna.

The business of the fort was simple enough. Outside, the town was peculiarly tensed. Moving, working, going about its parochial affairs, but yet somehow poised and waiting. These were the Days of Salt, the period of purification before the sacrifice.

In four days' time they would give her to their god on the end of a knife.

Cailo had been definite:

"You'd be advised to post men round the temple square. Not that they'll be necessary, but it's protocol. The temple building is to the north of the town; the square opens off three ways, closed on the temple side. A rotten area to contain in a skirmish, but fortunately you won't need to. They'll be gentle as lambs, and afterward they get drunk, and the girls are generous to a fault. No taboos at all. Take my counsel and let the men off the leash. It does no harm, and they like babies here. You won't get recriminations."

"And if there are recriminations, you'll be in Remusa."

"Trouble at Thraistum is like the rain falling before Novemia. It never does. Just leave their religion alone, Marsus. The rest takes care of itself. This is going to be the nicest year of your army life. You'll go soft. Enjoy it."

The heat had drawn over like a curtain behind Cailo and the line of marching men and horses.

Inside the curtain Thraistum cooked, and the dust lay like cinnamon on the air. The grainfields seemed to be smoking beneath the flat purple fresco of the hills, the blatant sky.

Days of Salt. Salt in the wound. (A sword cut at Samaia, salt rubbed in at a makeshift hospital post, to staunch the bleeding; the smart searing to the bone, the backs of the ears, the groin, making him vomit with pain.)

The crickets had a different sound by day.

"Don't drink any water unless you mix it one-third with wine. It's not bad water exactly. Just native water. Full of red clay from the hills."

Cailo's imparted information had been comradely, endless.

He had a homily for every event.

The crickets tortured the grass.

The fortress should have been cool, its walls ten feet thick, in spots more. But the walls sweated and were not cool.

In the middle of the afternoon they brought the girl into the town from the hill precinct.

There were twenty priests, white linen and shaved heads, like the avatars of Aigum. There were subsidiary girls, too. They wore their hair long and unbound. In the middle of the procession two white she-asses pulled a little gilded car. The girl was in the car, motionless, and a child held a fringed sunshade over her head. The girl's hair too was unbound, plaited with flowers. Her wrists were ringed with silver, reminiscent of shackles.

Standing on the gate tower, he watched them pass through. People stood noiselessly in the street. The stillness had become symbolic.

He had the urge to shout.

Beneath the parasol, darkened, her hair appeared almost blue. She looked only before her. She did not seem afraid. Of course, she had been promised paradise.

Salt in the wound. It didn't matter.

II

"But I thought you spoke the language well," he said to the adjutant.

"Sufficient to barter, sir. To make myself plain. But not good enough for this, sir."

"Good enough? Where do you imagine we're going? The plaster-and-lathe temple of some crackpot god. Gloria Remusa, soldier. Remusans go where they wish and speak to whom they wish, in whatever manner they wish. It devolves on our subject peoples to learn our tongue; we do not learn theirs. Do you see?"

Seteva spoke in mockery of an attitude. The adjutant, missing, naturally, the mockery, tried to reason with him.

"Yes, sir. The priests do have an adequate command of Remine, sir. But for this—"

"*This?* What is so special?"

"There could be—misunderstandings."

"And so?"

"I took the liberty—"

"Did you," Seteva said.

The adjutant flushed. He said, "A caravaneer from Mareuna, versed in many languages. A rogue, but reliable if well paid. He's been supplying the garrison at Thraistum for years with—different commodities."

"I know the sort. All right. Where is he?"

The adjutant hurried out and came back with the caravaneer. Cailo had mentioned him, too, a tall, wiry swarthy man with a gold nugget in his left ear and oiled black curls springing across his shoulders under the wound head-cloth. He had bought Remusan citizenship and had donned a Remusan name to match.

"So you're Nylerus."

Nylerus bowed. His face held all the loving, compassionate wickedness of six generations of desert nomads commingled five generations more with the serpentine city folk of the East.

"The Kastor requires an interpreter. I am his servant."

"The Kastor is not certain he requires an interpreter."

Nylerus smiled, resting, as he did so, one long, umber finger across his mouth, a parody of concealment.

"The Kastor knows best. Gloria Remusa. But I speak Trasint as fluently as Remine. As my own tongue."

"Trasint?" Seteva inquired.

"The native name, sir, for Thraistum," the adjutant broke in nervously.

"What business brings you to Thraistum?" Seteva asked the easterner casually.

Nylerus kept smiling. The smile said: *Illegal and barely legal business. But you will comprehend that, and pardon me. Remusans always comprehend how we second-class riffraff must scuff out our livings in this erroneous world. And we are quite useful to you, are we not?*

"Goods to sell, as ever, noble Kastor. My party leaves in three days—the morning of the sacrifice, to be exact. I dare not risk my men in the town longer. On sacrifice night there is a festival, a riot. Thus for three days, a portion less, my talents are at the worthy Kastor's disposal."

The temple was not as his mockery had fashioned it but a box of stone, older than the town, two or three centuries older than the fortress. A labyrinth of square courts opened into and out of each other. Daylight streamed in through high, blue-painted walls, falling in spotlights, like static rain pools. It was actually cold, icy almost, coming in from the baked town.

Scorpius and ten polished privates kicked their heels in an anteroom. Seteva stood, helmet under arm, shivering slightly in the dank shade, politely waiting for the High Priest of Thraistum-Trasint to advance through the curtain. And at Seteva's side, Nylerus, the decorous servitor.

Religion had always been a focal point for danger and dissent. More focal than the subdued potentates, the petty kings. The princes of the temples had the bit of spiritual power between their teeth, and all over the Remusan-conquered world, High Priests were reckoned a cipher for trouble. Save this one, apparently, in the backwoods of Thraistum. *So why in the gods' name am I here, seeking to stir the dregs at the bottom of the cask?*

The curtain moved on its rings.

The High Priest entered.

He looked immediately at his visitor. The priest seemed to know Seteva, to recognize him. In late middle years, a heavy, rambling decline of manhood beside the fine-honed soldier, the High Priest of Trasint, like the temple itself, had built, nevertheless, upon the foundation of his age.

The priest bowed to Seteva. It was pure courtesy, neither fawning nor ironic. The bow accepted Remusa as master, accepted and ignored it. It was no matter. The sun still rose, the moon waxed and waned.

Seteva stood there, not acknowledging the bow. He addressed himself to Nylerus. "Tell him."

Nylerus spoke in Thraistian to the priest, conveying the thanks of the garrison's commander, Marsus Seteva, for the interview. This being also a device: formal words in one mode, the arrogance of the Remusan standing by, stone-faced, in another, as if disowning them.

Seteva watched the priest closely. To Nylerus, Seteva said, "Now tell him I want the sacrifice stopped."

Nylerus blinked. He made no remonstrance; the blink said it all. Delicately Nylerus translated for the High Priest.

The High Priest, too, looked nowhere but at Seteva. His face unchanged, he enunciated levelly to Seteva in the outlandish tongue. Seteva grasped a couple of fragments he could identify. The phrase that meant a betrayal, and the phrase that likened a man to a dog.

There was a brief lacuna.

"Well?" Seteva said, looking at the priest, addressing Nylerus.

"The Patriarch says the ceremony has always been permitted in the past."

"That's not what he said. Explain to the Patriarch that I don't allow any man to call me a scavenging cur. Even a priest."

The High Priest spoke mildly, in a sudden hesitant Remine: "That was not—decidedly—my meaning, commander. My speech indicated—that even dogs cannot always obey their masters. We are—your dogs, commander. But we cannot obey."

"You handle Remine excellently," said Seteva. "You should be able, therefore, to absorb my decision firsthand. I don't intend this rite to occur while I am in Thraistum. Offer your god a pig or a sheep. Your women have other uses."

Still mild, the priest said, "You do not know our ways, commander. You must not expect to see sense in what you do not know. Under Remusa we have been allowed to follow our religion, always."

"As far as I am concerned," Seteva said, "to kill a woman on an altar is not merely barbarous, it poses a threat to law and order. While I am in command of the garrison, you will either suspend or discontinue the enterprise. That's my last word."

Now the priest stared. He uttered rapidly, once more in Trasint. Nylerus said, "The Patriarch vows the rite cannot be put aside. That it is unavoidable. That he must risk Remusa's displeasure."

"Remind the priest that Remusa, displeased, has been known to nail men on crosses. And no priesthood was ever exempt."

Seteva turned; one stride would take him back through the outer doorway. The priest said behind him, clear as a drop of water falling onto stone, "Commander, the girl is willing."

Seteva halted. "What did you say to me?"

"The girl is willing to die. I surmise this is what disturbs you, Commander. If you wish—with her own lips, she will assure you of the fact."

Seteva swallowed. Like an expert marksman the old man had pierced through officialdom, rage, Remusan arrogance, and struck the vital nerve. *I want to see the girl again. I want to hear her voice, touch her. I want to argue with her for her life, even though I can't do it in her own language. But. This is absurd.*

"The girl is nothing to me. Only a facet of your apparent refusal to abide by my order."

The priest spoke in Trasint.

"What does he say now?"

"Only that he is sorry, mighty Kastor, to offend you. And that the girl is in the adjacent courtyard."

It was becoming suggestive of a brothel, this insistence on the proximity of what he truly wanted. Except that, save in a very general way, that was not what he wanted. Nor what was offered.

Seteva's mouth was dry. A little breeze ruffled the

linen curtain and he saw a pale shadow pass over it, outside. The girl?

As if mesmerized, he found himself crossing the room, drawing aside the curtain.

The court was half-open to the sky, white with sun to its center, beyond that dyed blue by shade. There was a basin with static, transparent water in it. Doves were shooting up from about it like flung spears. The girl was seated on the lip of the basin.

She was combing her hair, slow shining motions, like waves running in over a smooth shore. There was no mark of death on her. Her stance conveyed a serenity of youth, gazing upon the endless vista of its future. That false dream of youth, which she, undeniably, could no longer possess.

Nylerus had reached him.

"No," Seteva said to him.

He moved out into the white sunlit half of the court and drove the curtain to with his fist as he passed, shutting the room into some other dimension that could neither see nor hear nor realize where he had gone, nor why.

The girl did not turn, but her hand with the comb sank away. Her hair was very long, covering her shoulders, falling like a silvery fringe almost into the water of the basin. Waterfall.

He walked toward her, around the basin. Her head was lowered, as if she examined the comb she held in her lap. The comb was ivory, bone, a mark of death after all. He could not see her face. He was the length of his arm from her when he spoke.

"Look up," he said. Perforce he used Remine, and she could not guess its meaning. But she did guess—the tone, perhaps—and raised her head.

Her eyes were wide and intent. Without modesty

and without invitation, they explored him. He saw
again that curious expression of amazement below
the surface of her eyes. He could not explain to himself what she represented. His heart hitting his breastbone, the sound of blood in his ears like the sea, he
thought, *Why did I never meet you on some marble
avenue in Remusa, why did I never see you in some
litter on the shoulders of slaves, going by, easy to follow? Why did I never meet you in the whorehouse at
Tynt, easy to buy? Why not on the road to Mareuna,
all those months kicking my heels, waiting for
transport? Twenty, thirty girls, not one of them you.
Why not that officer's wife at Samaia—I could have
killed him. Easy, easy. But this. Why now?*

She said something to him, softly, in Trasint.

"What?" he said, as softly. "I don't understand
you."

She had risen. She held up her hand before him,
palm open. It was the semantic tribal sign, current
the whole earth over: I am here without weapons.
Suddenly he fathomed what she meant, and, appalling him, his eyes stung with tears.

In Remine, concisely, a declaration she had
learned, she murmured, "I have consented. To die. I
will it."

"No." He caught himself struggling with the few
bits of Thraistian he had acquired. "We—I—can prevent—this."

She only looked at him. Probably he had not said
what he believed he had at all. Once more she said,
gently, "But I consent."

"In gods' name," he said in Remine. In Trasint he
sought and found the crucial word: "Why?"

Her eyes never left his face. She answered in Trasint, then in Remine she said: "There is no alternate way."

He could not offer the truth to her, gagged as he was, but he saw he did not need to. She knew, and in spite of the truth, she had said: *There is no alternate way.*

He turned only his head, and shouted across the court.

"Nylerus!"

The doves swirled up again, white wings like segments of the white stone of the courtyard exploded by friction. Nylerus came from the curtained door mouth, through the swirling of the doves.

"Kastor?"

"Say to her that she is under the protection of Remusa. That no one is going to kill her."

Nylerus bowed and translated the sentences to the girl.

A veil seemed to slip down across her face.

She spoke in Trasint.

Nylerus said, "She replies that she is grateful; but it is not within your power to promise her this. She is not afraid, and she asks that you leave her in peace."

Nylerus did not smile now, too clever to smile at this ludicrous spectacle, the Remusan commander sent packing by the foreign child-woman. The gaze of Nylerus slid silkenly beneath its antimony, simply observing, as the Remusan swung abruptly about and walked out of the court. Quiet as sand or snake, Nylerus poured himself in the conqueror's wake.

Sentries patrolled along the ramparts of the fortress. Periodically the challenge rang out, isolated by the hot, blue-black darkness, over the never-ceasing dazzle of the crickets. The stars burned inexhaust-

ibly, and in the huddled, heat-swilled mass of
dwellings below, the muddy lamps. Sometimes, from
the northern end of the town, a dull vibratory chanting. The temple.

"Nylerus is outside, Commander."

Seteva glanced up. A pile of parchments lay on the
table before him, brown withered leaves, the business
of the fort, unread. "All right."

Nylerus slipped into the room.

"I thought we'd paid for your services as interpreter."

"So you have, noble Kastor." Nylerus did not seem
to note the parchments on the table, nor the wine
jug. "I wonder if the Kastor will indulge me."

"I gather Cailo did. But I'm not Cailo."

"Indeed not, Commander. You must not suppose I
expect a welcome at your fortress. Though I have
been welcome."

"What do you want?"

"In the East . . ." Nylerus said. He had assumed
a storyteller's voice. He looked a second at Seteva, to
gauge his reaction. Seteva did not move. Nylerus
rested his hands on the air, lightly, expressively. "In
the East our holy books inform us that when the first
man had been made, the god breathed the divine
breath into him, which became his soul, and caused
him to become quick. It was then necessary to create
woman. But the god did not breathe life directly into
the woman. Instead he opened the man's body and
removed from it a piece of the soul, and this he gave
to the woman. Since then, for every man created, a
piece of his soul is subtracted to quicken a woman. In
memory of this deed the seed also passes from male to
female. But if a man finds by chance the woman who

contains that fraction of his own soul, he will know her, as he knows his own image in a mirror."

Outside something had caused the crickets to fall startlingly dumb.

"You gamble I have a weakness," Seteva said quietly. "You presume you can profit by it, just as you have profited here by Cailo's weaknesses."

"The Kastor misjudges me. Let me offer him the end of the story of the first man and the first woman who drew life from the same soul. Another god, jealous of the god who had quickened life in the bodies of Men, seduced the woman. He put on the form of a serpent and persuaded her away by his beauty. They fashioned a second race between them, half-human and half-snake."

"From which, no doubt, you can claim descent."

"The Kastor is too generous. With my people the snake is revered for its wisdom."

"Then be wise, Nylerus. Get out."

"Before I go, Kastor, my caravan. It leaves on the morning of the sacrifice, one hour before the woman dies on the altar."

"You forget. The temple will forego the sacrifice, by my order."

"Oh, mighty Kastor—" Nylerus laughed, musically and low. "These barbarians . . . Do you think they will obey you? In preference to their *god?*"

"They will if they decide to keep their liberty."

"They are not civilized enough to put liberty before religion. This is your stumbling block."

The crickets had started up again, like flints perpetually striking on the peppery flanks of the hills.

Seteva poured himself wine. The jug was almost empty, and the liquor had the sour stale taste of repetition.

"You'd better finish what you started to say to me."

"As the noble Kastor desires. I was about to postulate a theory. The men of my caravan—what are they? Villains, no more. The rubbish of the alleyways. And when they are in drink, gracious Kastor, neither god nor demon will deter them. Maybe they have seen a girl they fancy. What do they do? They abduct her, Kastor. They drag the poor wretch away with them, careless of whom she might belong to. And such a girl, once lost, is rarely recovered. For this cause I remove my caravan from Thraistum before the riotous celebration of the sacrifice is due. But possibly I am not quick enough. Possibly these dogs of mine have already espied some girl. Abductions can always be managed. Even a temple is not impregnable. And the priests. No match for jackals of the desert. There are a thousand crannies in these hills where such a theft might be hidden. I might detail for the noble Kastor the most likely concealments."

Seteva drained the cup and set it down among the parchments. "And the price?"

Nylerus touched one hand fleetingly to his brow, his heart. "To have the Kastor's friendship would be sufficient reward."

"I'm sorry to disappoint you," Seteva said. "I don't mean to be in your debt throughout the remainder of my time here. You've mistaken your man, Nylerus. Now, I can only reiterate my earlier proposal: Get out."

Nylerus bowed and moved toward the door. At the threshold he said, "On the day of the sacrifice, Kastor, I will leave thirteen men near the gate. They will be dressed in the manner of my people. You could not miss them, should you wish any service."

In the dark the crickets stopped again and again, for no obvious cause. Like a heart suddenly faltering. He remembered how his brother had died at Samaia, sliced in two, body bloodless, skin white as salt.

Salt in the wound.

Days of salt.

They had burned the dead at Samaia on one great pyre. The heat of it had spread like the heat of a summer day.

And the crickets began again. And again.

III

There was a woman in the town. She, or her Remusan clients, called her Pulcra, but she was ugly as forty years of whoring could make her. Her girls, younger, were a different matter.

In a minute cell of the scalding house, its walls painted with blue lotuses and red fruits, a girl the color of amber took the wooden combs from her hair and the garish clothes from her body. They lay down on the pallet and made something, not love, between them. Fire, perhaps.

When he had had her, she offered him wine, politely lingering, eager to please. The wine was local, honeyed and thick, like syrup.

She spoke Remine haltingly but correctly. Any time, she said, he would like her—or another girl, though she hoped it might be herself—they could come to him at the fort. There was a secret stair. Nylerus the Easterner knew the way. Jezit, the girl was named. The madam had told him. She would gladly come to him. Any night, save tonight.

"Why not tonight?" he asked her. He wasn't interested, but the sight of her eased him, the small flut-

tery trained movements she gave, like those of a
caged bird. Her accented, hesitant voice.

The light of day was already thickening like the
wine. The dense coppery glare which preceded sunset.

"Tonight is the night of the Passage of Sin. She
who is to die will sit before the temple. All who need
may go by, touching her. Through the touch we receive blessing. She takes our sins upon herself. I have
many sins."

"The men you couple with," he said noncommit-
tally.

But she merely lowered her lids. "No. They are not
my sins. It is no sin to couple."

"You'll have to find another formula, in any case.
Has no one told you? There will be no sacrifice."

The girl looked afraid. She whispered something in
Trasint and brushed at an amulet that had been
glued between them on her breast all the time he lay
over her.

In the narrow street the red rays of latter-day
stained the clay houses. The commander of the garrison stood, partially anonymous in the casual wear of
the fort, just a Remusan officer, his army cloak
wrapped loosely about him against the heat.

His feet walked him northward, through the sweet
stenches of dust, dung and spice, the odor of the town
at this hour.

What am I doing?

He waited for the sun to set, under the shadow of a
wall, across the temple square and facing toward the
temple building. There was a matte blot on the light
between him and the temple. It had not registered
with him before. A stone slab about the height of a
man, steps up to it, level across its surface.

No. This won't answer. I must have a reason for what I do. I have no reason. Nothing that has the guise of reason.

He had seen a man in one of the eastern villages five years ago. The man had run screaming through the village; he had eaten stones and drunk urine. When he uttered, it was gibberish. He was reckoned to be possessed by demons. That was, he had been motivated, without the power of his own will or sense, to perform acts injurious to himself and to others.

The sky altered from a wing of blood to a wing of indigo, and as the sky altered a crowd gathered along the edges of the square, as if the going of the sun had called it up.

Torches were flowing from the temple gate, droplets of fire running over the dusk.

There was no sound, no chanting. Voicelessly the crowd began to surge in on the gate, fulvously lit, then sinking forward into shadow.

The movements were such that he could not define their purpose.

Presently he also, muffled in the dark and in the cloak, joined the patient, slowly advancing crowd that pressed toward the gate.

Possessed.

By what?

A bit of his soul in her body. He had no soul; that was a dream of the East. The gods cared for a man simply while he was living. If there were gods.

Nobody stared at him or shrank aside disconcerted by this apparition of the Conqueror in their midst. They did not seem to notice.

Where the torches glared, he could see nothing.

Only the silhouetted black shapes of men and women, shuffling, pausing, eddying away.

Then, like a curtain, the crowd parted. He beheld the light, and in the center of the light, a creature in white robes, with a silver casque of hair; a blanched face, as if carved. A man knelt to her, contacting, with his fingertips, the hem of the robe, the silver-corded wrist. And next a woman, reaching to find the shoulder of the image. Sliding off into the shadow as the man had done, helplessly drawn to and thrust from the magnetic aura of the light.

It was the Remusan's turn now.

Take my sins. No. You are my sin, my stumble from the road of honor and duty. From sanity.

Did she remember him? The bleached face, white lips slightly parted, the eyes discs of jet, was raised to him like a mirror. But in the mirror nothing stirred.

There was a scent of incense and of drugs in the air.

He stood like a stone, a fold of his cloak over his head, hidden and unnamed.

The moment dissolved. Like a man stepping from a frieze, returned to flesh, he moved on into the shadow. Without touching her.

The girl, Jezit, sought him in the coal-black hour before dawn. Unsleeping, midway in the act of kindling the dish of oil, he heard a man laugh and a woman's protest. The sentry rapped on the door.

"One of Pulcra's daughters is here, Commander. She came in by the back stair and scratched at the postern." The man could barely restrain his amusement. Worse than Cailo, this new Kastor of the fort who could not leave the harlots alone.

Jezit poised in the dim yellow smudge of the lamp.

Her head bowed, she extended to Seteva, mutely, a cloth-bound package.

"What's this?"

"It was sent to me, but for you, Kastor."

"And Nylerus reminded you of the way in? Don't use that stair again without my leave."

She did not reply, and he unwrapped the package, and there was the ivory comb the girl had plied in the temple courtyard, and wound about it, trapped in its teeth, a slender rivulet of colorless, shining hair.

His heart seemed to congeal. She had sent to him the symbol of her death. No speech could be so final or so essentially pathetic. Like men drowning in some galley, casting their jewels from them, signets of their lives and office, to be swallowed by fish, perhaps, and discovered again a year later at the dinner table. His mother, when he was six years old, had recounted how his father's seal ring had come back to her that way, from the sea battle at Mentum. But even then, somehow, he had known she lied, that the ring was a copy. That nothing, not even the glory of a name, could absolutely survive death.

The little whore drooped her head.

Let it end, he thought. *I'm far from land, but still the harbor is in sight. Turn back. She's nothing to you. Pretend, as her priests do, that you never ordered them to forego their sacrifice.* These fools believed she died for them, their scapegoat. Too much hung on her death. She was condemned, for if she lived, their sins remained. Probably even the might of Remusa could not contain their spiritual panic and fury if they were cheated of their purging. He could not save her. But then, she was happy to die. Let her be happy. *One more death, what's that?* One more cup spilled on the ground.

He glanced at Jezit. "Well," he said. "Since you're here."

The hot shadows flared on the walls and sank, unappeased.

"It is a passing trouble," she said to him, consolingly, as if to a child. Doubtless she had seen men ashamed at their inability to fill her. He looked at the lamp glow and the quiescent shadows. The drought was not only in the world now, but within him. Dehydrated of water and of seed.

Die for me too, then, he thought. *Die for my sins, and give me back the rain, the water in the cup, my manhood and my soul.*

IV

"At noon," the adjutant said. "That's when they do it. To appease the sun, I think. Or to attract storms."

The hills seemed to be smoking. A brush of haze blurred the perimeter of the hard sky. Already the dust, momentarily laid by the flat black palm of night, was flouring the air, the ledges, the sills of the town, the sockets of the nostrils, eyes and lips of men and beasts. Just another feverish day. This fifth day.

"I won't risk this mob getting out of hand," Seteva said. "Whatever precautions Cailo took, I want them doubled. Trebled, if necessary. A century deployed in blocks of ten, thirty men on each of the three open sides of the square, and ten across the gate."

"Yes, sir."

Scorpius cleared his throat. "That's extravagant, Commander."

"Not quite. Cailo treated this place as a combined brothel and sanctuary. It's neither."

Scorpius and the adjutant skimmed a glance between them, a memento of the harlot who had come in by the secret stair.

"And who's to take charge of this modest deployment, Commander?"

"I'll see to it myself."

And I'll see her die. But he was ready for that. He was balanced, beyond the trivia of his emotion, his superstition. Beyond the reach of her and the effluvia of this compost heap of barbarism and self-blindness. He walked at his own elbow. Inflexible, and objective. Guiding, indifferent.

"Where's that Easterner? Away yet?"

"Nylerus?" Scorpius spat economically through the window. "He rode out early. Though I hear he's left thirteen of his pack rats near the gate. Selling, or trying to sell, horses. No one'll buy anything so close to the sacrifice. But, my god, who devised this system? A young, healthy girl to be butchered. Some decent farmer could have got sons on her. A waste, and no mistake."

"Pulcra could have found a use for her, at the very least," Seteva said.

They grinned, glad he would admit his weakness, reduce it thereby to the unimportant vice it was. The vice they thought it was.

Let from their cages, streamers of doves tangled across the cloudless sky.

The hundred men stood, sweating in their leather and iron. Scorpius, on the roan horse he had brought from Mareuna, sat by the temple gate.

The crowd pressed against the wall of shields and of Remusan soldiery. But hardly a sound came from the crowd. Once or twice a child, crying, was miraculously hushed. The dust was settling on the rims and folds and creases of the crowd, as if on statuary in a desert.

On his own face Seteva felt the pollen of the dust, while the black horse he rode became a gray dust horse.

He was tired, as if after a day's march. He ached, shut in the iron oven of heat and metal. His shadow lay on the ground under the hoofs of the horse. He wanted this to be over.

Inside the box of the temple a ram's horn moaned.

The gates swung open. From the well of shade into the bowl of sun, changing color and texture as the sun struck them, the linen-robed priests, shaved like the avatars of Aigum, flickered black to white, black to white. A sharp perfume of myrrh fanned from their censers, penetrating the nasal passages, seeming to pierce the dome of the brain.

Like high tide they washed in about the stone slab in the square, the slab that was the height of a man, steps up to it, level across its surface.

And now a girl came from the temple, also changing from black to white until, exposed in the force of noon, she too appeared to catch alight and to burn. She walked slowly, heavily, and observing her face, he saw that she was drugged, some poppy drink, to kill fear or to numb pain or simply to destroy the last vestige of the life-wish. She was very young. Life must be strong in her, despite her abnegation and her surrender to her god. She would need that drink.

He watched her face and felt nothing. She was a stranger, foreign-looking, not even actually beautiful. He could perceive now, as if from a high tower or across a vast distance, the gulf between them. She meant nothing. He was sorry for her, for her stupidity, for her death.

He had acted irrationally in this venture, and it could have become a worse irrationality if the more determined idiocy of these priests had not prevented it.

He had been within an arm's length of losing everything. And gaining what? Some provincial doxy who could not even speak to him coherently in his own tongue.

Her eyes were entirely darkened by the drug, and nearly closed. Her heavy movements were graceful, sensual almost, as she moved toward the stone. As though she swam through a glaucous river.

Two priests drew her up the steps tenderly. Yes, most certainly, with tenderness.

Through the mask of the dust Seteva's mouth fixed itself in a sneer, and he was aware of the dust cracking to form new lines.

She lay on the slab, against the sky, the slight profile—head, breast, the curious addendum of the up-pointed, naked feet.

(He had seen enough of those feet, upturned, corpses in ranks, piled on each other, ready for burning after the battle.)

The ram's horn groaned again from the temple.

The fat High Priest was emerging now, and before him a girl about thirteen years old with a bough of greenery across her hands and something flashing white on that green, like a long blade of water.

Seteva was thirsty. The local wine wasn't bad, once you were used to it. And it would have to be wine. The local water had a foul taste.

The High Priest mounted the steps. He was on the other side of the slab, confronting Seteva over the profiled body of the girl. The thirteen-year-old offered the green bough to the priest, and he raised from it a honed and burnished knife, holding it aloft for the crowd to see, and perhaps for his god to see it, too.

It would require two cups of wine, more, to wash this dust-dryness out of the throat. *When I get to the fortress—*

He found, with a sort of unsurprised bewilderment, that he had kneed the horse and was riding forward. Not fast, in fact rather leisurely. The High Priest had seen him and had paused, the knife still pointed toward the sky. The priest's face was blank. Seteva felt the same blankness on his own face.

Now all the priests were in his way.

Suddenly he was no longer riding leisurely but with a headlong violence. The linen-wrapped figures were toppling sideways, dividing, the slab loomed, horizontally spread with white, the fat, middle-aged man beyond it, and the silver blade abruptly tearing the sky with its motion.

The blade in his own hand, which he had not been conscious of till that instant, sheared through the High Priest.

The man's face was red now with his own blood, bloodily washed of its blankness, whirling backward—

Seteva pulled the white shape from the altar effortlessly. It was the first time he had touched her, but he did not think of it then, for she did not seem human, or real.

It was not quiet anymore.

He turned the horse, pulling on the bit to set the hoofs lashing, and plunged straight through the crowd. Women were screaming, and far off he heard, almost with nostalgia, the yammering yell of Scorpius. The soldiers had broken their formation. Seteva glimpsed three youths brawling over an armored man on his knees in the dust, and the army sword spitting

guts before the soldier went down. And he saw a
woman scratching her cheeks and tugging out hand-
fuls of her hair. And another soldier crawling in
circles. And another dead. But these things seemed removed, at a vast distance, or perceived from a high
tower.

He did not question his direction until he noticed
the way unhindered before him, the town gate standing unbarred, a scoop of ocher light in the clay-red
wall.

A sentry shouted from the wall as he clattered
through, the white swath, which was a woman,
clasped before him.

As the horse hit the wall of light beyond the wall
of clay, men on horseback foamed around him.

"With us, Kastor!"

A second called in the eastern language, and Seteva
identified the thirteen men Nylerus had left for his
"service."

The striped head cloths flapped over the black
fleeces of hair, and the gems seared, a perfect com-
ponent of this madness.

Seteva laughed, and all about the jackal teeth answered him, and the narrow eyes evaluated. They
rode together, galloping for the hills.

The town sank in their wake.

He sat the part-dead horse, the senseless woman a
leaden weight now on his arm. The sun had set, a sky
the color of apricots going out behind the land.

"Nylerus, I said," he repeated.

Despite their prologue of cries and the ride
through the hills, they did not speak Remine, or
would not. Nor did they appear to realize that their
own leader was the man he sought in the encamp-

ment. Of course, he himself had no authority left with them, or with anyone. The insignia of Remusa all over him, the gilded armor, the lion's-blood cloak, the crested helmet, the bronze-hilted blade—each had become the silliest and most unsavory kind of joke.

Yet he was not mad. It seemed quite reasonable, after all, that he should be here, with nothing, everything he had been reduced to a disaster and left behind him. Men he had known, whose lives were subject to his command, were scattered dead in that past. Reborn into chaos, only thus Marsus Seteva had entered the encampment in the hills. He had put himself into Nylerus's power as neatly as if Nylerus, some fictitious sorcerer of the East, had led him here. And now Nylerus was absent, the final tile left out of the wall. A chink in the reinvented, appalling structure of things as they had come to be. Strangely it was this, more than all else, which disturbed Seteva, provoking him to rage, so he shouted at the men about him: *Nylerus—Nylerus*—the only word they might logically be expected to grasp, but to which they refused to react.

Indeed, they had withdrawn from him, clearing a wide space about him as he sat there on the sodden horse, the white body of the girl leaden against his arm.

The sky faded, but the encampment fires rekindled the color of the afterglow.

Nylerus stood by the horse.

His hands were raised as if to receive some burden from the soldier on his exhausted beast.

"Your men professed not to remember you, Nylerus."

"It was not that, Kastor. You made them uneasy."

"No longer 'Kastor,' Nylerus."

"No longer 'Kastor.' Dismount now; the ride is over. I will take the girl."

Seteva sat on the horse, looking at him. Seteva did not move.

"Are there any women in your camp, Nylerus? I think she'll need women to tend her. Women who speak her own tongue. I can still pay for the service, Nylerus. Remusan capitas."

"No, Kastor. That is no matter. This was not the service I offered, Kastor."

"Damn you, stop calling me that."

"As you wish, Marsus Seteva. But still it was not this service."

"What are you talking about?"

"I am saying to you, Marsus Seteva, that I offered you a method whereby you might bring your girl from Trasint before the sacrifice."

"Split hairs, Nylerus."

"Not so. Examine what you have brought from the town, Marsus Seteva. Closely."

The space had widened further. Nylerus and the soldier and the horse and the limp form of the girl, ringed by fire-wash and shadow, by the settling canopy of darkness, by the men and their animals, but all a great way off.

He held her stiffly, like a heavy wooden bolster.

"They gave her a drug, to make her compliant," Seteva muttered. His arm no longer ached, holding her. His arm had grown into her body, become wooden as her body had become.

"She was compliant enough. Examine, Kastor. Examine."

Seteva glanced down.

Her face was tilted back, the bright hair gushing forth from the skull like spilling water from a tilted urn. Her eyes were open, dulled, opaque. Her lips did not meet. She stared at him as if about to speak.

A chill wind blew across the slopes, and the grass ran like the rollers of an ocean.

"Slow poison," Nylerus said softly, reciting to the lyre of the grass wind. "No harm in it, when they are to die anyway, their blood freed for the god. And it affords them a fair crossing from this earth into their paradise."

"She's dead," Seteva said.

"Yes, Kastor. From the moment she drank it. Dying even as she walked toward the stone. You cheated Trasint of her blood, but not of her death. Oh, they will not forgive it, Kastor. They will rebel and throw off the shackles Remusa put on them. Fresh soldiery will have to be sent to Thraistum. Men will need to be hanged, and crucified. Women raped. The temple burned. The fields salted. Afterward, peace again. The peace of Remusa; quiescence beneath the booted heel. And you, Kastor, your own kind will hunt you like a dog. But all this is, ultimately, very little. Their god has what he desires. If he loves them, the rain will fall. The sun will rise. The moon will wax and wane. I am sorry, Marsus Seteva. I am sorry for you."

Seteva lowered the girl. Her bare feet met the grass of the hillside, and he let her go. She flopped like an emptied water sack, unhuman and spent, soulless, to the ground.

His arm, reprieved, began to pain him, prolonged runnels of pain flowing from the joints and sinews. He massaged the arm absently.

"What now?" Nylerus whispered to him.

"The end of the world," Seteva said. He pulled off the helmet of gilded iron, with its raw red comb, and dropped it by the white sack on the grass.

"Your world, Kastor."

"My world."

Seteva touched the horse, and tiredly, resignedly, it resumed the trained parade walk of the march.

"Wait," said Nylerus. "Where are you going?"

But horse and rider went by him, between the fires, and through the circle of firelit men, up the spine of one hill, descending from sight over another.

"The Remusan is going to Tophiteth, the place of burning," one of the men said malevolently. He spoke in the eastern language, his words striking on the quiet of the young night, scoring it like writing on a wall. "The Remusan is going to Hell."

DREAM SNAKE

Vonda N. McIntyre

"Rich in character, background and incident—
unusually absorbing and moving."

Publishers Weekly

"This is an exciting future-dream with real
characters, a believable mythos and, what's
more important, an excellent readable story."

Frank Herbert

The *"haunting, rich and tender novel"** of a
unique healer and her strange ordeal.

* Robert Silverberg

A Dell Book $2.25   (11729-1)

Award-Winning Science Fiction

Dell Bestsellers